The Boarding School Quilts

a novel by
Jan Cerney

American Quilter's Society
www.AmericanQuilter.com

Located in Paducah, Kentucky, the American Quilter's Society (AQS) is dedicated to promoting the accomplishments of today's quilters. Through its publications and events, AQS strives to honor today's quiltmakers and their work and to inspire future creativity and innovation in quiltmaking.

EXECUTIVE BOOK EDITOR: ELAINE H. BRELSFORD
EDITOR: NATE M. BRELSFORD
COPY EDITOR: JOANN TREECE
PROOFREADER: ADRIANA FITCH
GRAPHIC DESIGN: SARAH BOZONE
COVER DESIGN: MICHAEL BUCKINGHAM
PHOTOGRAPHY: CHARLES R. LYNCH

This book is a work of fiction. The people, places, and events described in it are either imaginary or fictitiously presented. Any resemblance they bear to reality is entirely coincidental.

American Quilter's Society
www.AmericanQuilter.com

Additional copies of this book may be ordered from the American Quilter's Society, PO Box 3290, Paducah, KY 42002-3290, or online at www.AmericanQuilter.com.

Text © 2014, by Author, Jan Cerney
Artwork © 2014 American Quilter's Society

Library of Congress Cataloging-in-Publication Data

Cerney, Janice Brozik.
 The boarding school quilts : a novel / by Jan Cerney.
  pages cm
  ISBN 978-1-60460-162-6 (alk. paper)
  1. Quilting--Fiction. 2. Women missionaries--Fiction. I. Title.
  PS3603.E74B63 2014
  813'.6--dc23
           2014031988

CHAPTER 1

Cheyenne River Mission, 1899

The dry, summer grass shattered under Evangeline's feet as she walked toward the mission church. The day she had left to return to Boston, the church had been fragrant with new pine boards and had gleamed with fresh, white paint. Now, over the years she had been away, harsh storms and intense heat had beaten against the church's sides, peeling its paint to expose raw, battered boards. The church's salvation was its windows, an odd pairing of vibrant glass and weathered wood. The afternoon sun ignited brilliant colors in the recently added stained glass windows.

Evangeline paused near the door, drew in a deep breath, and tiptoed into the building to surprise Elijah. Her eyes adjusted to the glow the stained glass cast over the altar and pews. Leaning over his Bible and a tablet, Elijah Fletcher appeared to be working on a sermon in a side room. She could see his face had matured and was a bit fuller than she had remembered. His hair no longer gleamed like black coal, but was cut short the way she liked it. He wore spectacles, which distinguished him, she thought, like the scholar he was. She stood silently, nearly breathless for a few moments, until he felt a presence and looked up from his work. Then he slowly rose from the chair and walked over to her.

"I thought you were a vision." He touched her arm as if to make sure she were real. "Evangeline, you're here. I didn't expect to see you."

"I know this must be quite a shock. Your mother asked me to come back. She told me I was needed here." She waited for him to validate her reason for coming.

"I didn't know she was intending to ask you. I...I'm just so surprised, so unprepared. Please sit down." He pulled out a chair for her before placing his spectacles on the writing table and sitting across from her, shyly glancing her way. "You look well, Evangeline. I can't believe you've been gone for six years. You look exactly the same as when you left."

She laughed. "I have changed. You just don't want to admit it."

He brushed a lock of hair from his forehead. "You do seem surer of yourself."

Evangeline bristled some. "Was I unsure of myself?" Then she relaxed with a slight laugh. "Well, maybe I was. I'm not that young girl anymore."

Elijah's dark, brooding eyes remained serious. "I have an image of you that will never change, even when your blonde hair grays. Evangeline, you'll always be that idealistic, innocent, caring, and beautiful young girl."

The way he enunciated every syllable of her name sparked a struggling ember within her. "I'll remind you of that someday."

He tilted his head. "You look well."

"Thank you." She cleared her throat. "Cassandra and Morning Star's visit lifted my spirits." She smiled and willed herself not to reveal more. She wasn't ready to confess how low she had sunk before her friends' visit. True, they had lifted her spirits some, but she wasn't yet healed from grief. Coming here to begin again required every ounce of her courage.

His eyes held compassion. "I'm so sorry about James. It must have been painful for you."

"It was." She stopped herself short. Yes, spilling every hurt to him would be inappropriate now. Or maybe ever.

"I would have come myself. I just couldn't get away."

"I know. It's all right." Elijah was dedicated to his mission. She knew that all too well, but she could live with that, now.

Elijah grabbed his glasses from the writing table and awkwardly fumbled with them. "How was your trip? How are your parents?"

"The trip was just fine, and my parents are well. They send their best."

"How did they feel about you leaving?"

"They were worried about me and only wanted what would make me happy." Again, Evangeline felt a sharp, inward pain. She hadn't wanted to leave home either, but there was nothing for her in Boston anymore. Though her parents were precious to her, they couldn't help her now. They couldn't fill the void.

"Has coming here made you happy?"

She glanced at the timepiece attached to her lapel. "I've only been here a half hour."

"And you found me already?" He laughed.

"I did. I was anxious to see you. Have you been well?"

"I have, other than being too busy keeping the mission going. I hope you're here for more than a visit?"

"I'd like to stay and finish my original commitment. I hope coming to the mission will give me a purpose."

"A purpose?"

Her voice strained. "I can't seem to find myself, Elijah."

"I hope you won't be disappointed."

"Why would I be?" She wiped away the tears pooling in the corners of her eyes.

"You might be expecting too much from us. You know you have the answers within you—in your faith."

"I've tried that. It doesn't work."

"Perhaps you just need more time." He held up his hands, palms open. "Now don't get me wrong. We have missed you, Evangeline. You had a special way with the children."

"I have missed the mission, too. You don't know how many times I thought of you all."

He shook his head. "It is difficult to keep steady help, and there are new challenges every day."

She laughed. "I wasn't exactly steady help. I was here only a year."

"Was that all? You made such an impression on all of us that I thought it was longer."

"Elijah, you're too kind. I was a spoiled girl, only concerned with myself."

"That's not entirely true. You did care about the mission and the students."

"I'm ashamed of the way I behaved toward you, even acting like one of the students. It's hard to believe that you used to make me so angry when you didn't pay attention to me."

His tone warmed. "I'm sorry for that, too, but I didn't really think I should have. I didn't want to lead you into something you would regret, and I had the mission to think about." Elijah paused in thought. "Besides, James loved you, and I knew he'd give you what I never could. I'm flattered that you cared for me."

"I still do."

"And I for you." He smiled and touched her hand. "Let me show you around. The mission hasn't changed all that much, except for the addition."

"You don't have to. I don't want to disturb what you're doing."

"I'm just working on a sermon. It can wait." He tucked the notes he was working on in the Bible and reached again for her hand. She felt his warmth and strength flow into her own soul, but he dropped her hand all too soon to point out the altar and caress its smooth surface. "This is the altar and these are the pews your acquaintances Sadie and George provided."

"Very nice." She caressed it too, as if to draw his strength secondhand. Then she noticed a colorful star quilt hanging where the Jacob's Ladder quilt had been placed years ago. The quilt's diamond pattern radiated from the single star's center, bursting to its points. Elijah followed her gaze.

"This quilt symbolizes a new day, a new beginning for the Lakota people. It's a new day for you, Evangeline, and perhaps a new beginning."

"It's so beautiful." She stood still, transfixed on the colors and pattern, Elijah watched her as he opened the door to lead her outside. "I feel it." She stepped out into the warm, late afternoon sunshine and took a deep breath, feeling the warmth of familiarity. Elijah drew her attention to the new stained glass windows, explaining they were also gifts from George and Sadie.

"I didn't know they were still supporting the mission," Evangeline said.

"Every year they provide something for us. We're thankful for such generous people."

"And to think it came about from a casual conversation on the train." She remembered how the couple had filled those fretful hours on the train when she first made the journey to the mission.

"You never know when something good might come from what you say or do. Let me show you the new addition where the female members of the staff stay."

"Cassandra told me one of the missionaries returned to the East for more schooling."

Elijah nodded. "I live in the old chapel, the room my mother used." He pointed, saying, "She lives in the new addition now." He shuffled his feet. "I smell supper cooking. Shall we join them?"

———————

Cassandra looked up from the pot she was stirring, perspiration beading on her forehead. Her eyes scoured

Elijah and Evangeline as they entered the kitchen. Elijah embraced her.

"I'm so happy to see you, Mother. I'm thankful for your safe trip," he said.

"Good to see you, too, son," said Cassandra. "Judging by the state of this kitchen, I don't know how you got along without me and Morning Star."

He grinned. "I managed, but I'm looking forward to a good meal. Where is Morning Star, anyway?"

Hearing her name pronounced by the voice she knew so well, the young woman hurried into the kitchen. She threw her arms around Elijah and Evangeline. They shared a few hurried yet heartfelt words of greeting, and Morning Star resumed meal preparation by carrying the dishes from the cupboard to the table.

Evangeline savored the aromas filling the kitchen and distinctly recognized each one: cooking meat, onions, peppers, basil, and something sweet baking in the oven. Oh, how she loved this kitchen.

"Here, let me help you, Morning Star," Evangeline offered. The kitchen was still the same, and Evangeline remembered where to find the silverware.

Cassandra placed a bowl of fragrant soup and freshly baked biscuits in the center of the table. Evangeline anticipated the fine meal, so much like all the meals they had shared in this very kitchen years ago. Those were happy times. How she had missed her friends at the Cheyenne River Mission. Cassandra and Evangeline had endured a particularly difficult relationship until Cassandra and Morning Star visited her in Boston to ask her to return to the mission.

Elijah said grace, and they each dished up the food. "The three of you have much explaining to do," he said. "Did you enjoy your time in Boston?"

The three women shared a moment of nervous expectation. When their silence became unbearable, Cassandra started: "I faced one of my greatest fears there. I have kept a secret from you, Elijah. I wanted to wait until we were alone, but Evangeline and Morning Star already know. I need them here with us. We're all family."

Elijah stared at her. "What is it?"

"I never told you that I lived in an orphanage in Boston until I was old enough to leave and become a missionary. Evangeline's father drove us to that orphanage in Boston. It's falling down and no longer in use."

Elijah dropped his spoon. "You were given away? Did you ever know your parents?"

"I was told I was taken there by my mother when I was about a year old. That's all I know."

"Was it a bad experience?"

"I felt unloved and lost, but I survived. The good side of it all is that I learned to sew."

"So that's why you never talked about your family. You never knew them. Why did you keep that secret from me?"

"It was just too painful to talk about. I should have told you and your father."

Elijah nodded. "We would have been more supportive if we had known."

"I'm so much better now. Evangeline helped me see that I could put those experiences behind me."

"I'm so sorry, Mother, but I think it would have been

easier for us all if you had said something."

"It's not your fault. I faced the ghosts of the past and I'm better now."

"I didn't realize I was asking such an emotional question." He shook his head in disbelief.

Cassandra edged her hand toward his and touched him. "We'll talk more about it later, Elijah. For now, let's talk about something else. Morning Star, do you have something to ask Elijah?"

Morning Star cleared her throat. "Elijah, is it all right if I change my name to Sara?"

"This is another surprise. Why the change?"

"I just think it would be better for me to have a different name if I ever go away to school."

"Of course, it's okay with me. How did you come up with Sara?"

"It's Evangeline's middle name."

"I see. I believe it's a good choice," he said, glancing at Evangeline. "From now on, we'll call you Sara. But you'll have to forgive me if I still call you Morning Star from time to time."

"Have you decided on Evangeline's duties at the mission, Elijah?" Cassandra suddenly blurted.

"We haven't talked about that yet. Would you like to continue teaching, Evangeline?"

"I would, if there's a place for me."

"We've lost one teacher. We need to replace her. Interested?"

"I am."

He smiled. "Then it's settled." Elijah pushed back his chair. "Another fine meal, ladies. I'll help you clear the table and then read for a while."

Evangeline began stacking the plates. "I'll help Cassandra and Morning...um...Sara with the cleaning."

Sara glanced at Cassandra and tugged at Evangeline's hand. "We have something to show you first," Sara said.

Evangeline looked to Elijah for an explanation. He only shrugged and continued cleaning. Neither Sara nor Cassandra explained as they led Evangeline to a small, clean, and sparsely furnished room in the new addition. On the bed was a colorful Job's Tears quilt. Evangeline recognized it from the time she, Cassandra, and others at the mission had studied biblical quilt patterns. She hadn't quilted that pattern yet, but Evangeline knew that the four points on each block represented tears overlaid with a cross to represent his fractured life and Job was represented by the square in the center.

Stunned, she turned toward Cassandra. "Did you make this quilt?"

"Morning Star—I mean Sara—made it with me."

Sara laughed at the sound of her new name.

"You might think this pattern is an odd choice," Cassandra explained. "But we made it with the three of us in mind. We have all cried many tears in our hearts, and we're going to let go of the sorrow. The quilt is yours to keep."

Evangeline stroked the softness of the new quilt. "Yes... yes, we are going to put that sadness behind us. Thank you so much for this wonderful gift. I will certainly treasure it." They returned to the kitchen, and Evangeline told Elijah about the surprise gift.

"I knew they were up to something, but they never shared what it was," He said.

A moment later, Evangeline squinted and tilted her head to the side. "How did you know I would come back to the mission?" she asked Cassandra.

Cassandra shrugged. "I just prayed with all my might. I had no doubt my prayers would be answered."

———————

The next morning, Evangeline awoke with a lighter heart. There was a place for her here. Elijah had accepted her. She dressed and practically skipped to the kitchen where she found Cassandra busy with the usual tasks.

"Here, have some coffee." Cassandra poured a cup and put it in front of her. "I have bread toasting in the oven. Elijah left for the church, and Sara is out taking care of the hens."

"Thanks."

"Elijah asked me to send you to the church after breakfast."

"What do you suppose he wants?"

"I don't have any idea."

Evangeline finished her toast and coffee and left for the church as Elijah had requested. When she arrived, she noticed he hadn't slept well. Dark circles had formed under his eyes. His generally calm exterior appeared a little shaken when he stood up. Evangeline wondered what had changed him since yesterday. She knew him well enough to suspect something was bothering him. Evangeline peered into his office.

"You wanted to see me?"

"I do. Please come in and sit down." He pushed aside the book he was studying. "Remember when I told you the star quilt hanging here in the church means a new day, a new beginning?" Evangeline nodded. "Well, I didn't have the courage last night to tell you what else it means to me, mainly because I don't really know how you feel about...me."

"What are you trying to say?"

"I had no idea you were returning to the mission. You caught me off guard."

"I suppose that's true. But my being here shouldn't change things that much."

"Oh, but it does. I didn't sleep all night for thinking about this."

"About what?"

"The star quilt might also mean a new day for us." He cleared his throat. "I need a helpmate, someone to work by my side."

"I don't understand."

"I need more than just another teacher. I need someone to help me make important decisions and to plan the mission's direction. A...wife."

"A wife? Me? Why would you choose me? I couldn't even keep my commitment to the mission. I left Sara for you and Mary to look after. And I may not have even been a good wife to James."

Elijah drew back. "I thought this was what you wanted, why you came back."

"I admit I had these silly notions when I was nineteen. I came back for peace, to find out how to live again. I came back to see you, my dear friend."

"I'm so sorry I let you down. Sorry about James's passing. Sorry that I didn't come and give you my condolences myself. I haven't been much of a friend."

"It's been difficult for me, but Sara and Cassandra saved me by coming to Boston. It was Cassandra who asked me to come back. She said you needed me. I didn't know how she meant that." Evangeline looked deeply into his dark eyes for the truth.

He hesitated. "Yes, I have always needed you," he confessed. "There is a special connection between us, isn't there?"

She shook her head in disbelief. "Why didn't you tell me long ago?"

"Would it have made a difference?"

"I think so. I wouldn't have left."

"I didn't want you to be unhappy like my mother. I couldn't do that to you."

"I don't understand your reasoning. I wouldn't have been unhappy. Your mother has changed since she came to Boston. She told you her secret, and that was the main reason she was unhappy."

"But it wasn't just because of my mother I let you go. When James was here, he told me how much he cared for you. He was afraid I might persuade you to stay. But how could I? You would have had to give up so much to stay here with me. He loved you and could offer you so much. You were happy, weren't you?"

"Yes, James made me happy for most of our marriage, and I grew to love him. But there were pieces missing in my life, which was you, the mission, and Sara. Perhaps James knew that, but he never let on."

"And then there is another issue we never talked about."

"What is it?"

"Surely you know that marrying outside your race invites

bad comments, name calling, and such. You do read the papers?"

"Yes, I know. Some marriages end badly because of the criticism."

"Is that why you are turning me down?"

"No, it isn't. I'm not afraid of what people will say."

"You will stay, won't you?" Elijah asked in earnest. "I'm not scaring you away?"

"I'll stay if you want me to."

His dark eyes warmed. "I don't want to see you go. We can always use an extra teacher, and with you by my side, we can accomplish so much more. Even if you're not my wife."

She nodded. "I do need you as a friend. Marriage wouldn't be right just now. I'm not the same girl I once was. You may not like who I am now."

"I see." He hung his head. "You need time. You're still interested in teaching?"

"Most definitely. And your friendship."

––––––––

Evangeline spent hours going over the new teaching materials she would be using with her new students in several months. She felt a definite lift in spirit, knowing she would be back with her beloved pupils. She would have to earn their trust, just like she had that first year. It would be a challenge, but now she knew how to gain their confidence.

Focusing on something other than herself for the past few weeks had helped to remove the doubt from her mind. She still had flashbacks of her life with James, but the frequency had diminished. She was hopeful that in time, she might not feel the pain so sharply.

Elijah had been gone for several days, traveling the countryside far and wide to recruit students for the fall term. Evangeline finished her preparations for the day and was in the kitchen drinking a cup of tea when Elijah returned from his sojourn somewhat haggard and dusty.

"How did it go?" Evangeline asked. "Want something to eat or drink?"

"A glass of water, please. It's a hot one today. Too hot to eat." He wiped his brow, washed his hands, and took the glass of water she offered. "I didn't sign up as many students as I wished. Many families won't commit until later."

"At least we have some to begin with. Did you travel a great distance?"

"I did. The families are scattered hither and yon. I'm not sure I found them all."

"You must be worn out." She smiled affectionately.

"I am. I have some news, though." He pulled a letter from his pocket. "Mary wrote to me."

"Mary?" she shrieked. "Isn't she at Crow Creek with a man?"

"That's where she said she was going? I haven't heard from Mary in a long time. She says she's coming for a visit and has a big surprise."

"She's coming back alone?"

"I think so. It'll be good to see her again."

How could he say that? thought Evangeline. *Mary is trouble.* "Do you have a position for her?"

"Not really."

Evangeline hoped Elijah didn't hear her heart thumping against her chest. "When...when is she coming?"

"Well, let me reread this." Elijah scanned the letter. "She's coming within a week."

Evangeline couldn't believe what she was hearing. She wondered how Elijah could be eager to see her. *Doesn't he know Mary's goals are so different from those of the mission? Should I remind him that Mary was hostile to whites trying to transform the Lakota people? Or, does she have another motive for coming?* That thought gave Evangeline chills. *She's after Elijah.*

"Don't worry, Evangeline; you won't have to be her roommate."

"I didn't say anything," she countered.

"No, but the look on your face did."

"I can't deny that Mary and I disagreed about most things. I shouldn't be telling this to a pastor. If Minnie were here, she would scold me for being judgmental, but I can't help it. Thinking of it makes my heart race."

"Tell me. We're friends."

"I never told you about the time she accused me of turning Sara into a white girl. She made it sound like I was doing something terrible. I was sewing at the time, but after she left, I couldn't even finish what I was doing."

"Mary may have a different view of what we're trying to do here."

"It took me quite a while to get over her comments. In fact, I began to doubt our mission here."

"In what way?"

"We were expecting the Lakota to change to our way, just like that." She snapped her fingers.

"Is that why you left?"

"I thought I left for James, but maybe I left because I thought Mary had a point." She searched Elijah's truth-filled eyes. "I never considered that."

"But you're back. You must believe in our purpose."

"You're right. I must. But why does Mary want to come back?"

"I don't know. Maybe she had a change of heart. I have to give her a chance. You know we grew up together."

Evangeline frowned. "I remember you telling me."

"You still have a teaching job, regardless of Mary," Elijah said as he left the table. "See you at supper, and try not to worry."

While Evangeline washed the glass and cup and a few other dishes after dinner, she continued to think about Elijah's news. *I can't believe Mary is coming back. Why now, after I just turned down Elijah's marriage proposal? But I'm not ready for marriage, nor do I want Mary to have Elijah. Now what do I do?*

Cassandra came in carrying a laundry basket filled with freshly dried towels. "Was Elijah just here?"

"He returned from scouting for students."

Cassandra set the basket on the floor. "Did he find some?"

"He did. Not as many as he wished." Evangeline dried the last dish and placed it in the cupboard. "Do you know that Mary's coming back to the mission?"

"No, I didn't. How do you know?"

"She wrote to Elijah and told him she was coming. She has a surprise."

Cassandra lifted the towels from the basket and began to fold them. "I thought we had seen the last of her."

Evangeline reached for a towel to fold. "What kind of

hold does Mary have on Elijah?"

"What do you mean?"

"Elijah knows she's probably not the best influence for the mission, yet he feels he has to give her a chance."

"I suppose it goes back to when they were children," Cassandra suggested.

"That's what Elijah tells me. But I still don't understand why he has such loyalty."

"I remember her father had intended that she marry Elijah; Swift Bear always liked my son. Maybe the chief thought Elijah would be a good influence on Mary. She was called Running Fawn when she was young—a pretty girl, but very disruptive."

"She never approved of me. I guess I am too white for her taste." Evangeline was surprised at her own retort, realizing her bitterness had never completely left.

Cassandra flashed her a puzzled look. "Elijah may feel he has an obligation to her. She hasn't accepted our religion. She believes in the Old Way."

"I suppose that could be it. He doesn't have feelings for her, does he?"

"Oh, I don't think you have to worry about his feelings, but you may have to be on guard about hers."

————

The day Mary arrived, Evangeline was scouring kettles after dinner, thinking of Mary and the effect she would have on the mission. When Evangeline heard the approaching buggy, she dried her hands on a dish towel and peered out the window. Elijah heard the buggy, too, and was there to help Mary down.

Mary's upswept, raven hair was partially hidden by a fashionable, burgundy hat accented with tan feathers. Her formfitting traveling suit matched the hat perfectly. Evangeline had to admit that Mary was stunning. *Where had she been? she wondered. Certainly not on the Crow Creek Reservation.* She admonished herself for spying, but she simply had to know how Elijah was going to react. *What?* Mary kissed him on the cheek. She coyly opened her parasol. *Mary with a parasol?* Evangeline couldn't believe her eyes. She was beside herself when Cassandra joined her in the kitchen.

"What's going on? You look positively distraught," said Cassandra.

Evangeline pointed to the window. "Look."

Cassandra carefully pulled aside the curtains. "Oh, Mary's here. Elijah certainly seems interested."

"He is? Do you really think so?"

"Oops, sorry I said anything. Remember, they're old friends."

"Well, Elijah and I are old friends, too. Maybe not for as long as Elijah and Mary, but we're friends anyway."

"To be honest with you, I was hoping you and Elijah would become more than friends."

"He asked me to marry him."

Cassandra turned away from the window. "That's wonderful news. Why have you kept it secret?"

"I turned him down."

"You what?"

"I turned him down. I'm not ready for another marriage. I don't know if I love him, although I am very fond of him."

"Fond is a good place to start. Will he ask you again?"

"I don't know."

"If I were you, I'd keep an eye on Mary."

"Oh, dear! I can't seem to do anything right. And look at me. I look terrible. Could you take over while I run into my room and do something with myself?"

"Just remember to come back out."

Evangeline reached her room without being seen. Luckily, Elijah and Mary were still outside, but soon Elijah would be bringing Mary's things into the new addition, to the empty room next to Cassandra's.

Evangeline evaluated her appearance in the small, oval mirror above her washstand. Her stringy hair needed a good washing. She was going to put that off until she had cleaned the henhouse. She grabbed the milk glass water pitcher and shrieked with happiness when she saw there was enough to wash her hair. It wasn't warm, but she made do. She changed her dress and coiled her wet hair into a bun. It wasn't perfect, but it was better than how she had looked just moments before. How could she compete with Mary's elegant traveling outfit? Elijah had preached that beauty was skin deep and vain, but today she didn't want to test his beliefs.

Elijah and Mary made ample noise, alerting Evangeline to their whereabouts in the new addition. Evangeline waited until she heard them leave, opened the door of her room, and peeked out. She slinked back into the kitchen where she found Mary and Elijah drinking coffee with Cassandra. Evangeline's heart beat wildly, thinking of the confrontation with Mary years ago. She reminded herself she wasn't a young, vulnerable woman anymore. She straightened her shoulders and lifted her head.

"Hello, Mary. Welcome to the mission." She heard the words trip off her tongue, but she couldn't believe she had said them.

"Pour yourself a cup of coffee and join us," Cassandra said.

The three sat at the table, chatting and laughing just like old friends. Evangeline seethed inside. *Stop it,* she told herself. *I have no claim on Elijah or the mission. I gave it up when I said no to Elijah's proposal.* She crossed her arms and feigned joy over Mary's presence.

"Meet the new superintendent of schools," said Elijah, gesturing toward Mary.

Evangeline could barely respond. What she wanted to say wasn't appropriate. She hesitated, formulating a proper comeback. "Congratulations."

Elijah was apparently elated. He grinned and hung on Mary's every word. "Mary went back to school and graduated with an education degree at Hampton, Virginia. Then she secured this superintendent assignment."

Mary tilted her head slightly and smiled. "Oh, it was nothing, Elijah."

When Evangeline snapped out of her shock, she gathered enough courage to ask a few questions. "How long have you been employed at this assignment?"

"Just a short time."

"Do you evaluate both the religious and government schools?"

"Most definitely."

Evangeline wanted to ask about Mary's sudden attitude change—assuming she was not plotting to undermine the government's assimilation policy of civilizing the Indian population.

"My main concern is student abuse. I can now understand that training students in the whites' culture is essential, but the students do not have to be abused in the process."

Elijah's attention focused on Mary. "I totally agree. Certainly a worthy cause. Mary will be staying with us to go over some program changes. Evangeline and Mother, could you free up some time to meet with Mary while she's here? Maybe this afternoon." Evangeline wasn't sure of Mary's motives, but she had clearly charmed Elijah.

"Certainly. How long are you staying, Mary?" Cassandra asked.

"A week or so. This might be a good place to rest from my hectic schedule."

––––––

Evangeline and Cassandra had finished cleaning the kitchen and were waiting for Mary to meet them in the classroom. Evangeline paced the floor while Cassandra sharpened pencils. She handed one to Evangeline.

"Relax, Evangeline. There's no use getting worked up over Mary." Cassandra rummaged around in the cupboard. "Where did I put those lesson books?"

"I can't help it. It's even worse now. She's the superintendent. She has the upper hand."

"Ah, here they are." Cassandra placed the lesson books on the table. "We can listen to what she has to say, but there are ways around a problem."

"She's a big problem in my estimation, and I see no way around her." Mary had not only upset Evangeline's personal life, but now she was encroaching on her teaching methods.

She reminded herself to be strong, not to cower like she once had.

"Here she comes. Remember, I'm on your side," Cassandra muttered.

Mary entered the classroom like a judge, minus the black robe. "Good, I see you have set out the lesson books." She settled in a chair, opened one of the books, and flipped through its pages. "My major concern is student abuse. That's why I worked so hard to get this job. Abuse is a bigger problem in other schools, but I will also make a few instructional adjustments here." Mary scanned Cassandra's entries in the lesson book. "I especially like the details you included, Cassandra. This other one, Susan's, is quite sparse. I understand she returned to the East."

"She did. She was only here a year," Cassandra explained.

"And Evangeline, you have no lesson books to show me yet."

Evangeline grimaced. She didn't like the sound of that *yet.*

"My father, Swift Bear, believed Lakota children should learn white ways. I didn't agree with him at first. But I have come to understand the desire to learn the new ways." Mary spent the next hour making suggestions on teaching techniques while Evangeline fretted. Mary even made suggestions for Cassandra's sewing class. "I think you should let the students design their own quilts. They shouldn't be told which design and pattern to use. The Lakota are very creative."

"I know," said Cassandra.

"Enough for today. I promised Elijah I would join him on a walk to the cemetery and visit my parents' graves."

After Mary left, Evangeline let out her pent-up anger. "She acts as though I've never taught before! Who does she think she is?"

"She probably does have a point about letting the girls design their own quilts," Cassandra admitted.

"You're agreeing with her?"

"Well, I'm not going to disagree if she makes a good suggestion. You know the girls like to draw their own designs. I see no harm. But right now, I need to start supper."

"I'll join you shortly." Evangeline put the lesson books away and admired the afterglow of the summer evening. Mourning doves cooed their sad melody, serenading the world into a peaceful slumber. She espied Elijah and Mary walking side by side to the cemetery, huddled together, perhaps deep in conversation. Loneliness suddenly invaded her heart.

CHAPTER 2

The Friday after Mary left the mission, Elijah asked Evangeline to go with him to visit his friends and parishioners, Sol and Lily. Evangeline accepted, surprised that he had even asked her. She fretted over what she would wear and decided on a perky, apple green and white gingham summer dress and a small-brimmed, beige straw hat.

On the first hill outside the mission, Elijah pulled the horses and buggy to a stop that overlooked what was left of Swift Bear's camp.

"Where is everyone?" Evangeline asked, lifting her hand to shade her eyes from the intense Dakota sun. She frowned as she looked down on the old Indian camp near the banks of the running river. "Most of the tepees are gone. The log houses look deserted."

Elijah relaxed the reins and leaned back against the buggy seat. "Since Swift Bear died, no one takes the children to the mission school. The allotment agents have been talking with the Lakota, trying to get them to settle their allotments, farm the land, and raise livestock like the law says. That has taken people away from the camp."

"Do you think it's a good idea for the Lakota to leave the main camp? How can you possibly run the mission school with no children?" Elijah jumped down from the buggy and extended his hand to help Evangeline disembark.

She removed her hat, and the wind blew through her blonde tresses. She liked the feel of the prairie breeze caressing her face. She stooped and plucked a blade of grass and began to chew its stem.

Elijah shrugged. "That's what the government wants. I hate to complain, Evangeline, but the government doesn't always know what's best for Lakota people."

"I know you become frustrated with their Indian policies. Remember, you're one against many."

"The Lakota live together as one big family. We like to have our own land, our own space. I'm afraid the whites don't understand that, nor do they want to. Many of the Lakota don't want to farm. They think it's beneath them. You should have seen the wagonloads of plows the government brought into the agency." He shook his head. "I just don't think it's going to work. This land isn't good for farming." Elijah extended his arm toward the horizon. "Just look around. The worst part of all this is that the allotment law divides the reservation into units, and what isn't allotted will be sold to non-Indian people."

Evangeline gasped. "They will lose their land, won't they?"

"They will. I don't know what all will happen, Evangeline.

This community has been their way of life for as long as they can remember."

Once again, she shaded her eyes with her hand and squinted. "It's strange not to see dogs yapping or children running around. Is anyone still living in the old camp?"

"Alvina and Josephine and some of the older couples chose to remain. The young ones have been convinced to try farming or raising livestock."

"Have they been successful?"

"Not in farming; it's too dry here. Raising a few cattle has worked for them, but the allotments are too small for large herds. It's not their way of life. Oh well, I guess we can't do anything about it. Sol has a small spread a few miles to the north. He does quite well." Elijah helped her into the buggy. He clucked to the horses and they followed the northbound trail.

"What about the mission, Elijah? Are you sure we'll have enough pupils?"

"As a day school, the mission is in trouble. The children have too far to come. I've been thinking of offering places at the mission for students to stay."

"Like a boarding school? I thought that was taboo. Jeremiah vehemently opposed it, and I thought you did, too."

"We still don't care for the idea, but we seem to have no other choice, unless we close everything down. And there's another problem. The government has cut back on funds. Donations are keeping us going. Minnie and Jeremiah send an annual check from their fund-raising efforts. Your old friends, George and Sadie, send money every year, too. But it isn't enough."

"What about the book you wrote on Swift Bear's life? Doesn't that bring in money?"

"The royalties don't pay that well and book sales are down."

"Don't tell me the mission's going to fold!" Evangeline's eyes widened with concern.

"The school might, but the attendance at church is fairly good. Some of the cattlemen in the area come to church, and I expect homesteaders will be coming into the area soon." He gazed across the countryside. "The Lakota with allotments come when they can, but their workhorses can't do double duty. The horses have to rest sometime."

Evangeline sighed. "It seems like we can't escape change. I thought I would be returning to what I had left, but that was foolish of me. I don't want to see the school close."

"Life is constant change. We just have to accept it. Besides, change can be good." He turned to her. "After hearing all this, do you still want to stay?"

"Of course I do." She laughed. "Now, let's not repeat those old mistakes from the first time I was working here at the mission."

Elijah smiled. "You're right. It *is* going to be different."

"I suppose you won't need as many teachers as you used to have."

"You're right. Mother doesn't want to teach anymore, except for sewing, so that would leave you and me and maybe Sara someday. I think we will send her to Santee, Nebraska, this fall. How do you feel about that?"

"I feel it's a good idea if she wants to go. She may want to go farther from home, but I don't want her to!"

"Don't worry. She doesn't like to leave home, and believe it or not, she has become fond of Mother. They spend hours sewing together."

"I'm glad Sara has found some contentment. I felt so bad for deserting her." Up ahead, cattle blocked the trail. Elijah waved his hat and yelled at them until they moved out of the way. "I don't remember seeing so many cattle before," Evangeline said.

"More all the time. Some white men have married Indian women, which entitles them to their allotments. They stock their land tracts with cattle. Of course, the Lakota have some cattle, too. They all run together on this open range." Elijah pointed to a group of log-and-sod buildings. "There's Sol's place up ahead."

Irregularly cut cottonwood and cedar poles formed a corral some distance from the low, log house. A crowd of men rimmed the corral, shouting and waving hats to cheer on a young rider doing his best to stay on a bucking bronco. When they arrived, Elijah and Evangeline left the buggy and walked toward the corral.

"Hello Pastor!" Ruben ambled toward him and extended his hand in greeting. "What brings you out here?"

"We were out for a drive and thought we'd stop in and see how things are going. You remember Evangeline?"

"I do. It's been a long while. Didn't think I'd ever see you again," he said bashfully.

Evangeline smiled at Elijah. "I'm back to stay."

Returning her smile, he asked Ruben, "Who's riding the bronc?"

"Oh, that's Sol. Yeah, we like to get together, rope a few calves, ride a few broncs, and maybe even try riding some wild bulls. Looky there!" Ruben turned toward Sol. "He did it! Yippee!" he whooped, waving his hat in the air. Sol had ridden the bucking horse, but lost his felt western hat in the process. He stooped to pick it up, dusted off his backside, and walked over to where Elijah, Evangeline, and Ruben were still cheering.

Elijah patted him on the back. "Good ride. Sol, do you remember Evangeline?" Sol tipped his hat and nodded.

"I see you don't wear ties anymore," she kidded, remembering he liked the ties sent in the annual Christmas barrels full of donations they received from churches in the East. In fact, she was totally surprised by his transformation to western garb.

"Nope, I traded them for kerchiefs." He twisted the blue one he was wearing around his neck.

"How's the cattle business?" Elijah asked.

"I guess we're doing alright. Could use rain for the grass, though."

"It never rains enough here, does it? I'll pray for some on Sunday," Elijah said.

"Thanks. Maybe I'll get to church."

"I've been thinking about coming out and holding services at different homes every Saturday or so. I know it's a long way to come for church every Sunday."

"You can come here whenever you wish."

Elijah nodded. "Thanks for your offer. Would it be too late to make arrangements for tomorrow?"

"Certainly not! In the meantime, want to see the babies?" Sol folded his arms to contain his pride, but it eked out as he blushed and looked over his left shoulder at the simple cabin, smoke streaming from its crooked chimney.

Evangeline's eyes twinkled. "Babies! You have babies?"

"A boy and a girl. Come to the house and meet Lily, my wife, and Sally and Howey."

"I married Sol and Lily four years ago," Elijah told Evangeline. As they strode to the small house, Evangeline detected the aroma of baking cookies. Their tantalizing scent made her mouth water. She noticed Lily's house was sparsely furnished, yet tidy. She was pleased that Lily's home reflected the mission training. Handmade quilts covered a couch and a rather rickety chair. Lily was feeding the children when Sol brought them inside.

"Lily, this is Evangeline," Sol said. "You should remember her from school several years back."

"Oh, I remember. Please come in and sit down. I just took some oatmeal cookies out of the oven. How about one?"

"Thank you." Evangeline bent down and softly spoke to the little girl who could not have been more than two years old. "I noticed your quilts."

"Oh, yes. They're not very good and almost worn out. I did those when I went to the mission school," Lily said.

"Have you been attending the sewing circles at the mission?"

Lily shook her head. "I've been too busy with the children. But I would like to."

"We'll have to arrange for you to attend this year," Evangeline said.

Lily smiled. "I would like that." Howey began crying in his high chair. Lily lifted him out and held him. "This is Howey. He's nine months old."

Evangeline held out her arms. "How adorable. May I hold him?" Lily transferred the pudgy, little boy to her. Evangeline cuddled him in her arms. His softness reminded her how she had wanted a baby of her own. *Will I be able to have children?* Regret stabbed her heart. She held Howey closely until he became fussy and then passed him back to his mother. She tried to converse with Sally, who hid behind Lily's skirts.

After they ate the cookies and played with the babies, Elijah suggested that he and Evangeline depart. "I'm sure Sol needs to get back to the corral."

Evangeline said good-bye to Lily, patted the little ones on their heads, and promised to come back for another visit. Sally peeked around her mother and waved. Evangeline laughed and waved back.

"Thanks for stopping by," Sol said as he walked them to their buggy.

Evangeline took hold of Elijah's hand. He helped her up to the buggy seat. "What a nice little family. Thanks for inviting me to come along with you. I really enjoyed the day."

"You're welcome. You can come along some other time if you want. In fact, I will need help when I hold services on Saturday."

"What would I do?"

"You're good at music. There won't be a piano or organ, but you could lead the hymns."

"I would like that," she said.

"I arranged with Sol to conduct the first Saturday worship service at his home. In the meantime, I'll turn the music portion of the service over to you."

Evangeline nodded, hoping she wouldn't botch her assignment.

———————

Evangeline breathed a sigh of relief on that bright Saturday morning. Mary had left the day before with promises to return in a month. Evangeline scurried to place the hymns she had organized for the Saturday gathering in a large envelope. Elijah hadn't told her the order of the service, but no matter what it was, she was confident she was ready. Cassandra had made sandwiches and cake to contribute to the luncheon and packed them in a basket, which now dangled from Evangeline's arm.

Evangeline climbed into the awaiting buggy with Elijah, who was not particularly talkative that morning. She shrugged inwardly; she had her own thoughts to mull over. He launched the horses into a trot and she settled in for the long ride.

As they neared Sol's ranch, Elijah initiated snippets of conversation. "Sorry I was so quiet."

"Something bothering you?"

"I've been doing some thinking. Trying to come to a solution. I'll tell you about it after the service."

She wondered at his serious tone. *What could be brooding in that head of his?* She didn't have time to worry, as people were already gathered for the service. The attendance seemed to have surprised everyone.

"We'll start with a prayer and then a hymn," Elijah told her. Sol stepped out to help her descend from the buggy. She held the envelope of hymns tightly and followed Elijah to the arbor that had been constructed for the occasion. She appreciated the scent of coffee boiling over a fire. She would have liked a cup but knew she would have to wait until after the service.

Elijah said the prayer and Evangeline led the gathering in a hymn without any musical accompaniment. Elijah's sermon was uplifting. After the service, the congregants remained to share a midafternoon meal. Evangeline added Cassandra's cake and sandwiches to the table that held a variety of other food contributions. During lunch, Evangeline conversed with the women, promising she would be out to visit some of them soon. Meanwhile, the children explored Sol's ranch together.

"Thanks for helping out," Elijah said to Evangeline when they were on their way back to the mission.

Evangeline noticed Elijah had loosened up since the early morning ride to Sol's ranch. *Perhaps he had been concentrating on the service—or was it Mary's departure that caused him to be pensive?* She had to ask him about Mary. *What have I to lose? I can't make matters any worse than they are.*

They had driven a great distance before she mustered her courage. "What...what about Mary?"

"Mary?"

"Yes, Mary. Is she important to you?" Evangeline flinched at her own audacity.

Elijah chewed the corner of his lip. "If you weren't my good friend, I would refrain from telling you anything. I need someone by my side. I thought since Mary and I had been childhood friends, she might be the one."

Evangeline's heart wrenched against her chest. "Is she?"

"I found out after you left for Boston that she thought so differently than I. She was bitter and didn't want anything to do with the white people who were taking Lakota land and heritage. I stifled our relationship when I found that out."

"And this time?"

"She says she has changed."

"You believe her?"

"Why do you ask? Don't you think she's truthful?"

"I don't know. I guess it's not for me to decide."

Elijah turned toward her. "Mary wants to marry me."

Evangeline sat rigidly beside him. "You asked her?"

"No, she asked me."

Evangeline began to tremble and gripped the buggy seat to steady herself, but Elijah couldn't see her anguish. *I was so stupid to reject his proposal. What was I trying to prove, anyway? That I am strong enough to be alone for the rest of my life? That I was afraid to risk happiness again?*

"Evangeline, are you all right?"

She nodded, unable to speak, her eyes searching him for the truth. *Could he possibly love Mary?*

He stared ahead, seeming not to notice her. "We made plans before she left. Mary will be back in a month. We will marry then."

Dizziness overtook Evangeline. Her worst fear was coming true. "Here?"

"Yes, it only makes sense we should marry here."

Evangeline fought for composure. "You love her, then?"

"Like I said, Evangeline, I need a helpmate."

Relief. He didn't love Mary, but that admission wasn't a victory for Evangeline. "Have you told Cassandra?"

"No, not yet, but I will soon."

Evangeline wanted to tell someone. It couldn't be Cassandra; a mother had to accept her son's choice. But how could she keep this secret bottled up?

CHAPTER 3

Jeremiah and Minnie arrived at the mission in June. Both had become considerably grayer, and though approaching their seventies, they were as enthusiastic as school children and still in love. Jeremiah's ruddy face shone whenever he caught a glimpse of his wife. Minnie fussed at his constant attention.

Evangeline couldn't evade the way Jeremiah looked at Minnie, the way he held her hand. *This kind of happiness will never come to me,* she thought, *especially now that Mary is going to wed Elijah.* James had never showered her with that kind of attention. Oh, maybe when they were first married, but it didn't last.

The mission friends had so much to talk about that they kept on for hours around the supper table. Jeremiah's eyes shone. "Minnie and I have been busy with our church in Iowa and fund-raising for the Cheyenne River Mission, but we have missed being here with all of you."

"Morning Star...oh, I mean Sara!" Minnie laughed at her blunder. "I haven't gotten used to your name change. I will miss calling you Morning Star. What a beautiful girl you have become, and you've grown up so quickly."

"I'm going to Santee, Nebraska, this fall to study to be a teacher," Sara said.

"But you're so young! Fifteen now, right?"

"Yes, I'm ahead in my classes."

"A wonderful choice, then," Minnie said.

Sara beamed delightedly. The mission had been her home since the death of Red Bird, her grandmother; Sara had lost her parents when she was very young. Elijah and Cassandra had been the only ones left to care for Sara once Evangeline had left for Boston to marry James, and Minnie and Jeremiah had moved to Iowa. Sara had blossomed under their guidance.

Elijah had been abnormally quiet since Minnie and Jeremiah's arrival. Evangeline cast him furtive glances and fidgeted about the news he hadn't yet revealed. *Here it comes,* she thought. Evangeline stiffened with dread. Elijah cleared his throat.

"I haven't announced this yet, but Mary and I plan to be married in a month." Silence. Everyone at the table exchanged glances. Evangeline thought she heard someone moan—or was it her own? Cassandra turned pale, and Minnie's smile faded.

Cassandra's voice thickened. "A month?"

"Yes. Mary and I will make a good team. She has furthered her studies at Hampton, Virginia, in the past few years. She's now a superintendent of education and will be a valuable asset to our mission."

"I see." Cassandra stole a glimpse at Evangeline. "Sounds like a good business deal," she said as she left the table.

Jeremiah stirred. "Minnie and I should probably unpack."

"We should," Minnie agreed. "Evangeline, want to give me some help?" Minnie had been Evangeline's best friend and confidant seven years ago. Minnie had given her invaluable advice then. As they walked toward their cabin out of earshot, Minnie asked, "What's going on here, Evangeline? I always thought you and Elijah had some sort of connection."

"Oh, Minnie, I have made such a mess of things."

"I guess you have. Come on in. Explain everything to me." Minnie closed the cabin door and and Jeremiah excused himself while muttering that he was going to tend to the horses. Evangeline immediately burst into uncontrollable tears. She sobbed for some time before she was able to explain what had gone awry. Evangeline shared with Minnie all the details about James's death, her inconsolable grief, Cassandra and Sara's visit, her return to the mission, and rejecting Elijah's proposal. "You turned him down? Seven years ago, you would have jumped at that chance. What happened between then and now?"

"I'm afraid of being devastated again, of commitment, of pain."

"I can understand that. But some opportunities never come again. Do you still love him?"

"Still?"

"I know you better than you think. Remember when you were trying to decide between Elijah and James?"

"I do. What a silly girl I was then."

"Silly? No. Confused, yes."

"I do still care for Elijah a great deal, but I didn't know how much until he told me about Mary. Now it's too late. I can't believe I'm faced with the same dilemma again. When they marry, I won't be able to stay here." She dropped her head into her hands.

"Talk to Elijah and tell him the truth, once and for all."

"I can't do that. Elijah's an honorable man. He will never go back on his vow to Mary. Telling him the truth would complicate the situation."

"Do you think he loves Mary?"

"I don't believe so, but he wants a wife."

––––––

Evangeline avoided Elijah during the weekdays, but she still continued to accompany him on his Saturday services. Conversation had been difficult between them. This Saturday morning, Elijah asked Evangeline to be ready earlier than usual. He didn't explain why; Evangeline simply complied with his request and joined him in the buggy. *What was there to discuss, if not the wedding?* she thought.

"Evangeline, I can't help but notice that you appear to be very sad—so very different from your attitude when you first came. Are you feeling well?"

Evangeline knew she couldn't cover up her returning depression, weight loss, or the dark circles under her eyes. "I guess not. I was wrong to come back. I can't seem to get it right."

"It's Mary, isn't it?"

She nodded.

Elijah pulled the horses to a stop. "I asked you to be ready early for a reason. I have something to tell you," he said in a sobering tone. "I wanted you to be the first to know." He rested his arms on his knees and concentrated on the view ahead of him.

"Do you remember when I saw you in Boston?" Evangeline nodded. Elijah turned toward her. "It was very difficult to leave you behind...with James."

"Really!" Her luminous, green eyes met his. "It wasn't easy for me, either. I wanted to throw my arms around you, but felt I had no right to do so." Evangeline's face saddened.

"I didn't propose to you very well." Elijah slowly reached toward her, stroked her blonde, glistening hair, and looked toward the floor of the buggy. "I do care for you a great deal, Evangeline, and I want you to stay."

Evangeline melted under his touch. "You do care for me."

"I do. I always have."

"I care for you, too. But...but you're going to be Mary's husband."

"No, I'm not."

"What happened?"

"Mary wrote to me that she changed her mind."

"How could she possibly change her mind so fast?"

"I suppose she found someone who suited her better. To be honest with you, I don't think a marriage would have worked. She's not committed to the church like a pastor's wife should be."

"I agree."

"I'm sorry I was so pigheaded in the past," Elijah said, carefully placing his arms around her. I really thought it was

40

best for you to be with James."

"We *were* happy together and I missed him after he was gone."

"Does it bother you to talk about him? Should we avoid the subject?"

"It's important to talk. James will be with us in spirit for some time. We can't pretend he never existed."

"Will you marry me?" She couldn't believe he was asking her again. This time, there was no doubt in her mind. She slowly raised her hand and stroked his high cheekbones that displayed his Lakota blood.

"I will. I should have accepted the first time you asked. You have no idea what agony I have gone through."

"I haven't been happy, either," he admitted.

"I'm sorry we have hurt each other so needlessly."

"When do you want to announce our marriage—or do we announce our engagement?" Elijah became flustered. "I don't have a ring. What do we do about that?"

Evangeline glowed with the prospect of marriage. "Don't worry. We don't have to be formal about anything. I would like a wedding band, but an engagement ring is unnecessary, don't you think?"

"I suppose. Are we engaged?"

"Yes, we're engaged." She laid her head on his shoulder. "I think we should tell everyone at the mission. I can't keep this a secret."

Elijah laughed. "I hope I can concentrate on my sermon. Just don't look at me with those beautiful eyes of yours."

Evangeline grinned. "You like my eyes?"

"I like everything about you. Do you realize I haven't even kissed you?"

"A kiss would be nice to seal our engagement." She closed her eyes and lifted her face to his, just like a schoolgirl would. His kiss was warm and silky, not passionate, but she hadn't expected it to be. During the Saturday service, Evangeline could hardly contain the news that she and Elijah were finally engaged, but Elijah wanted to tell the family the news first.

————

Back at the mission, Elijah surprised everyone at the evening meal with the news that he and Mary had broken off their engagement. "But there's one more piece of news. Evangeline and I are getting married instead." Instantly, cheers went up from the crowded table. Sara leaned over to hug Evangeline.

"I've dreamed of this forever," Sara said. "You'll be living with us always." Evangeline warmed to her happiness and smiled, recalling the first time she had seen Sara—a child with full cheeks, downcast eyes, and neatly braided hair. She had always regretted leaving that child behind when she returned to Boston to marry James.

"When is the big day?" Cassandra reached across the table and squeezed Evangeline's hand.

"It depends on when Jeremiah can marry us," Elijah said.

Jeremiah beamed. "I would be happy to marry you whenever you want, even this evening!" But Minnie insisted they plan a ceremony.

"A simple wedding," Evangeline suggested.

Minnie smiled. "Just like I wanted?" she reminded them. "Glory be! We wouldn't have missed this for the world. Will your parents be able to come?"

"I don't think Mama is up to the trip just now."

"I want to be here for the wedding," Sara insisted.

"You shall be. We wouldn't be married without you." Evangeline reassured Sara with a wink. The rest of the dinner was filled with wedding talk, and Elijah eventually took hold of Evangeline's hand.

"Excuse us," he said, "but we have plans to make." As soon as they were outside, Elijah slipped his hand around her waist. "Let's talk about where we're going to live."

"Isn't there room in the old chapel?"

"All the available space has been taken for classrooms and the boarding students. I was thinking of our own house."

"A house! Isn't that a little extravagant for a pastor and his wife?" Evangeline asked.

"Not if we do most of the work ourselves. We can begin right away."

"What about money?"

"Oh, I have a little put away."

Evangeline decided to allow the money concerns to simmer. She knew she would have to tell him about the inheritance. James had always been evasive about his parents. She knew they had died when he was young, but after James's death she had learned of his father's wealth. With plenty of money to keep the mission going and to build a house, she wondered if Elijah would let her help.

Like an excited little boy, Elijah yanked her away from the mission. "Let's pick a spot for our house and we can talk about the wedding at the same time."

"I think you have a place picked out already," she teased him.

Elijah nodded. "I do, but I should give you a chance to choose, too."

"You probably know best. But I'm thinking it shouldn't be too far away from the church. Let me look this over. There, east of the church." She pointed to a spot for the house.

"Good girl. You're very close. Here, let me show you the dimensions." He stepped off the size of the house with her at his side.

"It's going to be a long time before our house will be ready. Where will we stay until then? None of the rooms in the addition are large enough for us."

"I was just going to have you move in with me." He blushed.

"What about the cabin where I used to stay? I know it's used for storage, but maybe I can clean it out. I have such good memories of my stay there."

"That's an idea. I'll take a look at it later."

Evangeline smiled at his exuberance. *Can this really be happening?* she asked herself. *Another chance at happiness? But what kind of marriage will we have together without romantic love?*

––––––

The sun rose in a yellow blaze on the Sunday wedding day. The ceremony was to be held in conjunction with the typical church service. Cheyenne River Mission hummed with activity.

Since Elijah and Evangeline's announcement, Cassandra had busied herself with wedding preparation. She found enough periwinkle material in the sewing cupboard for Evangeline's wedding dress. With Sara's help, she worked her sewing magic to make it into an elegant dress with a flowing skirt, long sleeves, with white lace at the collar and cuffs. For Sara, Evangeline's bridesmaid, Cassandra had ordered pale yellow material and lace. She crafted it into a frivolous dress with short sleeves and a gathered skirt. The best man, Sol, was selected with Sara's youth in mind; neither Evangeline nor Elijah wanted her to look too much out of place. They had no reason to worry, because Cassandra had styled Sara's dress to fit the occasion.

Cassandra was also hard at work in the kitchen. She baked three cake layers the day before, and had yet to decorate the cake on this cool morning of the wedding. She wanted to avoid the midday heat that would prevent the frosting from setting—a lesson she had learned in preparing Minnie's cake six Junes ago. Cassandra rose early to complete the cake and found Minnie already in the kitchen making sandwiches.

With so much help from her friends, all Evangeline needed to do this morning was to be ready before the nine o'clock service. During her ablutions, she thought back to her first wedding. Her mother had insisted on a fabulous affair with Victorian fanfare. Perhaps it was best her mother wasn't here to fuss that Evangeline's dress wasn't Boston's finest or that they lacked attendants. Evangeline slipped into her periwinkle gown, which flowed from bodice to floor like cool, gentle rain. A matching fascinator completed her ensemble. She shuddered upon remembering she had nearly lost Elijah to Mary. Now she felt certain that marrying Elijah was a part of the divine plan. She shook her head realizing how long it had taken to arrive at this point in her life.

By nine, the congregation had assembled in quiet anticipation of the ceremony. After a musical prelude, Sara appeared in the doorway. She glided down the aisle in her yellow dress, her dark braids twisted in an upswept style and carrying a nosegay of yellow and lavender coneflowers tied with a wide, white ribbon. Evangeline's smile lit the church as she entered, carrying a black Bible ornamented with waxy, white yucca flowers. She and Elijah joined hands at the altar. He grinned, and his dark, shining eyes caught Evangeline's for a moment.

Jeremiah smiled while he performed the entire ceremony. Having pronounced the bride and groom as husband and wife, the wedding party sat in the front pew. Jeremiah eased into the rest of the service, after which the wedding party led the congregation out of the church.

Elijah, arm in arm with Evangeline, led the group to the north side of the church. Evangeline stopped short and covered her open mouth with both hands. "What is this?" she gasped. Before her stood a new gazebo. The white paint was still fresh, and its fragrance commingled with that of the crackly prairie grass. "When and where did you make it? Why did I not see it before?"

He laughed at the success of his scheme. "We did our best to keep you from going over to this side of the church. We assembled it in pieces at Swift Bear's old camp, and last night at about midnight we brought it over and the men put it together as silently as we could. But before you enter it, we need to drive a few more nails. We were afraid you would catch on if we did too much pounding. This is your wedding gift from all of us."

Evangeline smiled at their expression of love. She sat and watched the men finish the gazebo. *A perfect wedding,* she mused to herself. *Simple, but full of love and the best of wishes.* She only hoped that she and Elijah would meet life's tests together, not letting the trials tear them apart.

Cassandra and Minnie nabbed a couple of the men to haul the kitchen table to the center of the gazebo. Then they placed the food on the table, including the three-tiered cake trimmed in delicate, lavender swirls atop white frosting. A small vase of fresh wildflowers sat atop the confection. As soon as the wedding cake emerged from the kitchen, Evangeline followed the women into the gazebo.

"Everything is beautiful, Cassandra. Thank you so much for all you've done."

"You are most welcome," said Cassandra. "I wanted to do something special for you and Elijah, and this is all I could come up with."

As the crowd drew closer to the gazebo, Minnie handed a knife tied with ribbon to Evangeline and Elijah. The crowd clapped as they cut the first slice of cake. The couple giggled when she fed him the first bite and swiped a dot of stray frosting from his nose.

Shortly thereafter, Alvina and Lily entered the gazebo and ceremoniously draped a red and white star quilt on the happy couple. Evangeline recognized the gesture as the highest compliment the Lakota could bestow on a person. She was humbled that she and Elijah had earned their respect, and thought back to her first day at the mission with the native children. She was scared to death, but her friends had told her to be patient. They were right. Over time, Evangeline had become comfortable with Lakota culture and had even earned their trust. However, Mary had shaken her to the core. She questioned Evangeline's motives for being at the mission, accusing her of trying to obliterate the Old Way. Much had happened since then, but now Evangeline was certain that she was needed here at the mission with Elijah. It was destiny.

"Oh, Elijah, this is all so extravagant!" Evangeline gushed.

Elijah smiled. "We can use this gazebo for every special occasion to come."

Evangeline's eyes warmed. "And there will be many." She hoped with all her heart and soul that she was right.

————

Several weeks after the wedding, Evangeline opened a letter from her mother. She had anticipated well-wishes, but her smile faded before she finished the first page. She resisted the urge to crumple it and toss it into the garbage. Her heart raced and her hand shook as she placed the scented stationery back into the crisp envelope. *Elijah must never read this,* she determined. What Maud had written would devastate him. At least Maud had the compassion not to send the newspaper clipping along with her letter.

What Evangeline had secretly feared had come to pass. She had hoped her marriage to a mixed-blood would not cause a scandal like it had for others who had married on the reservations. Missionary women sometimes married educated native men, and even though some of those marriages prospered, they almost always produced scandal. She had read newspapers that criticized mixed marriages. The comments were downright ugly and probably not even true.

How could people be so cruel? Elijah was a good man, much better than the ones who wrote the lies just to sell papers, she thought. Her trembling turned to anger. Just because her parents were prominent Boston citizens, someone had to bring them down with scandalous gossip. Maud had accepted Elijah and Sara when they had visited Boston before Evangeline had married James. Maud hadn't been worried about what her own friends would say, but now she was undoubtedly shunned from society. Maybe, then, her mother secretly had not approved of her daughter's marriage to a mixed-blood. Evangeline pushed that thought out of her mind and paced the room, trying her best to calm herself.

Elijah was on his way home. *Is this something I should keep from him?* she wondered. She couldn't decide what to do. They would be leaving for their honeymoon shortly, and she didn't want to spoil it with ugly gossip.

Later that evening while packing her belongings in satchels, Evangeline asked Elijah, "Are you sure we should be away from the mission this long?"

"Evangeline, I thought we agreed to have a honeymoon. Now that school's out for the summer, it's alright to take a break. Rest is good. Even Scripture says rest is necessary."

"I suppose you're right, but I don't know if we should go so far away. It took me years to get back here to you and the mission, and now I am leaving again."

"We'll be back," Elijah said with finality as he finished his packing in short order.

Evangeline's anxiety was returning. "How do you know? Maybe something will happen to us while we are gone. We might drown in the river, or the stagecoach could wreck."

"You are worrying needlessly."

"I know it's silly to worry. But I am so happy, I'm afraid

something will happen to ruin this new life we have finally begun." She thought of the letter she was keeping from him.

Elijah took her in his arms to reassure her. "Enough of this doubt," he said quietly. "Finish packing. Think of our leaving as a chance to be alone with no one to interfere. A pastor's life isn't his own. You will see that you are going to have to share me with everyone."

"I never thought of it that way," Evangeline admitted. "I am so thankful that Jeremiah was able to marry us. We did have a nice, simple wedding, didn't we?"

"Yes, we did. And I'm thankful that Jeremiah and Minnie decided to remain at the mission while we take our trip."

"It's so great to have them back again. I wish they would stay forever," Evangeline said. She regarded the older couple not only as mentors but also as second parents. She had often sought their consolation and advice.

"I like having them around, too. When we get back, maybe we can convince them to stay longer."

Evangeline gently broke free of Elijah's embrace, her worry and fear returning. "What if Minnie and Jeremiah need us while we are gone? What about Morning Star...I mean Sara?" Calling her friend by her new name was difficult for Evangeline. She had always loved the name Morning Star, which suited the young girl perfectly. Sara had been a bright star for both Evangeline and Elijah.

"Sara will be just fine with my mother and Minnie," Elijah reassured her.

"I'll have to admit that Cassandra has changed since her trip to Boston, and she seems quite fond of Sara."

"See, there's no need to worry." He gave her another hug before he turned to leave. "I'm going to go over some things with Jeremiah at the church. I'll be back."

Evangeline returned to her packing, wishing she had a few more stylish clothes to take along. She had reduced her wardrobe drastically when she had left Boston. *I'll just have to make do,* she told herself. She admonished herself for preferring to stay and enjoy the mission. She knew that wouldn't be fair to Elijah, who could never get away. Something about leaving the mission bothered her. The outside world intimidated her, and now the newspapers were spreading lies about their mixed marriage. What if Elijah picked up one of those newspapers? Evangeline closed the satchels, satisfied that she had everything she would need. They would leave in the morning to meet the train, and she was almost ready.

Evangeline left the cabin and went to the kitchen to help the women prepare supper. She would have liked a separate kitchen. She wanted to cook for her husband and talk with him privately. She longed for a house of their own, no matter how simple, but she had to be patient.

"What are you cooking for supper?" Elijah asked as he entered the kitchen an hour later.

"Your favorite—venison and potatoes," she told him, placing the gravy beside the potatoes on the table. The staff gathered at the table and waited for Elijah to say the evening prayer. After the final amen, Elijah reached for the venison steak and cut off a bite before dishing up his potatoes and gravy. Evangeline set aside her unhappiness about leaving. She was thankful to be once again surrounded by her friends. Never in all her imagination did she dream she would be back at the mission, reunited with everyone she loved.

"I, for one, am looking forward to our trip tomorrow," Elijah said.

Evangeline couldn't agree with Elijah wholeheartedly, so she attempted a change of subject. "I can't believe the railroad still hasn't reached this side of the Missouri River."

"We'll just have to take the stagecoach from Pierre and travel down the Fort Pierre-Deadwood trail, just like everyone else who wants to go out West," Elijah said.

"Mention my name," Minnie said, "and maybe they'll treat you extra nice when you get out on the trail. I wonder if anyone will remember me," she laughed. Minnie had freighted the trail with her first husband, Abe. After he had died, she had worked on the trail by herself until it had become too difficult for her. Then she came to the mission and found employment as a cook.

Jeremiah took a last forkful of venison, saying, "We wish you the best. Don't worry about a thing while you're gone."

After Evangeline helped with the dishes, they all retired to their rooms. She tossed and turned in bed that night, worrying about leaving everyone behind. The night seemed endless, but finally the sun peeked through their east window and splashed its light across the bedcovers. She left the bed to quietly begin the coffee and care for the chickens. When she returned to the kitchen, Elijah was already frying pancakes. "I thought we could breakfast alone before everyone gets up," he said.

"You're such a good husband," she said after they kissed. "I didn't know you could cook. I suppose I will learn a lot about you as the years go by." She smiled at her musing. He dished three fluffy cakes on a plate and motioned for her to sit after she poured the fragrant coffee. She sipped at the rich, dark brew, savoring its satisfying lift. She watched her husband, hardly believing that they were enjoying such simple moments together. If only time could stand still, preserving this moment forever.

"You look a little tired this morning, Evangeline. Didn't you sleep well?"

"No, not really. I wish I could settle down and not be so anxious about everything."

"James's death turned your world upside down." Elijah helped himself to another pancake and smeared it with freshly churned butter. "It will take time. Just try to be patient, and I'm sure you will feel better after a while." He placed his hand on hers.

"I sure hope so. I want to be me again—not this jumpy, nervous person I have become."

"This trip will do you some good. I'll start packing the buckboard while you clean up the kitchen," Elijah said after his last bite. He placed his dishes in the dishpan and left.

A slight tear tickled Evangeline's cheeks as she joined Elijah to load their luggage into the buggy. They were startled by a voice that came from behind them.

"You two sure are up early." It was Minnie, walking toward the kitchen.

"There's pancake batter on the counter," Evangeline said. "Elijah made us breakfast. Oh, yes, I took care of the chickens, but I guess you can see that."

"Well, isn't that nice. Thanks. I could use that leftover batter." But before Minnie had gone the rest of the way to the kitchen, Cassandra and Sara gathered around the buckboard to wish the honeymooners a safe trip. Jeremiah, who was to drive the buckboard to the boat landing and back, was inspecting the rig with Elijah one last time. Evangeline hugged each and every one of them with promises to return soon.

"Now, don't you worry," Jeremiah reminded her, wiping a tear from her cheek before helping her climb into the buggy.

"Don't mind me," Evangeline said. She scooted closer to Elijah when Jeremiah launched the buggy across the grassy plain, and the couple bid their final farewell to their friends. The women shouted their best wishes and waved the happy couple out of sight.

"Are you feeling better about making the trip?" Elijah asked Evangeline.

"Now that we have actually left, yes, I do feel better. It's just that after James died, I learned how fragile and precious life is. Happiness can end in the blink of an eye. It makes me feel so insecure and afraid." Elijah reached for her hand and held it.

After some time, they reached the boat landing where a stern-wheeler was waiting. Jeremiah deposited them and their luggage, said one more emotional good-bye, and drove back the way they had come with the assurance that there would be some means of transportation for them in about two weeks' time.

A thick, ghostly fog draped the trees and the riverbank as they boarded the boat with cowboys, homesteaders, and reservation Indians, all heading downstream. Once they settled, Elijah and Evangeline relaxed to the rhythm of the lapping water as they glided by the hazy hills.

"Every year this country changes," Elijah reflected. "This wild, free land is being scrutinized by more and more people on the move, people looking for ways to turn it into profit."

"How to do mean?"

"There's more cattle along the river now than when you were here before." He looked over his shoulder and whispered, "The cattlemen are in it to make money, and the homesteaders look for land to farm."

"More people means increased attendance at the church, right?"

"No, not really. A few cowboys come by from time to time, but most don't have families, or they don't bring them."

"I see what you mean," she said. The fog began to lift, revealing the herds grazing the hillsides along the river. "Do all the cattle belong to one ranch?"

"No, they belong to different ranches, but without fences, they mix together eventually. Each ranch brands its cattle with different markings to show ownership."

"Brands?"

"They use hot irons to burn particular shapes or initials into the animal's hide."

She scrunched up her nose. "Oh, doesn't that hurt? It must smell terrible, too."

"Probably some, if it goes too deep. The critter lets out a bellow. And you're right, the stench of burning hair sticks to you until you scrub it off."

She shuddered at the thought. "But don't they become mixed up? The cattle, I mean?"

"They do, but they have roundups twice a year to separate the cattle. They brand the calves in the spring, and in the fall some of the younger steers are sorted out and sent to markets in the East—"

"By train," she interrupted. "I have seen cattle being loaded and unloaded in Pierre. How do you know all this?"

"Some of my Indian friends have run cattle together on the open range. Others have built up small ranches on land that was allotted to them. I used to help them out some when I was a little younger. I don't have much time for that anymore."

"Would you rather be a rancher?" she teased.

"No, I would rather round up souls for the Lord," he said with a grin.

When they arrived in Pierre, Elijah immediatly checked the stagecoach schedule for Rapid City. After studying it for a while, he said, "Looks like we will have to spend the night here and catch the stage in the morning." They had no difficulty finding lodging, for the city had grown considerably since Evangeline had first walked its streets. "I'm hungry. Let's check in and then find some supper," Elijah suggested.

"I could eat something, too. But before we do, I'd like to go visit the general store. As soon as the weather turns cold, Minnie and Cassandra will be looking for quilting materials."

"Don't you usually use scraps for that?"

"We do, but I thought it would be nice to have some extra lengths of material. Besides, they become so excited over pieces of cloth."

"Do they?"

"Oh, yes. Their eyes light up, and you know they are already thinking about their designs. That's quite a skill, something I haven't yet acquired."

"I'm sure there's more than one store around here. I'm ready if you are."

Evangeline had no difficulty locating a store stocked with fabrics. Evangeline walked back and forth between the bolts of cloth. Finding the patterns she thought Cassandra and Minnie would appreciate was going to take much longer than she had imagined.

"I didn't realize this task would be so hard. I think it's best to choose equal amounts of light and dark. Cassandra loves contrast. Oh, is that your stomach rumbling, dear?"

Elijah nodded.

"I'm sorry I'm taking so long. As soon as the clerk cuts the lengths, we'll go find supper."

Half an hour later, a waiter escorted Evangeline and Elijah to a quiet table in the corner of the dining room. They ordered the house special and lingered over coffee.

"Tomorrow will be quite an adventure. Are you up to it?" Elijah asked, those dark eyes showing his concern.

"I am," Evangeline said, smiling warmly. "I was being silly. Please forgive me. I should know that as long as I'm with you, everything will be just fine."

CHAPTER 4

The next morning, Elijah and Evangeline arrived at the stagecoach stop to board for Rapid City. She frowned inwardly at the run-down stagecoach and hoped it would be able to make another trip. It seemed like everything out here had seen better days. Evangeline had never ridden in one before and thought it was a queer contraption. She held the skirt of her simple, gray dress and stepped into it. The driver hefted their luggage to the top of the coach and fastened it with rope. The inside of the coach was already crowded with four other people. Luckily, there was still room for her and Elijah.

In such confinement, Evangeline thought it was best that Elijah introduce them to the people with whom they would share a number of hours. She nudged him with her elbow and whispered for him to initiate the introductions. A distinguished gentleman and two ladies sat across from them. Another prosperous-looking man sat to the left of Elijah.

Elijah hesitantly began. "Hello, I'm Elijah Fletcher, pastor from Cheyenne River Mission. And this is my wife, Evangeline." He extended his hand first to the man sitting near him, then to the man across from him, and finally bowed his head toward the ladies. Evangeline nodded her perky, plum hat with matching feathers.

"Pleased to meet y'all," the distinguished man wearing a black Stetson hat drawled. "I'm Tex McMurray. No need to tell y'all where I'm from," he laughed. "This here's my daughter, Netty," he said, gesturing toward the woman beside him. Netty was dressed in a stylish, blue traveling suit. Evangeline guessed she was not quite twenty.

"Call me Kat," said the lady seated on the other side of Tex, dressed in flamboyant red, the same shade as her painted fingernails and lips. "I'm on my way to Deadwood." She adjusted her black hat, which matched the trim on her dress.

The tall, lean, middle-aged man at Elijah's left removed his brown bowler hat. "I'm Jet Black. I'm going to Deadwood, too." He stroked his black, wavy hair and stared at Kat from across the stage. Her hat's red feathers danced as the stagecoach lurched forward. It wasn't long before the stage, pulled by six sleek, black horses, began to climb the river breaks onto the prairie above.

Evangeline looked out the open window to see the Missouri River unfurling like a glistening ribbon in the distance. Except for their stage, all evidence of civilization soon disappeared, and she turned her attention to her fellow passengers.

Kat whipped out a deck of cards from her small, black purse and shuffled them with little effort. "Anyone want to play a game of poker with me? This trip gets long and tiresome. I've learned to bring some entertainment along."

Everyone declined except Jet. "Sure, go ahead and deal," he said. "Name your game."

"Three-card high," Kat announced.

Tex watched them for a while, then shook his head. "I've learned to give up cards. I've lost too much at the tables in the past. This trip is purely for business. Netty's going to make sure of that." He looked at his daughter and patted her hand.

"Where are you heading—if I may?" Elijah asked.

"I've been in Pierre looking at the cattle prospects, and now we're on our way to Belle Fourche. Good cattle country there. We have about a thousand head near the Belle Fourche River. I used to bring cattle up the Western Cattle Trail through Belle Fourche and on to Fort Buford. Those were rough and rugged days. Have y'all been to the Belle Fourche country?"

"No," Elijah said.

Jet shook his head vigorously.

"I have a few stories I could tell about them days." He slid his hat toward the back of his head and rubbed the crease on his forehead. "The railroad changed all that. I'm getting a little old to be sitting on a saddle for days at a time, anyway. We can bring in the cattle by train now, but it also brings settlers. I'm meeting my son in Belle Fourche. We're having trouble with rustlers, and I've come back to meet with some of the cattlemen to come up with a plan to stop those ornery thieves. I also need more grazing range. The homesteaders are moving in and taking the open ranges. Now, where did y'all say you're from?"

"The Cheyenne River Reservation. I've lived there all my life. I guess I don't know much outside the reservation. My wife's from Boston."

"Boston? Can't say I've ever been there. I've spent all my years here in the West, mostly in Texas and on the old cattle trails. When I was young, I saw the likes of San Antonio, Dodge City, Sedalia, and Ogallala, to name a few. I hardly had a dime in my pocket then. I found some grazing land west of your reservation. I'm going to talk to my son about it."

"Some of my Indian friends have small ranches along the Cheyenne River," Elijah said. "Herds sometimes travel over to the reservation from nearby cattle ranches."

"Bet they have conniptions about that! It appears to be good cattle country. How about the winters?"

"There are miles and miles of good grass. The winters can be hard on livestock, though. "

Kat interrupted. "Sure you don't want to join us?" She snapped the cards as she dealt them. To liven up the card game, Kat pulled coins from her purse. Jet reached in his pocket.

"No, thanks," Elijah said, turning his attention back to Tex.

Evangeline was captivated by Kat's dexterity. She watched as each snap of a card dictated an ensuing bet. She still kept an ear to what Elijah and Tex were saying.

"Hard winters, you say?" Tex moved his hat back to his brow. "I know about them. I had cattle on the northern ranges in 1886 when the big blizzard hit. Lost nearly half my stock. Chased a lot of the big operators out of the country. Shoot! I managed to hang on."

Evangeline imagined all those cattle dying in a snowstorm. *What a tragic waste!* she thought. *Didn't these men know how to care for their stock animals?*

All of a sudden, the driver yelled, "Yip-yip-yip-yi-yi!"

Evangeline's heart began to race at the sound. She could not discern what would warrant such a fuss. She was sure it couldn't be Indians; they were peacefully settled on the reservations. She looked at Elijah for an explanation. Elijah's eyes were on Tex, who craned his neck to see out the window.

"Looks like a stop up ahead," Tex reported. "We'll be changing horses here. The driver was just letting the stage tenders know that we are on our way in."

Such commotion for a simple stop, Evangeline thought.

The stagecoach descended a hill and crossed a makeshift bridge over a creek. A crude shanty served as a stage stop, and Evangeline was eager to get out and stretch. When the stage came to an abrupt halt, the driver informed the party not to stray too far; this stop would be brief.

"They don't offer anything to eat here, but the next stop will," Kat explained as she gathered her cards and the greater share of the coins.

When Evangeline got off the stage she took the opportunity to speak to Netty, whose complexion seemed too fair to have spent as much time on the trail as her father. "Have you been out West before?"

"Not this far north. Daddy says the West is pretty much settled, so he brought me along this time. I like to travel and see some of the country."

"We're on our way to Denver. Have you ever been there?"

"Yes, I went when I was much younger. I don't remember much of it, but my mother really liked it. We stayed in a beautiful hotel, and the food was so good."

"Your mother stayed behind this time?" Evangeline asked, somewhat concerned that she was prying.

"My mother passed away several years ago."

"I'm sorry to hear that."

"Thank you, but I'm getting used to it. I still think about her every day. Do you have relatives in Denver?"

"No, we decided to spend our honeymoon in Denver and see a Wild West show while we're there."

"I see. Congratulations on your marriage."

"Thank you. Well, I suppose we should tend to our needs before we have to get back on that stage," Evangeline suggested.

Within the half hour, the driver yelled again, announcing to his passengers it was time to leave. Another stage had pulled into the station from the other direction just as they embarked. The party assumed the same spots in the stage and settled in as best they could. "How long does it usually take to get to Rapid City?" Elijah asked Tex.

Kat interjected, "It takes about two days with a night stop—unless it rains, and then who knows how long it could take." Evangeline checked the sky for clouds, but she didn't see any. Rain would be unlikely this time of year. She really didn't want this adventure to be prolonged more than necessary.

Kat had retrieved a mirror from her purse and applied more lipstick and primped her hair. Evangeline wilted from the heat and dust and wind entering through the open windows and was too weary to worry about her looks. She wondered what Kat did for a living. She knew by Kat's appearance and actions that she didn't lead a simple, common life.

"Want to play some more cards, Jet?" Kat asked.

"No, I think I'll try for a nap." Jet placed his hat over his face and folded his arms.

Occasionally, they passed wagons and other conveyances on the wide, rugged trail, but regardless of traffic, they maintained a steady speed.

"There are no freighters on the trail anymore?" Evangeline asked Tex, thinking of Minnie and Abe's freighting days.

"No, the railroad came up from Nebraska to Rapid City in 1886. It nearly ended freighting on this trail. Oh, once in a while, y'all will see people hauling freight, but it's nothing like it used to be. They say the freighters and their wagons stretched out for miles in those early days. I wasn't on this trail in its heyday, but I seen plenty of freighters in other parts of the West."

Eventually, the conversation dwindled and the rocking and rolling of the stage lolled almost everyone into a sleepy state, regardless of heads bobbing at every bump. The lurching prevented Evangeline from napping and continued to upset her stomach. As they neared the next station, Elijah took hold of Evangeline's arm and asked if she were hungry.

"No, not really," she replied. "All the bouncing around in this coach has made me queasy. I think maybe coffee will do me just fine."

"How's the grub at this place, Kat?" Tex asked when they rolled to a halt.

"No guarantees, but it's better than it used to be. Travelers would always complain about the stale bacon they had to eat at the stage stops on their way to Deadwood."

The station dining area wasn't crowded and the passengers had no trouble finding a spot at a long table that could accommodate their number. Evangeline glanced around and saw that the place was fairly clean, but an odor of stale grease permeated the air. A rather disheveled woman served them meat covered with fatty gravy, boiled potatoes, and a few vegetables from a nearby garden. The black coffee was bitter, but Evangeline poured cream and sugar to dilute its bite. She drank it with a piece of coarse bread, hoping to revive her stamina.

The driver gave them about forty minutes before hustling them back onto the stagecoach. About a mile down the road, conversation ceased. Most in the party closed their eyes and slept the best they could, bobbing in rhythm to the jolting trail. By nightfall, they had approached the Cheyenne River breaks, and the party was reawakening.

"Sometimes crossing this river can be treacherous, especially after a good rain or snow melt," Kat said through a stifled yawn.

"We shouldn't have any problem," Tex said, "unless it rained upriver somewhere."

Evangeline relaxed at his reassurance and enjoyed the changing view. Even with darkness approaching, she thought the river breaks and the way the cedar trees covered the hillsides were rather pretty. It was a nice change from the stretch of prairie over which they had traveled. The driver followed the ridge above the river until heading downward toward the pebbled bottom of the Cheyenne.

Tex strained to look out the window. "Let's see if the men on the other side mark out the crossings with signal lights."

Evangeline felt the steep decline to the river bottom and heard the grinding of the brake. She grabbed the edge of her seat in alarm, fearful that they would descend too fast. When they reached the bottom, Evangeline poked her head out the window and saw faint lights twinkling in the distance.

"There, I see them," she said.

"Sure 'nuff," Tex agreed.

The driver and his messenger approached the river cautiously, stopped the stage, and descended from their perch. They checked the crossing marked by the signal lights and came over to the door of the coach. They seemed determined.

"The river looks rather deep. I think we can cross, but don't be surprised if water comes in the coach. Be prepared," the driver warned.

"Oh, my," Evangeline gasped involuntarily.

"I've been here when the water was so deep that they had to take us across in a scow. You might want to raise your feet off the floor," Kat advised.

They heard the driver urging the unwilling horses forward. Evangeline hung on tightly and put her feet on the opposing seat, fearing the worst. The stage seemed to tip to one side, and she heard the horses thrashing in the water. She closed her eyes and sent up a silent prayer. The driver cursed the horses onward; stopping midstream would be disastrous.

Evangeline stared at Elijah in fright. He held her hand, and they prayed for the best. All of a sudden, water poured into the coach, rising to the edge of her seat. Finally, she felt the horses lifting the coach upon the riverbank. The water stopped rising, but the fringes of her skirt were soaking wet. As soon as the stage was pulled to safety, the passengers cheered and opened the doors for the water to escape.

"Mrs. Fletcher, how did you like your first day on the trail?" Tex asked, laughing as she stepped down from the coach at the stage station.

"I had no idea riding in a stagecoach would be so adventuresome," was all she managed to say. She saw that Netty and Kat had also gotten wet, but they seemed not to be too perturbed by the inconveniences of frontier travel.

"I'm starving," Kat announced. "Let's find something to eat."

They entered the dimly lit eating area to find a number of rough-looking characters crowded around the tables. These strangers were apparently brought by other stages that had pulled in for the night. Evangeline hadn't eaten much all day, and she knew she had to put something in her stomach. Her furtive glances toward the food on the table confirmed her suspicions of an ill-prepared meal. She spooned canned tomatoes into a sauce dish and ate a few mashed potatoes. The meat appeared questionable, so she left it for someone else to consume.

After they had eaten, Evangeline nervously inspected their sleeping accommodations. She was used to the finest hotels and had no idea what she would find at this rustic establishment.

"Be grateful you won't have to sleep with a stranger,"

Elijah said when he saw her scrutinizing the accommodations with a frown.

"A stranger?"

Elijah shrugged. "Sometimes there are simply not enough private rooms or beds, so people just have to double up and make the best of a situation."

"I simply wouldn't sleep a wink," she admitted as she inspected the bedding. "I doubt this bedding has been washed." Wrinkling her nose, she lifted the mattress to look for bedbugs. She had heard that bedbugs, lice, and fleas infest hotels, and she shuddered at that thought. "I brought along an extra sheet, just in case." She pulled it out of her satchel and spread it on the bed.

Kat knocked at the door. "I'm afraid Netty and I have to share a room with you." She surveyed the room. "The three of us will share a bed, and Elijah will have to sleep elsewhere."

"This small bed?" Evangeline asked, incredulous.

Without complaint, Elijah settled on the floor and wrapped himself in Evangeline's spare sheet.

At least, she thought, *I can sleep in the same room with my husband.* Resigning to fate, Evangeline slept sandwiched between Kat and Netty, barely able to breathe.

––––––

The next morning, after a simple breakfast, the sleepy traveling companions went outside to board the stage once again. They expected to see the horses harnessed and ready to go, but there seemed to be some confusion. Kat, Evangeline, and Netty went back inside to wait while the men stood around watching the driver help hitch up the team.

"Why the delay?" Elijah asked Tex.

"I don't know. There seems to be a problem harnessing the team."

After some time, the stage was ready to roll, and the travelers climbed inside. The stagecoach tipped and groaned during the steep, uphill climb out of the river bottom. Evangeline released her hold on the seat and sighed with relief as they made it to the top without mishap. At last, they were out on the flat. She was just relaxing and closing her eyes when another stage pulled up beside them so closely that she could have reached through the window and touched its side.

Elijah drew back against his seat. "What's going on?"

Tex looked out the window. "The drivers are passing a bottle back and forth between them. Well, I'm fit to be tied!"

"They're drunk," Kat said with a frown.

"But alcohol isn't allowed on the reservation," Elijah protested.

"That doesn't make any difference," Kat said.

Jet became alarmed. "He's going to turn this stage over and kill us all!"

Evangeline braced herself again. "What should we do?"

"Hang on tight until the next stage stop. We'll report him and demand a new driver," Tex suggested, holding Netty's hand tightly.

"That's if he doesn't dump us out on the prairie first," Elijah reminded them in a huff.

The stages parted company and raced until the other one surged ahead. They heard laughter and cursing until finally their stage slowed to a normal pace. The next eight or nine miles seemed endless to the anxious passengers. Luckily, this length of the trail was relatively flat, which meant less danger before arriving at the stop to change horses.

When they reached the next station, Tex hastily jumped out to apprehend the driver and his messenger. He grabbed the driver by his shirt collar and interrogated him while the others stood back and watched. The two employees slunk away when Tex got through lecturing them.

Tex rejoined his fellow passengers and said, "Both reeked of whiskey. How did they think they would get away with drinking? Ordinarily, the stage lines watch out for passengers' safety."

A new driver took up the reins with fresh horses and they departed. Confident that this leg of the journey was in good hands, Tex drew Jet and Kat into his conversation. Evangeline guessed that his curiosity was getting the best of him by now.

"How long have you been in Deadwood, Kat?" Tex asked.

"Let me think on that one a minute. Hmm . . . I guess it's been about seventeen years. I came around 1880 when I was just a young teenager and stayed ever since."

"And you, Jet, have you been there long?"

Jet, seemingly startled by the question, replied, "Just a couple of years. I originally came from Cheyenne. I'm a ... tailor by trade."

"That's good to know. So if I need a new suit, you're the man for the job?" Tex kidded him.

"Sure, that's what I do best." Jet flashed a rare smile.

"Do you have a family?"

"No." Jet turned his hat brim around with his hand. "I'm not the settling-down type, I guess."

70

Tex shifted his attention to Evangeline and Elijah. "Netty tells me you two are headed to Denver?"

"That's our plan," Elijah replied.

"Denver's an interesting place, but so is Rapid City. It's on the edge of the Black Hills." Tex pointed westward. "We'll see it over yonder soon."

"We haven't been to Rapid City, either," Elijah said.

"Do you have a place to stay when we get there?" Tex asked.

"No, do you have any recommendations?" Evangeline responded rather wearily.

"We like the International Hotel. Why don't y'all get a room there? We four will have supper together." Tex turned to Kat and Jet. "Will you be staying over, too?"

"No, I plan to go on to Deadwood." Kat was dealing herself a hand of solitaire.

"Same," Jet muttered.

"What a shame. It would be great if we all could eat together and get to know one another over a good meal and a glass of wine," Tex said.

Netty interrupted him, pointing. "Look, Father. Is that the Black Hills in the distance?"

"Yeah, it sure is."

Evangeline peered out the window and saw that the far hills deserved their name. In the distance, they appeared dark against the blue sky. Her spirits lifted, knowing they would soon enjoy a fine meal, pleasant accommodations, and hopefully a good night's sleep, all thanks to Tex.

After a few more stops to change horses, and one more stop for their noon meal, the coach pulled into Rapid City, a bustling town on the edge of the Black Hills. The driver pulled the stage to a stop at the International Hotel, where the passengers unceremoniously parted ways. Kat and Jet left to board the stage to Deadwood. Evangeline, Elijah, Tex, and Netty went inside the hotel to check in.

A porch with repetitive arches and a second-story balcony added some interest to the otherwise plain building. However, the elegant interior surprised Elijah and Evangeline. Tasteful cabbage rose, floral wallpaper, and furniture upholstered in rich greens added an aura of Victorian opulence. As Elijah signed the guest register, the driver of the stage rushed into the hotel carrying a small object. He approached Evangeline.

"Is this yours? I found it in the stage."

"No, I believe it belongs to Kat, the lady who took the stage to Deadwood," Evangeline said. "She took it out of her purse when we were in the stage. Has she left already?"

"Long gone." He waved his hand. "Just keep it. I don't want to bother with it."

"Oh, alright." When the driver left, she turned it over in her hand and recognized it as a powder compact—an expensive one. On the silver front was a hand-painted lady dressed in dark pink. It held the powder and puff, but an additional compartment held a picture of Kat, another woman, and a child. *Gosh,* she thought to herself. *I must get this back to Kat. This photograph undoubtedly means something to her.*

"What do you have there?" said Elijah, having just checked them into the hotel.

"The driver found it. It's Kat's, and I don't even know her last name. We should get this to her." They decided to spend part of the next morning investigating Kat's whereabouts as they went to their room at the top of the stairs.

"Oh, this is nice," Evangeline remarked when they stepped through the door. "I do enjoy nicely decorated hotel rooms." Her eyes feasted on the delicate rosebud wallpaper and matching red bedspread. She sat on the bed, testing the springs. "This isn't bad either. I'll unpack a few things and let the wrinkles hang out of them before morning. But first, I am going to bathe and change clothes before dining. If you don't want to wait around, go and see some of the town."

"I might take a short walk to look for a newspaper and catch up on the area news. See you after a while."

As soon as he left, Evangeline suddenly reconsidered what he had said. *A newspaper?* She paced the room in worry, hoping with all her might that there wasn't anything about them in the papers that would ruin their vacation. She laid out something more frivolous than the gray traveling suit she had been wearing the last two days. By the time Elijah returned, she had bathed and changed into a coral frock trimmed in white lace.

"I saw Tex and Netty in the lobby. I told them we would join them in a few minutes," Elijah said as he tossed the newspaper on a side table.

"Did you find anything interesting in the newspaper?"

"No, not really. It's mostly about the growing area and mining activity."

Evangeline sighed with relief, and her spirits lifted. "I'm ready."

"You look as fresh as a flower. I like your long hair." He kissed her loose, blonde tresses lightly. His compliment made her skin tingle. "Let me wash up a little, and then we'll go to dinner."

The happy couple came downstairs to find Tex and his daughter seated in two lounge chairs. Netty looked charming in her pale lavender dress. Tex had removed his hat for dining, revealing a handsomely rugged face tanned from hours in the wind and sun. His thinning hair was streaked with gray. "Ready for a tasty meal?" he asked them.

"You bet," Elijah answered.

"What about you, Evangeline?" Tex turned toward her.

"Yes, most definitely."

Tex led them toward the dining room, which was filling fast with guests. The foursome found a table near the window overlooking a busy street. A waitress dressed in a crisp, white-and-gray uniform with a perky, matching hat welcomed them and passed out menus.

"What do you recommend?" Tex asked her with a sly wink.

"Oh, everything is good here." She blushed and smiled.

"How about the steaks? Are they tender?" Tex asked unabashedly.

"Usually they are. Shall I order you one?"

"That's what I want. Make it medium well."

Elijah also ordered a steak. Evangeline and Netty perused the menu before settling on freshly caught fish.

"Oh, and bring us each a glass of wine," Tex quickly added.

"Thank you, but not for Evangeline and me. Coffee will be just fine," Elijah said.

"Sorry, I forgot. You probably don't drink anything fermented."

"Only during communion," Evangeline explained. "Thanks anyway, Tex, for treating us to the meal."

"You're most welcome. I have been thinking that the next time I come to western Dakota, I'm going to look you two up for a visit. The lawmakers in your fair state are trying to open up the reservation land and lease it to the cattlemen for grazing. They haven't passed anything yet, but I'll bet they're fixing to. I'd like to learn what it looks like out your way."

"Stop by. We aren't planning on going anywhere after we return from our honeymoon," Elijah said. The waitress approached their table balancing two glasses of red wine and two cups of coffee on a wooden tray. She placed a sparkling glass of ruby red wine in front of Tex, another beside Netty, and the coffees by Elijah and Evangeline. After she left the table, Tex raised his glass in a toast. "May we meet again," he said as they clinked the cups and the glasses together.

CHAPTER 5

Kat and Jet boarded the final stage of the day to Deadwood. She could have spent the night in Rapid City, but she wanted to get home. The trip had reminded her how much she dreaded traveling in a stagecoach. But before she claimed her seat inside, she checked to make sure the rattan birdcage she had purchased in Cleveland had made it on.

The stage filled to capacity and none of the passengers did much talking, which was fine with her. She had tired of chit chat. She once again sat across from Jet, but this time she paid him little heed. She wondered to herself why she hadn't seen him around Deadwood. It wasn't that big of a town, and in two years time she would have bumped into Jet somewhere! She had no call to visit the tailor shop, but surely he must come out to eat a meal or visit one of the saloons. Not that she had any particular interest in him other than he was rather tall, dark, and handsome, but it just seemed odd to her that she hadn't seen him before this trip.

Kat pulled her shawl around her, tilted her head back and closed her eyes, recalling the past few weeks while she had been away. Once a year, she made it a point to visit her sister in Cleveland. That was the only family she had, and she didn't want to lose the connection. Life could be lonely—that she knew well. Her sister had one little girl who she was rearing by herself. Her husband left her before the child had even been born. Kat had tried to convince Annabelle to return with her to Deadwood, but she would not leave Cleveland and the old family home. Maybe someday Annabelle would change her mind or maybe Kat should consider moving to Cleveland, she thought to herself. But no, she liked the Black Hills. No one there cared about a person's past or livelihood.

After several hours the coach pulled up to the Deadwood hotel. Kat had slept most of the way. When she awoke, she worked the kinks out of her neck before she got down from the stage. She gazed around the town, noticing that Deadwood hadn't changed since she left. Not that she was expecting it to, but it had changed since its early days. Fires had leveled the ramshackle buildings years ago, and brick structures had replaced them. Deadwood was almost respectable now, although there was plenty of action if one was willing to look for it.

Kat left her luggage at the hotel and wandered down to the Birdcage Saloon, carrying her new birdcage. It wasn't quite midnight yet and business there would still be going strong. She reached in her purse for the compact to check her face, but the compact wasn't there. *What could I have done with it,* she fretted to herself while rummaging around inside her purse. *Oh no! I probably left it on the stage!*

"Hello, Kat, glad you're back," greeted a dealer at one of the tables when she entered the saloon. "See you bought a new birdcage. Are you getting another bird?"

"Hi there, Jake, I'm happy to be back, too. You know how I like birdcages, but no, I don't think I'll get another bird just yet." She glanced around her establishment. "How are my birds?" she asked as she walked toward her parrots Marley and Scrooge.

"They're alive," Jake said.

Clem, the main bartender, scratched his balding head. "The cages need some cleaning, though. No one liked that job."

Kat chuckled. "I suppose not."

"How was Cleveland?" Clem asked while Jennie, the barmaid, waited for him to fill her tray. She tapped her feet impatiently.

Jennie smiled, "Hi, Kat. So glad you're back."

"Nice to be back. Cleveland is one busy place. My sister Annabelle and niece seem to be doing well, too. I would show you a recent picture of them, but I lost my compact. Annabelle gave it to me as a gift before I left. It had a place for a picture. It just makes me sick that I lost it."

Jennie commiserated, "Oh, that's too bad, Kat. Did you do some shopping while you were in Cleveland?"

"I did. Tomorrow, I'll show you some of the new clothes I bought. They have nothing as stylish in these parts."

"That's for sure," Jennie said, frowning as she lifted the tray full of drinks.

"How's business been since I have been gone?" Kat asked Clem.

"It's been about steady," he said wiping a glass. "No major bar room fights either. All in all, it's been pretty calm."

"That's good news. I just thought I'd stop by before I go home. I'll sleep easier knowing everything is okay. By the way, I brought you all something back from Cleveland."

Clem laughed at the thought. "Is it a new bar apron?"

She snapped her fingers at the idea. "No, but I wish I'd thought of that. Guess you'll have to wait and see."

Jennie returned for another tray of drinks. "I hope it's something fashionable. Then I can tell everyone it's from Cleveland."

"Oh, you'll like it, I'm sure. Thanks for watching the place for me while I was gone. I need one more favor though."

"You need a ride home?" Clem asked.

"If you don't mind. We'll have to stop at the hotel and pick up my luggage first."

"No problem. My buggy is out back. I'll pick you up in front."

Kat turned to her other employees and waved. "I'll see you later tomorrow," Kat said as she neared the door.

––––––

The next afternoon, Kat came to work carrying the gifts she had purchased in Cleveland for her faithful employees. She had wrapped them to make the gift giving a little more festive.

Jake and Clem opened up fancy new gold cuff links, and Jennie tore at her package tied with purple ribbon, opened it, and pulled out a high fashion frock the color of topaz.

"Oh, I love it!" Jennie exclaimed. "But it must have cost a fortune." She held the dress up to herself and turned toward

Kat.

"You're worth every penny."

"Thanks. I can't wait to wear it."

"Hope it fits. Go try it on."

"All right. I'll be back in a minute." Jennie dashed up the stairs.

Kat sat down at a table and absently shuffled a deck of cards. In a short time, Jennie came down the stairs in her new dress. "It fits perfectly. Now I have an excuse to buy a matching hat."

"You look great. I knew you would. Nothing like a new dress to lift one's spirits."

"Why do you say that?" Jennie asked her. "Haven't I seemed happy and in good spirits to you?"

"Oh, sure you have. Maybe it's me that needs to have my spirits lifted. I thought the trip to Cleveland would help. It did for a while, but I feel like I'm in a rut. My life's going nowhere."

"You're one of my best friends, but maybe you should consider moving to Cleveland to be close to your sister. We'd miss you, of course."

"I've thought about that a lot lately, but I don't know if it would help. My friends are here." Kat pushed the deck aside.

Jennie wrinkled her brow. "What do you feel you're missing?"

"If I knew, I would go after it, whatever that is. I just don't really know. I've been here for seventeen years and my life is about the same. Well, not quite. I've gathered enough money to buy a business. Besides, I'm getting old." Kat pushed herself away from the table. "Oh, never mind me. I'm just in a foul mood today."

"I'm sorry. I wish I could cheer you up, like you have me. And thanks so much for the dress. It's great."

"You're welcome." Kat took her shawl from the chair. "I think I'll go for a walk about town. Be back in awhile." She wrapped the shawl around her shoulders and left the saloon. At first, she walked aimlessly around the town. Then she came up with an idea to visit the tailor shops to see if anyone knew of Jet. She walked in the first one and looked around for the tall lean man but didn't see him anywhere. Kat then asked the clerk if he knew of Jet. No, he did not.

There was one more tailor shop in Deadwood. She walked over to it and entered, again looking for Jet, but she didn't see him in that shop either. She asked the shop's tailor if he had heard of Jet. He said he didn't know of anyone by that name or description.

Clearly defeated, she quit searching. *Where could he be?* she asked herself. Not that she really cared. But it all seemed mysterious to her. *Was he posing as someone else?* It was just a nagging hunch she had. He didn't really seem suited to the bowler hat or that suit he was wearing on the Deadwood stage. She remembered that his face was tanned and his hands were rough. She also recalled he said he was a tailor by trade, but that didn't mean that he was a tailor in Deadwood. Or, maybe he wasn't a tailor at all.

"Oh well," she mumbled to herself. "I guess it isn't important anyway."

CHAPTER 6

Elijah and Evangeline settled into their hard bench seats at Denver's Wild West show, not knowing what to expect. A band of musicians in colorful, western-style shirts, kerchiefs, and chaps of buffalo hide struck up the music. The crowd filtered in and filled every available seat.

"It's like we're at a circus," Evangeline said to Elijah, nodding toward the large arena.

"All we need is the popcorn. Would you like some?" he asked.

"Sure, why not? That's what people do when they go to a circus."

"I'd better go now, before it gets too crowded."

While Elijah was gone, Evangeline took in her surroundings. The Indian village on the outskirts of the arena didn't seem strange or out of the ordinary to her. She had been to an Indian camp many times and could speak some of their language. She didn't think she would be awed by what the show had to offer, but Elijah wanted to see for himself how the Indians were treated. He had told her about the missionaries who were worried that the natives were negatively impacted by show life, that they were being exploited. Some of the missionaries had been quite vocal about the poor treatment of Indian employees.

"Here you go." Elijah handed her the box of popcorn and eased in beside her.

"Tastes good," she said after sampling the salty and buttery treat. Before too long, they heard a drumroll and applauded as the mounted showmen charged out of a painted mountain backdrop. Evangeline focused on the Indians. Their horses quivered, expecting the chase. The colorful riders burst forth in formations and circled the grandiose arena—cowboys in western hats and spurs; Mexican *vaqueros* with fringed trousers; cavalry in dark uniforms; and Indians in feathers, headdresses, and war paint. "Doesn't that cowboy remind you of Tex?" Evangeline said, pointing.

"Maybe a little."

"Oh, there are cavalry men and Mexicans with their big, floppy hats."

"I think they call them sombreros," Elijah said.

Evangeline shrugged. "Here come the Indians. Do you think there are any from Swift Bear's camp?"

"I doubt it. I've never heard of any joining up."

"They are such beautiful horsemen." Evangeline admired the pattern of their movements. She had learned to appreciate fine horses and their riders while she was married to James. In the few years they were married, he had taught her a great deal about horses. Evangeline's heart beat with excitement when the riders broke formation and lined the grandstand, which was now filled with spectators.

A sudden trumpet blast heralded the appearance of Jack Benton, the owner of the show. The explosive sound startled her, causing her to spill some of her popcorn. She fumbled with the spilled kernels in her lap.

"I wasn't expecting that!" she said to Elijah. "He must be the impresario riding toward us on that magnificent palomino."

"I think you're right. He sure is dressed the part."

Jack rode out in front of the grandstand, dressed in his finest buckskins. His long hair flowed from under a beige Stetson. His palomino reared back as he waved to the audience. He took off his Stetson and the horse bowed on one knee. "Wild West, are you ready? Let the show begin!"

At that point, the riders broke the line and surged throughout the arena, yelling and demonstrating their riding abilities.

Evangeline shivered with excitement.

Most of the showmen then left the arena to prepare for the reenactment of western scenes, leaving only the mounted Indians who wore flowing warbonnets. A stagecoach, drawn by six racing mules, charged into the arena. Loud war-whooping Indians swarmed it, shooting rubber-tipped arrows at the driver and passengers. After a few minutes, a group of cowboys rode to the rescue at breakneck speed. As they fired blank cartridges, more downed horses and men were scattered across the arena floor. The crowd roared excitedly. Even Evangeline felt the intensity in her glowing cheeks. At the conclusion of the battle, the Indian showmen jumped up, waved, mounted their horses, and rode out of the arena, leaving the cowboys to flaunt their riding tricks and shooting stunts.

In the next scene, Indians chased bison into the arena. The crowd went wild when the show Indians entered with raised guns blasting. Others pulled back bowstrings, releasing arrows at the shaggy beasts. The blank cartridges and rubber-tipped arrows didn't do any real damage, but the audience was thrilled anyway. Then the horses and men drove the bison out of the arena, followed by more men performing sharpshooting and rope tricks.

"Look! The show is scaring those young children." Evangeline pointed toward a boy and girl hiding behind their mother.

"They ought to have known there would be shooting and hollering at a show like this. They'll get used to it," Elijah said in an attempt to alleviate her concern.

Evangeline felt that she, too, must get used to all the commotion. As the western scenes unfolded before her, she told Elijah time and again how she admired the riding skills of the participants.

"Is this really the history of the West?"

"I suppose you can look at it that way, although it may not be totally accurate. The crowd sure seems to be enjoying it, though. Evangeline, look at that Indian on the sorrel pony."

"I see him. What about him?"

"He's too far away, but I feel like I should know him."

"Oh, it's probably someone you met while you were traveling around the reservations," she said. "He sure does sit tall and straight."

"That's probably it. Maybe I can find him after the show when I'm visiting with some of the actors."

"You don't think they'll mind if we go back and visit the Indian village?"

"I'm sure they won't. Besides, I speak Lakota," Elijah reminded her.

"Yes, I remember," Evangeline said, laughing. "Wait! They're going to do the Ghost Dance next!" Evangeline hadn't been on the reservation to see the circle dance. The Missionary Society and her father advised her not to go until the frenzy and its aftermath ceased. She examined the event flier. "I see here that some of the dancers were at Wounded Knee when the massacre happened. Can you imagine what must be going through their minds while they're performing the dance that brought about so much suspicion and mistrust?"

"And death," Elijah added. "Did I ever tell you the survivors claim that the spirits of those killed at Wounded Knee inhabit their old campsites on the reservation?"

"No, you never did," Evangeline said, wide-eyed. "Do they bother anyone?"

"Oh, no, they are peaceful."

"Do we have any at our mission?"

"I've never heard of any. Besides, Evangeline, Christians don't believe in ghosts."

"You're right, but it's still kind of scary." She hesitated before asking, "What do they say the ghosts look like?"

"Some say they come back as deer or other animals."

"Well, that wouldn't be so bad." Elijah smiled at her. "You made that up, didn't you?"

"No, I didn't. That's the truth," Elijah said. "These dancers aren't wearing their ghost shirts."

"Why not?"

"Probably because they're sacred."

"What did the shirts look like?" Evangeline asked.

"They were flimsy and ornamented with eagle feathers. The dancers intended to bring back the buffalo, the old life—and to miraculously make the whites disappear."

The show's finale came all too quickly.

"I didn't expect to enjoy this event, but I can honestly say I did," Evangeline conceded.

"I enjoyed it, too."

All riders gathered and rode in the arena for a final round of applause, which the crowd stood to deliver.

"I'm glad we came. Now we can say we saw a Wild West show. It's quite a popular attraction, you know." Elijah retrieved his program from the bench. "Now, let's go back to the village and see what we can see."

Elijah and Evangeline followed the crowd out of the arena. Most of the crowd returned to town, but a few people walked toward the village. Evangeline linked her arm in Elijah's as they walked to the Indian village that had been erected for the Indian performers. White, canvas tepees along the perimeter of the arena provided lodging for the Indian showmen and their families and lent an aura of authenticity to the Wild West show.

Evangeline and Elijah approached the tepees painted with celestial, geometric, and animal designs. Elijah had no trouble locating a group of Lakota Indians. At first, he spoke their language, but after discovering they could speak English, he dropped the Lakota and asked, "Do you enjoy traveling with the show?" They nodded in agreement. Elijah explained who he was and where he was from, and they clasped hands. Others nodded in recognition of another Lakota brother.

"We're treated well, get paid, and get all we want to eat," said the oldest male in the group, Two Bears. He removed his warbonnet and handed it to his wife. "Sometimes on the reservation, there's not enough food for everyone. But my children do not have to go hungry while we are here."

"Do you work too hard?" Elijah asked.

"This is a better life than sitting around with nothing to do and not enough food to eat," said Two Bears, shaking his head. Two Bears went on to explain that Jack Benton usually hired Indian males with families. "The show Indians become like one family," Two Bears said. He then stood straight and puffed out his chest. "Jack likes the Lakota to perform in his shows."

"Why is that?"

"We are most often chosen because of our reputation as fearless warriors. We can bring back the old days while we are here."

After the couple parted with Two Bears, they walked all the way to the edge of the camp. She smiled as she watched the children happily skipping and darting around the camp. Evangeline turned toward Elijah. "So, what do you think?"

"That family seemed to be content," Elijah said. "I suppose there could be instances where the show Indians are taken advantage of, just like anything else. But I don't think I'll be one to stir up a ruckus about it." He paused. "I haven't yet seen that man I thought I recognized, the one who rode the sorrel. I wonder where he is."

"You know what kind of horse he rode. Ask someone," Evangeline prompted.

"Good idea. Let's give that a try." They walked back through the camp and approached an especially friendly couple with their inquiry.

"We know that man," the man said. "He lives in the small tepee over there." They pointed to a tepee with a large buffalo painted across it. Elijah thanked the couple and asked the name of the man they were looking for.

"His name is Ben," said the woman.

Her remark left Elijah and Evangeline momentarily stunned. Elijah thanked the couple again and slowly walked toward the dwelling with Evangeline closely beside him.

"That can't be," Elijah said to Evangeline. "It must be some sort of coincidence."

"We thought he was dead," Evangeline whispered.

"We just assumed that. I must speak with him."

"I know it isn't my concern, and we have only been married a short time, but do you know how you are going to feel when you see your father?" Evangeline asked quietly.

"Not really. I had no idea we'd ever find him."

"Are you bitter toward him?"

"You mean, have I forgiven him? I don't know. A pastor, of all people, should forgive, but there are so many unanswered questions."

"Yes, I know." She squeezed his arm to reassure him. When they reached the tepee, Elijah stopped.

"Now what do I do?"

"Call his name. It's hard to knock on a tepee flap," she said, trying to lighten the mood.

Elijah cleared his throat and called, "Ben...Ben Noisy

Hawk." They heard no response other than a little movement. Then, a tall man with a rough yet pleasant face came out of the tepee.

"Do I know you?" the man asked.

"Are you Ben Noisy Hawk?"

"Yes, that is my name."

"You don't know me?"

Ben bent toward Elijah, concentrating on his voice. His eyes swept over him. "You are my son."

"I *am* your son Elijah, and this is my wife, Evangeline."

"My son, what are you doing here?" Disbelief still clouded his deep voice.

"I had no idea you were here." Elijah stared at this man he hadn't seen in many years. "I...I have been looking for you for years with no luck," he stammered. "I can't believe I am standing in front of you now."

"I am without words," Ben said, standing straight and tall.

"Can we talk?"

"You want to talk with me?"

"I have many questions."

"I'm sure you have. Some I may not be able to answer."

Elijah shrugged. "We could give it a try."

Ben stepped aside. "Come into my tepee and sit." Elijah and Evangeline followed him into the dimly lit tepee and sat on mats near the doorway. "You are married," Ben said, "and you have turned your back on the Old Way?"

"Evangeline and I were married about two weeks ago. But I haven't turned my back on my people."

"I have nothing to offer you. I eat with a group of my friends at meal time."

"That's all right," Elijah said. "We had popcorn during the show. I'm surprised to find you in a Wild West show. How long have you been doing this?"

Evangeline relaxed some, thinking the question was a good starting point for their conversation. As she listened to them, she realized how important her father was to her. *How is Elijah feeling just now?* she wondered. She would never be able to comprehend growing up without a father.

"It's been about twelve years now. I suppose you are wondering what happened to me." Ben said.

"I am. Why did you leave us?" Elijah blurted out in a more accusatory tone than intended.

"I don't have an easy answer for you. I was confused and didn't know what road to take."

"Confused about what?"

"I didn't fit in with your mother's life or her people. I was walking the white man's road for a while, but I did not want to become one. I wanted to help my own people in my own way. That's why I went to Nevada with another man from Standing Rock to hear what a prophet had to say."

"You mean Wovoka?"

"No, this was before him. I saw another man who had a vision. We journeyed a long way to see him and spent many days talking. In the end, we decided that what he was saying could not be true; the Ghost Dance could not bring back the old life. When we came back, I knew I could not go to you or your mother. I don't think she would have wanted me anymore."

"But what about me, your son?"

"I didn't want to leave you, but I knew your mother had you in her grip. You were all she had, so I just let it be."

"Do you have another family?"

"I do not. The show has been my family for some time."

"And where did you join it?" Elijah asked.

"I was at Pine Ridge when I heard a showman was coming to Rushville looking for Indians to be in his Wild West show. I was still young then and thought I had a chance of being chosen. So I went with friends and got a job with the show. It was better than sitting around doing nothing or trying to be a farmer. Luckily, I have been chosen every year. I look good enough in a warbonnet and buckskin clothing," he said with pride. He reached into a wooden box and pulled out some photographs. "But I'm getting older, and I don't know how many more years I have left as a show Indian."

Evangeline took the photographs and saw why he had been chosen for the show. He stood tall and straight in his regalia, a feathered warbonnet trailing down his back. Dark, piercing eyes shone from a well-formed face.

Elijah said, "I have heard the reports of missionaries who say the Indian showmen are being taken advantage of."

"Some, perhaps. But I have found it to be a good life." Ben retrieved a leather bag in which he kept his money. He counted it in front of them. "As you can see, the pay has been good over the years, too. Many of the show Indians send their money home to their families. I don't have a family on the reservation anymore, so I've kept the money for myself."

"You *do* have a family," Elijah reminded him. "We are still at Cheyenne River Mission. I am the pastor of the mission. Evangeline teaches and helps run the mission. Mother teaches sewing now." Ben didn't respond; an awkward silence followed. Elijah spied a few pictures painted on a hide behind Ben. "You still paint?"

Ben nodded. "I sell a few during the shows."

"They're interesting," Evangeline murmured. Ben reached behind him and pulled out a book for them to see. They took the green ledger book and opened it. Inside were simple figures drawn in a hard outline and filled in with red, blue, green, and yellow. Evangeline studied the drawings with interest.

"My father has always painted on hides," Elijah explained. "It's the old Indian way of recording history—calendars, feats in battle, hunts, visions, or any other records they wanted to keep. Since we didn't have a written language, important events could be kept in this manner."

Ben added, "When we had no more hides, we used scraps of paper or accounting ledger books to make our drawings. Jack Benton hired me to make drawings of his show." Ben reached over to a box and produced a handful of colored pencils. "I use these to fill in my outlines."

Elijah and Evangeline continued turning the pages, appreciating the free-flowing artwork. The figures were rudimentary, but the flat, colored pictures seemed to fly off the page.

"This picture here looks exactly like what we saw today," Evangeline said, astonished. "Ben, you have captured the essence of the show—Mexicans wearing their sombreros, cowboys in their high-heeled boots, Indians wearing their headdresses, and even the American flags surrounding the arena."

"It's painted in my memory," Ben responded. Turning toward Elijah, he asked, "Do you paint or draw?"

"No, I don't seem to have the knack for it." Elijah looked up at Ben. "I remember the boys at Carlisle who drew on scrap paper every chance they got. They were so homesick. I suppose drawing whatever they left behind helped ease the loneliness."

"Your mother sent you to Carlisle?"

"Yes, but only for a few years. I remember some of my friends remained there nearly six years. Mother couldn't stand for me to be so far from home, so she brought me back to the mission."

Ben hesitated before asking his next question. "You thought I was dead?"

"I did give up hope."

"I wanted you to think so."

Evangeline sat quietly, letting father and son struggle through their past. She could see a resemblance between them, though Ben was darker and had heavier features. *No trace of white blood,* she thought.

"I have been looking for you for a long time," Elijah said. "I was told you went to Nevada, but I never found out any more than that. What did you do when the show wasn't playing?"

"I came back to Standing Rock for the winter."

"But I was looking for you there. I asked everyone around about Ben Noisy Hawk."

"I told them not to tell anyone where I was. It would be better that way," Ben explained.

"So you are never coming back to us?"

"My life is here until I become too old. Then I will just drift from camp to camp. Someone will watch out for me. That is our way."

"And Mother? Shouldn't she know?"

"It would just open the old wounds. I am sure she has healed by now."

"I'm not so sure about that," Elijah said. "Did you know she grew up in an orphanage from a very young age? Her mother gave her away."

"She never told me that. I knew she was sad and smiled little. We should have never married in the white man's church."

"Mother felt unloved and had a hard time loving—even me, her child."

"I know that. It is sad, but I cannot go back."

Evangeline realized nothing could convince Ben to return. The rift between Cassandra and Ben would not allow it.

"Your mother...how is she?"

"She has been at Cheyenne River Mission since you left. Like I said, she cooks and teaches. Of course, she cannot remarry. She is still married to you under the white law."

"That is true. Does she want to be married to someone else?"

"No, she doesn't have anyone else."

"I see. The white man's word is divorce?"

"Yes, that is what they call it," Elijah answered.

"Since everyone thinks I am dead, there would be no problem. She could remarry if she wanted."

"I see you've made up your mind not to return." Elijah stood. "I will keep your secret if you wish, but I pray you change your mind. I would like to see you again sometime."

"Come to Standing Rock in the winter. Ask for Fast Arrow. They will know who I am."

"I will."

Evangeline and Elijah reluctantly left Ben Noisy Hawk. Evangeline twined her arm around his and leaned against him.

"I hoped I could convince him to come back to us," Elijah said to Evangeline.

"It's a start. At least you found him and he answered most of your questions." After meeting Elijah's father and listening to the revealing conversation, she felt closer to Elijah than ever before.

"But he wants no part of our life."

"That probably would be too much to ask. You seem to have little in common anymore."

"I suppose you're right. I wasn't expecting such an end to our honeymoon. How about we go home in the morning?" he asked, kissing her forehead.

"I would like that very much."

———

"Oh, there's the mission!" Evangeline pointed. "I'm so happy to get back to our little home."

"You really are glad to be back?" Elijah asked in surprise.

"Yes, yes, I truly am."

"You are amazing. Most women would run from this kind of life."

"What kind of life do you mean?"

"Well, you know, none of the things you enjoy in Boston."

"Most women don't know that *you're* here."

"Are you saying you wouldn't be here if I wasn't?"

"That's mostly right."

"Evangeline, you are a treasure."

"Aren't you glad to be back?"

"I am," Elijah said with a nod. "It's always nice to see some of the world, but coming home is even better." It wasn't long before they pulled up in front of the mission. Sara was the first to run out to meet them.

"I'm so happy to see you both," she said, embracing Evangeline.

"We missed you, too," Evangeline said earnestly. The rest of their friends greeted them joyously and were eager to hear all about their trip to Denver. They came into the mission and sat around the kitchen table.

Just like old times, Evangeline thought, watching Minnie and Cassandra bustling around the kitchen like they had years ago, making the coffee and preparing a wonderful meal for them all. She wished the good parts of life would never change. There was comfort in sameness. She said a silent prayer of thanksgiving for her dear friends and for Elijah.

"Well, what did you see?" Jeremiah was brimming with curiosity.

"We visited museums and bookstores, of course. We tried some of the famous restaurants and took long walks. We even took a trip to the mountains by train and visited the mining boom town of Leadville," Elijah told them.

"I even talked Elijah into seeing an opera in one of the finest opera houses in the West," Evangeline added.

"Sounds like a wonderful trip," Sara mused, clearing the dishes from the table.

"Next time, we'll take you with us," Evangeline promised.

Elijah scooted away from the table. "Jeremiah, would you help me carry in our luggage?"

"Sure, I also have a few church matters to discuss with you," he said, leaving the kitchen with Elijah.

Cassandra poured hot water into the dishpan. "I'm so happy you had a nice honeymoon, but it just wasn't the same around here without you."

"That's nice of you to say," Evangeline said with a smile. "Here, let me help."

"No, just sit and tell us more about your trip."

"How was the trail to Deadwood?" Minnie asked as she scraped the kettles. "It's been years since I have been over it."

"The stage is not my favorite mode of transportation," Evangeline said. "At the time, I wasn't in a laughing mood, but when I look back at it all, being packed in a coach like sardines for endless hours seems funny to me now. I hope we can travel by rail next time. I don't know how you did it, Minnie—freighting through such inhospitable land."

"I was younger then, and didn't know any better. Like I told you before, I would have followed my husband anywhere. Sounds like I was a fool then," Minnie said, continuing to wipe the dishes.

"Let me at least put the dishes in the cupboard," Evangeline said.

"No, I'm doing that," Sara insisted.

"Oh, alright. But tomorrow I'm going to start doing my share around here," Evangeline said.

"Did you meet anyone interesting on the trail?" Minnie asked.

"Yes, we did. There was a friendly fellow, Tex, and his daughter, Netty. He was a cattleman from Texas looking for more grazing land. There was also a woman who called herself Kat, a fancy lady. She wore makeup and flashy clothes.

A man by the name of Jet Black sat beside Elijah. Jet said he was a tailor, but he was quiet and kept to himself."

"Yeah, you meet all sorts of people on the trail. When I was helping my husband whacking bull teams, we ran across desperados as well as plain, ordinary folk. I was never afraid because Abe could take care of us."

"I wasn't aware of any desperados on the trip, but was I ever glad to get to Rapid City. We had a scare at the Cheyenne River. I thought we were going to tip over into the river, but the driver got us through. I thought the crusty-looking gent did a good job and seemed concerned about our safety. Oh, and there was another driver who was drunk. He scared me half to death. We reported him."

"I'll bet he doesn't have a job with the stage lines anymore," Minnie said.

"The last driver was very helpful, though. When we were checking into the hotel in Rapid City, the driver came into the hotel with a lost compact. He thought it might have been mine, but it wasn't. I think it belonged to Kat. She had already left for Deadwood by then. We were going to try to get it back to her, but in our haste the next morning, we forgot all about it. It's a nice one. I think I have it in my purse." Evangeline grabbed her purse from the chair, opened it, and with some rummaging produced the compact. "See, isn't it pretty?" The ladies stopped what they were doing and came over to inspect the compact.

"It's silver—and look at those stones! Do you suppose this one could be a real diamond?" Cassandra asked, handling it carefully.

"I suppose so. I feel that this is an expensive piece. Let me show you something interesting on the inside." She flipped it open to reveal the additional compartment that held the portrait.

"Nice-looking people," Cassandra remarked.

"Here, let me look." Minnie took the compact from Cassandra. "Why, this woman looks familiar," she said, pointing at Kat.

"That's Kat," Evangeline told her.

"I don't know anyone by that name. Let me think a minute." Minnie squinted and pressed her temple, deep in thought. "She sure does look familiar."

"I don't even know her last name. All she said was to call her Kat. She knew her cards, though. I never saw anyone shuffle and deal cards the way she did. Not that I have been around much card playing," Evangeline added. By now, all the ladies were sitting at the table, totally fascinated by the portrait. The dish water was getting cold.

"Do you know where she lives?" Sara asked.

"She and Jet took a stage to Deadwood, and I remember her saying that she had lived in Deadwood for quite a while."

"I'll bet she's one of those card dealers at a saloon," Cassandra said.

"She did look the part," Evangeline said. "That might explain this expensive compact. She was somewhat vain. She opened it several times to check how she looked and must have dropped it the last time she used it."

"You know, I remember now. This picture resembles a woman I knew in Deadwood—a little younger, though. Her name was Kathryn Spencer. She never called herself Kat, but I suppose she could have shortened her name," Minnie said.

Cassandra tapped at the picture. "You knew a saloon girl? How did you meet her?"

"Like I said, I lived a different life back then."

"We met on the trail when I was helping my husband. At that time, I was doing the cooking. Kathryn was just a young girl then, maybe in her teens. She told me she had caught a ride with a freighter coming from Pierre. I don't think she had any money for the stage or she wouldn't have been traveling the way she was. One night, she came to our camp and asked for food. She certainly wasn't wearing any fancy clothes then. She was willing to help me with the camp chores in exchange for sharing a few meals together. I don't think the freighter she caught a ride with fed her very well. I felt sorry for her, so I said it would be fine with me."

"Did she say where she was from?" Evangeline asked.

"I think she told me she was from St. Louis. Or was it Cleveland? My memory isn't what it used to be," Minnie complained. "Anyway, she looked soft. You know what I mean? She hadn't had to work too hard, maybe had an easy life. She told me she was going to Deadwood to look for work. I didn't like the sounds of that. Work for women in Deadwood usually had something to do with saloons unless you wanted to sweat it out in a laundry or a hot kitchen."

"Where did she go when you got to Deadwood?" Cassandra asked.

"I don't know. I was so busy checking the invoices when we unloaded freight. I never saw her after that. But I have always wondered what happened to her. Let me see that picture again." Minnie gave one more scrutinizing glance. "Yes, I think this is her."

"Do you suppose if I send this compact to Kat Spencer, addressed to Deadwood, then she might get it?" Evangeline asked.

"It certainly would be worth a try. It sure would be something if she were really Kathryn." Minnie said.

"I'll wrap it up and send it with Elijah the next time he goes for the mail." *How strange,* Evangeline thought, *that Minnie would know someone she'd met on the stagecoach. Cassandra is probably right. Kat is a saloon girl.*

Minnie said, "I'll write a short note to go with it. I'd like to see if she writes back to me, her old friend, Minnie."

CHAPTER 7

After their stay in the International Hotel, Tex and Netty left from Rapid City for Spearfish. They boarded the stage to take them there to meet Curt, Tex's son.

Netty settled into the coach beside her father. "I can't wait to see Curt," she said. "It's been so long since he left Texas, it seems, even though it's just been a year."

"I'm looking forward to seeing him, too, and to hear what he has to say about our cattle operation here in the Black Hills." He drew in a long breath. "Smell that pure, mountain air."

A naturally gregarious man, Tex visited with everyone aboard the stage once all had boarded. Two of the passengers were homesteaders looking for land. Tex did his best to be polite, but he spent most of his time talking to another cattleman who had a small herd near the Belle Fourche River. The two men kept their conversation to cattle and horse thieves, avoiding the subject of the encroaching homesteader.

The spectacular, pine-covered hills rose from the velvety, green valley. Netty kept her eyes glued to the landscape. "Wouldn't it be nice to live here?" she remarked to her father. "Look how green and lush it still is here."

"Yeah, it's nice. The bottom land's good for cattle."

"Oh, Father, all you think about is cattle. Can't you see the beauty in this country?"

"I see it." He chucked her under the chin.

When the stage delivered them to Main Street in Spearfish, Netty slid to the edge of her seat. She immediately spotted her brother sauntering across the street to the hotel. He wore dark trousers, a blue flannel shirt, and a scarf knotted around his neck. A soiled, felt cowboy hat shaded his brow, and a gun belt and pistol slung on his hip.

"He's wearing a gun. I had no idea he would need one here."

"Now, don't be concerned. I'm sure he has a good reason." Tex and Netty were the first ones out of the stage.

"Curt! Curt!" she called as she ran to him. He took off his hat, grabbed her, and lifted her off her feet. Curt stood just a little taller than Netty. She reached up and ruffled his curly brown hair, which had grown a little longer than he used to wear it when he lived in Texas. He swung her around one more time and shook his father's hand.

"So good to see you, son." Tex's deep voice boomed.

"Why don't we go find ourselves a cup of coffee while I catch you up on everything that has happened around here." He picked up their luggage, which the driver had tossed on the ground, and loaded the buckboard he had brought to town. "It should be all right in here while we drink our coffee." He led them into a rather nice hotel with a small dining area. Curt waved to the waitress who came over. She gave the handsome cowboy a sly smile.

"What can I get for you?" she asked.

"Coffee, please," Curt said, not paying any special attention to her. "How was your trip across country?" He asked.

"Actually, it wasn't too bad. Met some interesting people along the way," his father answered. "Now, what can you tell me about our cattle business here?"

"The day before yesterday, I took the stage to Deadwood to a cattle thieving trial. The cattlemen 'round here think we should all show up at these trials so that some kind of justice will be served. It seems to work. There have been several convictions lately," Curt explained.

"Have we lost cattle to thieves?"

"We'll see after the roundup. It's hard to tell until we bring 'em all in."

"And the homesteaders?"

"They're moving in every day, crowding us out. You'll see their sod houses and shacks and the plowed fields taking over the prime grassland. The way I see it, we have to find more grass somewhere."

"I've been looking ever since I got to Dakota. There might be some grazing around Pierre. If they'd open up the reservation to lease, that would sure help us out." Tex tipped up the last mouthful of coffee.

"Ma'am, bring us more coffee," Curt said, waving the waitress over again.

"Please," Netty said in an accusatory whisper. "Have you forgotten your manners?"

"Yeah, I guess I have." Netty's reprimand caused Curt to blush.

"You need a woman to remind you, to whip you into shape." She smiled at her brother.

"Ah, I ain't got no time for women. Besides, they all seem to belong to one homesteader or another."

"And what's the matter with a farmer's daughter?" she asked.

"I'm a cattleman, plain and simple. No dirt farming for me."

Netty looked down at his sidearm. "By the way, why do you wear a gun?"

"Mostly for wild animals and rattlesnakes. But one never knows 'bout these rustlers." Having finished their coffee, Tex and Netty climbed into the buckboard. Curt unwound the reins from the hitching rail and mounted his horse. "The range headquarters isn't too far, only a few miles out of town," he said from the saddle.

After several miles of pine-filled scenery, they came to the ranch, a cluster of log buildings: a house, a barn, a bunkhouse, and the crudely fashioned corrals. They approached a long, low house. The fence out front was draped with the antlers of elk and deer. Two dogs barked and raced back and forth. Several mowing machines, almost hidden by the high grass, stood outside the log fence.

"Welcome to what I have called home for the last few years," Curt told them as he led them through a heavy door and into the building's dark interior. He unbuckled his gun belt, hung it on a hook by the door, removed his hat, and tossed it on a leather-covered chair.

Tex smiled as he surveyed the setup. "Looks good, son. How many men stay here?"

"Just the cook, Tater, and myself. The hired cowboys have their own bunkhouse."

"Tater?"

"Yeah, we call him Tater. I think his real name is Harold. But what kind of name is that for a cook? He'll be the one driving the chuck wagon and doing the cooking during the round up. He does wonders with a few spuds and a skillet. You'll see tonight."

Tex and Netty squinted to compensate for the trickle of light coming through the small windows. More antlers, once possessed by prize animals, lined the walls along with tanned animal skins. Massive furniture made of pine and leather filled the long room. A fireplace on the outer wall was worn by many roaring fires. Tex ran his hand over its rocky surface. "Who does the hunting around here?"

"Tater, mostly." Curt pointed to a rack of five points. "These are mine. Got them last winter."

"I did a lot of hunting in my day. Had to supply meat for the family. We were so poor that Pa couldn't afford nothing."

Curt nodded, knowingly. "We'll eat good tonight. Tater's gone to town for supplies for the roundup. I told him to be back in time to cook us up some nice steaks for supper."

"Where do you want us to put our bags?" Tex picked up the valise and satchel at his feet.

"There's only three bedrooms. Tater has his off the kitchen, and there's two off the end of the hall. You and me will bunk together, and Netty can have the one across from it."

"I'm anxious to see the herd. Netty, would you mind if we left for a while?"

"Go right ahead. I'll unpack and settle in."

Tex was content to sit in a saddle again as he and his son rode through the pastures, rimmed by the piney hills. "This sure is beautiful cattle country," Tex remarked. "Netty would be annoyed to hear me say that," he laughed. "She thinks the only thing I'm interested in is cattle and money."

"Well, aren't you?"

"Yeah, I guess I am," Tex confessed." He drew his horse to a stop on a ridge overlooking acres of prime grassland. "I've spent too many years being poor. I've invested everything I have in this operation."

"Yeah, I know. You won't notice any difference from last year. Now, if we could fence the pastures and buy some Hereford bulls, we might be able to put some meat on them critters. They'd be as shiny as a new penny."

"Some of the big cattlemen are fencing and getting away with it. As you know, I'm considering moving our herd east. Right now, it's dry out there. If we can file on land on the outer perimeters of the range, we'd be able to fence off a large block of land. Then we could bring in Hereford bulls."

"But that's illegal," Curt insisted as they continued to ride.

"Maybe according to the law books, but it hasn't been enforced. I'll be darned if them homesteaders plow up prime grassland and ruin the country." Tex surveyed the landscape. "The grass looks good, but a little shorter than I expected."

"We've been a little short of rain. The cattle numbers keep climbing. Soon there won't be enough grass to go around," Curt said. "I have a strong feeling this paradise isn't going to last forever. Change is coming. The homesteaders want this land, too, and we aren't going to be able to keep them out."

"We'll hang on as long as we can. I plan on going back to the Cheyenne River Reservation and look around. We can't graze it yet, but I have a feeling the legislature will give us the leases in time. I want to be ready."

"What about those leases?"

"Well, you know the legislature tends to lean toward the homesteader over the cattleman in land deals. The newspapers do the same thing. So I wouldn't count on them giving us leases on reservation land any time soon. Guess we'll just hope for the best," Tex said.

"We're going to be crowded out of our pastures here before long," Curt said, stroking his chin.

"It'd be a shame to leave this nice place, but we'll have to. Like I said, after the roundup, I'm going back to Cheyenne River country near the reservation. There's got to be some grazing space there. When the leases open up—and I say *when* because I really believe it will happen—we will be that much closer to the prime grass."

Curt nodded toward the rippling stream and the pine-covered ridges of the ranch. "I won't like leaving here. This here's what they call 'God's country.' He took special care when he made this land. I can see why the homesteaders want to settle here."

"You sound like Netty." Tex smirked as he looked off toward the hills. He pointed to a herd of cattle about a quarter mile away. "Over there, I see some of the cattle."

"They look good, don't you think?" Curt pointed to an array of longhorns speckling the rich, green meadows as they came closer.

Tex nodded. "The grass and water's good here. I just hope we don't turn up short at roundup." The men rode over the land for another hour, spotting small herds of cattle grazing and watering at the rivers and water holes.

"How long are you planning on staying?" Curt asked his father.

"I'll stay around here for a month or so, then ride back to the Cheyenne River country and look it over. If I find enough grass, we'll move the cattle before winter."

"Do you want me to ride along?" Curt asked.

"There's no need. You'd probably better stay here and keep an eye on things—rustlers in particular. I sure hate to lose cattle to thieves. I'll take Netty to Rapid City when I'm ready to meet the train, and then strike out from there." The men continued riding until they came upon an area that had been rutted with hoof prints. Curt dismounted for closer inspection. Tex joined him. "Looks like there's been a number of beeves milling about here. See that trail? Let's follow it a ways and see where it leads us." The men mounted their horses and rode to the southeast.

"Looks like rustlers, don't it?" Curt asked.

Tex nodded. "I wonder how many they got away with, the scoundrels."

"I'd say they headed toward rocky ground so as not to make a trail."

"You're probably right. Wonder when they made their move? When's the last time you been out here?"

"It's been a few days. Them and the cattle are long gone by now. Sorry, I should have noticed sooner," Curt said.

"It isn't your fault. There's no way you can keep track of hundreds of head of cattle, especially when they can wander anywhere they want. After roundup, we'll know more. We just have to cut our losses for now. Don't talk about the rustling in front of Netty. She'll just get upset."

———————

Back at the ranch, Tex and Curt unsaddled their horses and joined Netty on the porch.

"How was your ride?"

"Just fine. Did you get lonely without us?" Curt jested.

Netty frowned. "Don't flatter yourself."

Tex glanced at the yard surrounding the house. "I see you have a couple of mowing machines. I suppose after the round up, you'll get to haying."

"Yeah, the hired hands would rather ride than hay, but it has to be done."

"Investors and cattlemen sure learned the hard way. The range cattle need that extra feed during the hard winters," Tex said. Netty left the men and returned indoors to read.

The western horizon was streaked with pink by the time Tater rumbled in the yard and pulled up in front of the porch. The wagon was loaded with supplies for the roundup.

"Come and meet my family," Curt called. He slid off the bench to make introductions.

Tater reached the topmost step of the porch, extended his hand toward Tex, and drawled, "Pleased to meet you."

"My sister's here, too. Wait a minute, and I'll get her." Curt opened the screen door, stuck his head in the doorway and called, "Netty, come on out. I want you to meet someone." Netty approached the doorway and peeked through the screen before she stepped out onto the porch. "This here's my sister, Netty."

"Pleased to meet you," said Tater. He had removed his hat, uncovering a mop of graying hair. I hope y'all like your stay here."

"Thank you, I'm sure I will," said Netty.

Tex laughed in amusement. "I'll bet you're from Texas, Tater."

"Sure am. Came up with a cattle drive once. Been here ever since. Not enough cooks in these parts. Curt here wouldn't let me go back." Tater laughed and turned toward Curt. "I suppose y'all be wanting supper?"

"We're thinking of some steaks and your famous fried potatoes."

Tater's gaze trailed off toward the dogs, which were sniffing the wagon. He scratched his gray, wiry beard before he spoke. "Well. I'm supposin' we'd better unload the wagon before them dogs get a notion to help themselves to the grub." Curt and Tex nodded in agreement and helped carry the supplies into the house for safekeeping. Tater soon had steaks sizzling in one frying pan, and in another, he fried the potatoes and onions in bacon drippings. After a while, he shouted, "Come and dish up. I'm too tuckered out to put on anything fancy."

───────

After a scrumptious meal, Tex, Netty, Tater and Curt sat out on the porch listening to howling coyotes piercing the still night air with their mournful cries.

"It wouldn't be the West without coyotes," Netty said.

"They'd better leave the stock alone, or I'll shoot them dead," said Curt.

"Oh, men. All they think about is their cattle," Netty retorted. "How about the sound of croaking frogs?"

"Oh, they'd make good fried frog legs." Curt licked his lips mockingly.

"And the comforting sound of crickets?"

"They keep me awake at night. I squash them with my boot." Curt laughed.

"I don't care what you say." She glared at her brother. "It's certainly a peaceful evening. And look at that sunset," she sighed. "All seems right with the world."

Tex hardly agreed with Netty's optimism. Life was hard. At least Netty didn't remember how he and his wife had struggled to raise two children on his meager income as a cowhand in Texas. After his wife died, he had bought a ranch of his own. He and Curt had profited on it. Tex had sunk all his savings and teamed up with English investors in this cattle operation. He couldn't afford to make any mistakes as their manager.

CHAPTER 8

The wind whispered high among the pines as Jet gathered kindling for his fire. He picked up dry pinecones and twigs and carried them back to an open spot near a stream. Secluded by the banks of the creek, Jet filled his gray, graniteware coffeepot. The water from the rapidly babbling creek was crystal clear. He built a fire under a grate and placed the pot on top to bring the water to a boil. He then took a frying pan and a slab of bacon from his saddlebags. Taking a knife, he sliced the bacon into strips, and laid them in the skillet. While the bacon sizzled, he opened two cans of beans, which he placed on the fire next to the skillet. The bacon had just begun to crisp when two men rode into camp.

"No one followed you, did they, Tom?" Jet said to the older man.

Tom, a short man with long, straggly hair, dismounted and approached Jet.

"Nah, I don't think there's anyone around for a few miles anyway. Bacon sure smells good. Haven't had anything since breakfast." He watched Jet take up the bacon before it burned, then add flour to the drippings in the pan to make gravy for the hardtack he had taken from his saddlebag.

"You're just in time to eat," said Jet. "You and Bill take care of the horses, and supper will be ready," Jet said.

Bill, who was just a young lad, led their mounts over to a grassy knoll near the stream and hobbled them. When they returned to camp, Jet had the bacon, beans, hardtack, and gravy dished up on tin plates. The coffee had already been poured into tin cups.

"No one got hurt, did they?" Jet's voice was etched with concern.

Tom sat and began to eat. Through a mouthful of beans, he answered, "Nah, everything went good."

"I'm glad to hear that. You know how I feel about killing," Jet reminded them.

"We know." Tom swallowed another mouthful of food before speaking again. "Bill and I are thinking we should lay low for a while."

"Why do you say that?" Jet poured himself another cup of coffee.

"Those range detectives are like fleas on a mangy dog. Ain't like it used to be ten years ago. You weren't around these parts then, but it was easier. The law wasn't always dogging us. A fellow could get away with a lot more."

"Maybe. But then if you got caught, you were invited to a necktie party whether you wanted to go or not," Jet said.

"Yeah, but them hangings didn't happen that much."

Bill finally spoke up. "I'm too young to rot in prison or dangle from a rope. I agree with Tom. Let's not push a good thing."

"How about just moving on to somewhere else?" Jet placed his plate on the ground and reached into his pocket for his tobacco pouch and cigarette papers.

"Where you thinking?" Tom waited for an answer as Jet turned up the edges of the thin paper between his fingers and filled it with tobacco from the pouch. He rolled it and licked the ends to seal the cigarette. Then he touched the end with a match, inhaled, and blew the smoke toward the treetops.

"How about farther east, toward the reservations? Maybe the range detectives aren't as bad there." He passed the tobacco and cigarette papers to Tom.

"Let's think on that awhile." Tom rolled his own cigarette as he spoke.

"How did the boys get on with the cattle?" Jet asked.

"They should be somewhere in the southern hills by now. My boy, Jed, will make sure they get loaded on a train to market. He'll get our money to us. We're supposed to meet them in Deadwood the day after tomorrow with our share of the money."

"Good. Maybe you're right," Jet said. "Let's meet the boys as planned, and tell them to split up for a while. We don't want to hang around together and look suspicious."

After eating, the men washed the plates and skillet in the cold stream and played several games of cards before turning in for the night. Jet enjoyed a winning streak that made Tom hopping mad.

"Ah, you're a poor loser. I'm going to bed," he told Tom. Jet threw down the cards and crawled into his bedroll.

––––––

The next day they lazed around camp, biding their time. They played more cards, against Jet's better judgment. Bill won, and Jet could see the anger building in Tom. He wasn't surprised when Tom pulled a gun on Bill and accused him of cheating.

"Wait a minute, fellers!" Jet said, stepping between them. "This has gone far enough. We'd all better find something else to do." Tom stomped off toward the woods and Bill stood, clearly shaken, still holding the winning cards in his hand. "It's best not to rile Tom," Jet advised. Bill nodded.

The night passed with no more card playing or commotion. Everyone rose in good spirits the next morning. Tom had forgotten about his surliness and nearly split in two when he saw Jet at breakfast.

"It's called a disguise," Jet said, offended at Tom's laughter. "You might think up one yourself."

"What for?"

"Would you take me for a cattle rustler if I came to town like this?"

"Probably not, but a bowler hat and a suit? You look like one of them drummers."

"Well, good. That's the idea. My disguise is working. It worked when I came from Pierre to Rapid City on the stage. I said I am a tailor by trade."

Tom slapped his leg and began another round of laughter, exposing his tobacco-stained teeth. "And they believed you?"

"Why shouldn't they? I kept my mouth shut and played cards with this woman who looked like she could have been a saloon girl. Let her win, too. Maybe I did see her in Deadwood once." He rubbed the stubble on his chin. "Can't remember."

"Was she pretty?" Bill leaned forward.

"Yeah, if you like redheads," Jet said.

"We'll each ride into town alone," Tom said. "We don't want to be seen together in Deadwood. Pass the word to the boys that we're moving on. How about the Fort Pierre country? We'll meet there within a month." Jet and Bill shrugged. "Jet, go on ahead and take the stage to Fort Pierre. When you get there, look the country over. Be at the Fort Pierre hotel within the month."

"Clean up a little when you come looking for me, Tom," Jet said. "Your looks are suspicious enough."

"What's the matter with my looks?" Tom jammed his thumbs in his gun belt.

"You look like you've been sleeping in the cattle pens, that's what." Jet regretted the remark as soon as he said it, but Tom was really starting to irritate him.

"Remember...I'm the boss of this outfit, not you," Tom ranted. "I'll do whatever, whenever."

"Maybe so, but I don't want to get caught and thrown in jail."

Tom flashed him a fiery glance. "You haven't yet, have you? Just listen to me, and nothing's going to happen." With that, the three men parted company and Jet rode into Deadwood.

———————

Kat woke up late, as she always did. Her business kept her up until the wee hours of the morning, and she rarely woke before noon. She rubbed her eyes, which still burned from last night's cigarette smoke, eased out of bed, and went to her small kitchen to start the fire and make herself a cup of coffee. While the coffee was boiling on the stove, she stepped outside on her small porch to let the cat in and get the mail. Immediately, she saw a small package in the mailbox. The return address of Evangeline Fletcher was beautifully written in the upper left-hand corner.

"I wonder what this is all about?" she asked aloud.

When she got back into the house, she poured herself the first cup of coffee of the day and took a long sip. Sitting at her small table, she opened the brown parcel. Out fell her compact onto the tablecloth. *Oh my!* She thought, *I must have left it on the stagecoach, and Evangeline found it.* Just then, Kat realized she hadn't even told Evangeline good-bye when they parted. But there was no point in it; the two women had nothing in common. They knew they would never see one another again, as it was highly unlikely that Evangeline would walk into her saloon.

She opened the compact to see the portrait still in its compartment. Then she pulled out a note she found tucked in the package. She opened it and read the short missive.

"Minnie!" she blurted out to her cat, which was lapping up her morning milk from a saucer. "She's the one who recognized me? It's incredible that she would be connected with this. She remembered me!" She was so excited to get her compact back and hear from Minnie that she decided to celebrate by frying herself a couple of eggs and bacon. Ordinarily, she limited herself to coffee and a bowl of oatmeal.

While she made her breakfast, she mused on Minnie's note. Minnie was now a missionary—married to a preacher at that! She could hardly believe it. She knew Minnie as the wife of a tough freighter, but she had been so kind to Kat when she needed someone.

It seemed only yesterday to Kat when she had run away from home and her father who was so insistent that Kat marry his best friend's son. No way was she going to tie herself down to that fool that called himself a man. She probably would have stayed if her mother had stood up to her husband and took Kat's side, but her mother wasn't strong enough to take the consequences. Well, her daughter was certainly strong enough, but leaving had been difficult, and to survive, she had had to do things she would not have ordinarily done.

The cat had curled up on a chair by the time Kat finished her noon breakfast and coffee. She wasn't in the mood to go to work today, but she had to do her part to keep the business going. She bathed, put on the yellow dress from Cleveland, applied her makeup, and piled her red hair high on her head. She looked at her final efforts in the mirror and decided it was the best she could do—not what you would call pretty, but what men would find attractive. Finding her compact and wearing her new dress had perked up her spirits, and she felt she was ready to live the day, no matter what it had to offer.

She put the cat outside, left her little Victorian house perched precariously on the hillside, and walked to the

Birdcage Saloon. Clem had just opened up the double doors of the saloon when she arrived. This wouldn't have been her first choice of occupation, but this was where she could make the most money.

The previous owner had given her a deal on the saloon as well as the house, and she felt she couldn't turn it down. She had worked her way up from waitressing and card dealing and by observing everything around her. She had decided that she could run a saloon. Managing a business seemed to come naturally, and in Deadwood, nearly everyone would rather drink and play cards than eat.

"Good morning, Clem," she said as she removed her hat and placed it behind the bar. "I almost forgot the smell of stale beer and sweeping compound," she said, wrinkling her nose.

"Oh, come, now. Admit you love this place," Clem said, kidding her. She didn't answer, but instead frowned and took out the box of bar receipts and looked them over. "Looks like business was about normal while I was away, except for one day I see here," she remarked to Clem while adding up the receipts.

"Oh, yeah, that was the day they tried a cattle thief. There were lots of people in town. After the trial, all the cattlemen hit the bars."

"Did they convict him?"

"Gave him two years in the pen."

"I guess that was better for him than getting hung from the nearest tree," she said absently as she placed the sale records under the counter.

"Want to deal the cards this afternoon? I'll take the second table if we need to start another."

"Sure, it helps to pass the time." She sat at the table, broke out a new deck of cards, and shuffled them to soften them up a bit. Soon, a few men approached the table looking for a game of poker. They sat down and bought some chips. She began to deal the cards as if it were second nature to her. She snapped the deck and dealt the afternoon away.

At about five o'clock, she went home to eat a bite and rest before returning for the evening. As she sat at her kitchen table with a sandwich she had made for herself, she picked up the note from Minnie and read it again. *I would enjoy a talk with Minnie now,* she thought.

Minnie had a way of making a person feel that someone cared. Kat really had no one in her life but her sister and niece. Deadwood wasn't the place to meet men she wanted to keep. She had entered a few relationships here and there, but she had been cautious about associating with someone who would just complicate her life.

Kat took a piece of paper and pencil out of her desk drawer and began to write Minnie a reply. She felt inhibited in the beginning, knowing that Minnie was now a pastor's wife, so she chose her words more carefully than she ordinarily would have. But as she wrote, she realized she was telling Minnie everything about her rise to success and the emptiness she felt in spite of it. She reread her letter and thought maybe she shouldn't send it, but she didn't want to write another. She would never see Minnie anyway, so what would it hurt? Taking a stamp from the drawer, she moistened it, put it on the addressed envelope, and placed it in her mailbox.

After cleaning the kitchen and fixing her makeup, she returned to the saloon to catch up on her paperwork. After several hours of shuffling papers and adding entries to her books, she stepped outside to get a breath of fresh air. That was when she saw a man in a bowler hat and suit ride down the street in front of her establishment.

Kat looked again and then called out, "Jet! Jet Black, is that you?" The man turned briefly and kept on riding. *I know that was Jet,* she thought. She hurriedly followed him down the street, hoping he would stop, but he continued riding and soon disappeared. She placed her hands on her hips. *Well, I'll be. That had to have been Jet. I'd have known that ill-fitting suit anywhere. I wonder why he didn't stop?*

CHAPTER 9

Jet arrived in Fort Pierre three days after he boarded the stage in Deadwood. A muddy trail had delayed his progress and frayed his nerves. He had ruined his shoes and probably his trousers, too, when he had assisted the stagecoach driver in digging mud from the wheel spokes.

It was evening when Jet arrived, and after scraping the mud off his shoes and trousers, he checked into a hotel for the night. He ignored the strange looks from the clerk and took the Pierre newspaper from the hotel lobby to his room to read the latest news in the area. The notices of roundups in western South Dakota caught his attention. One was just beginning northwest of Pierre. He calculated that by the time he reached the area, he might be able to see the roundup in progress.

The next morning, he swapped his suit and hat for his usual work clothes and threw his shoes in the trash. He strapped on his gun, checked out of the hotel, and walked to the nearest livery stable, where he bought a black horse that appeared sound. At the nearby general store, he purchased enough food and supplies to last a week or two and rode north out of town on what promised to be a sunny day.

He imagined that a man could get lost in the vastness of these wide, open spaces. At first, the thought of riding as far as he could appealed to him, but out of habit he found himself searching the landscape for hiding places. Ever since his first rustling escapade, he felt vulnerable and in need of cover, like an animal camouflaging itself to evade predators. But out here, he could see no trees, no deep gorges, and no rocky hills. He sighed, realizing he was growing tired of living on the edge of the law. If only he hadn't been down on his luck the day he had met Tom, he would never have turned to rustling. Now, he had no idea how to change the direction of his life. He was caught in a snare, and there seemed no way out. Tom just wouldn't accept no for an answer.

Cattle, pasture land, roundup wagons, and a multitude of cowboys filled his vision as he rode. He tried to count the cattle, but determined there were too many. Seeing cattle grazing contentedly had always warmed his heart. They were at peace; he wasn't.

The spring roundup crews were scouring the hillsides and ravines for cattle. He waved to a crew now and then, just to be friendly and divert any suspicion. He congratulated himself on his timing. After the spring roundups, the cattlemen most likely wouldn't check on their herds until the fall roundups. This would give Jet, Tom, and the men time to pick up the unbranded strays left behind.

After several hours of riding, he stopped to brew a cup of coffee and heat up a can of beans for a mid-morning lunch. There was no hurry. He had almost a month to come up with a plan. In the meantime, he had to learn the lay of the land and perhaps observe some of the cattlemen in the area. He listened to the bawling cattle and yipping cowboys. While enjoying the last of the coffee in the pot, he watched as two men rode up to him. He felt uneasy and stood up with his hand close to the butt of his gun.

"Howdy, there," called one of the men. "We couldn't help notice you riding across the prairie. You passed us up there a ways back. You seem like a friendly fellow. We're looking for some help. One of our men fell with his horse and is laid up, and another one is suffering something terrible from a stomach ache."

"What kind of help are you needing?" Jet eyed them suspiciously.

"You probably noticed there's a lot of cattle scattered all over the prairie and in the ravines and gullies 'round here. Had a bad winter up north. Lots of ice," one of the men said. "The cattle drifted to the southeast to find grazing. We think more than usual drifted out of their home range and it will take a lot of hands to round up them cattle. Got a late start for the spring roundup. If you see your way to help, the boss would pay you well for the day's work. You got some experience with cattle?"

"Yeah, some." Jet relaxed. He didn't really want a job, but this might be an opportunity to learn about the cattlemen in the area and their dealings. He could help for a day or so and then move on. "I suppose I could help you out today."

The man bent down, crossing his hands and resting his arms near the saddle's pommel. As he explained their plan, he moved just his hands in abbreviated gestures, indicating the circular roundup. "We all met at a certain point on a creek back there a ways. Now we are fanning out, looking for cattle. We'll eventually end up near the mouth of the creek. Half the men were dropped off at different places on one half of the circle on the left and half were dropped off at other places on the right side. We're moving in, flushing out the cattle, and driving them to the designated gathering spot."

"Yeah, I get it. The stream is the line that runs through the circle."

"Right. Now, meet us at the ridge over there. By the way, my name is Hal," said the tall, slim one with a hollowed face. "And this is Bert," he said with a nod toward the shorter man.

Jet nodded toward them, shoveled dirt on his dying fire, buckled on his chaps, packed up his cooking utensils, and rode after the two men. As he rode, he was concocting a story that would explain his lonesome presence on the prairie. He wondered if he should give them a fake name, too. Oh, how he disliked lying to keep himself safe. Sometimes he nearly became caught up in his own fibs. His mama had taught him to tell the truth, but he hadn't been doing that lately.

"Now you take those canyons over on the west side, and Bert and I will follow behind to bring out what you might miss. Bring them cattle up on the flat and keep them bunched."

Jet did what he was told. He knew exactly what to do; he had rounded up cattle many times, but for different purposes. His horse seemed like he had been around cows enough, so that made his task even easier. He was careful not to be too efficient.

Jet rode into the ravines, searching through the brush and gullies for calves. The briars and thickets raked against his chaps, and he pulled his hat on tighter so the low branches wouldn't dislodge it. After a time, he brought many steers, cows and their calves out of the brush and up to the flat, purposely leaving behind a few that were well concealed. Hal and Bert joined him a few minutes later with the few stranglers.

"Looks like I missed a few. Sorry about that," Jet said.

"Oh, that's all right. That's why we followed you up. You stay up here with the herd, and we'll check the other ravine over there," Hal said.

Jet watched them ride off and rolled a cigarette while he waited for them to return. He rode slowly around the cattle, keeping them bunched. He expertly located and read the brands, knowing exactly how he would cut out the cattle and sort them. He hoped his horse was up to it, but again, he knew he didn't want to look like a rustler.

In about half an hour, the men brought more cattle out of the ravine. And soon as they were assimilated, the three men drove them to meet the other bunches that had been gathered that morning. With the sun glaring straight over them, they knew it was time for lunch. When they located the mess wagon and the other bunches of cattle, they rode straight over to them.

"Say, boss, I found some help," called Hal when he spotted Ed.

"Get him something to eat, and then we'll put him to work. I'll be over in a bit."

"I really don't need to eat," Jet protested. "I've already had some beans."

Hal handed Jet a plate. "Grub is part of the deal. Besides, you get to taste Pepper's stew. He makes the best around. Don't worry, you'll earn it." Having no other choice, Jet accepted the chunky, brown stew filled with canned vegetables. The men filled their plates with grub, sat for a few minutes of respite, and turned their attention to devouring the meal.

"Oh, sorry—in our haste, I forgot to get your name," Hal said.

"Yeah, I guess I didn't give it. Just call me Jet Black," he said, coughing and sputtering after several bites of stew.

Hal laughed. "Now you know why we call our cook Pepper?"

Jet nodded then got up to get more coffee. While filling his cup, he counted about twenty riders in addition to the horse wranglers, the nighthawk, and the cook. He hadn't even counted the day herders who were out holding the bunched cattle.

"Hope we didn't interfere with your plans," Bert said as he limped over with his tin plate.

"Oh, no. I was just on my way to visit some relatives." Jet hoped he didn't have to explain any more.

"You're darn good with a horse, Jet," Bert said, seemingly satisfied with the brief story. "You could have a job here for a long time if you wanted."

"Oh, I don't know. I'm the drifting kind, just like these open-range cattle. When a situation becomes too boring or complicated, I move on, looking for better eating, better shelter, better weather. You know, these cowmen have it made. It doesn't cost them much to run cattle on this open range. And look at the profits!"

"Not all have been lucky," said Bert. "The blizzards in the 1880s wiped some of the big outfits off the map. And I hear the cowmen talk about the rising cost of keeping cattle. Some are starting to hay their cattle in winter, plowing fireguards, and putting up windmills. The cost is beginning to add up."

Jet nodded. "I guess that's so, but if I had backing, I'd try it."

"You like cattle?"

"Yeah, I guess I do—horses, too."

"I'll never get enough money together to start a ranch. Guess I'll always be a cowboy," Bert reflected. He scratched the stubble on his chin. "It's hard work with little sleep. I'm thinking a man has to be a half-wit to do this for a living."

"I guess you're right," Jet said, laughing. "But there are worse jobs, I imagine."

Bert scraped up the last of his stew before speaking. "I've done some of 'em. I cleaned livery barns as a boy but always dreamed of trailing cattle. Spent more time leaning on a pitchfork, wishing I were older. I started trailing cattle when I was thirteen like lots of young cowboys in them days. Nah, I've always been a cowpuncher. That will never change until the day I die."

By the time Jet finished the pie that Hal foisted on him, the boss came over and introduced himself. "My name is Ed Reynolds. I'm the boss for this roundup and manager for Bar Double B Cattle Company."

Jet extended his hand. "Pleased to meet you. Just call me Jet Black."

"Well then, Jet, the boys will outfit you if you are in need of anything, and we'll see you at the end of the day at camp."

"You heard the boss. What are you in need of?" Hal asked.

"Nothing much. I guess another rope. Otherwise, I think I'm ready. I have a bedroll with me. Don't know if my horse will be up to a roundup, but I guess we'll see." He placed the rope on his saddle pommel and signaled that he was ready.

"We have plenty horses in the remuda. If you need a different mount, the horse wrangler will help you pick out something. You'll have to change horses every once in a while. They get tuckered out awfully fast."

Jet took the advice and changed horses before joining the men as they rode off with their circle bosses to work another circle. This time, Jet was left off alone about a half mile from Bert. The chuck wagon proceeded over a hill to another roundup camp where there was plenty grass and water.

Jet directed his new mount toward the cattle, driving them to the center of the circle. As he did so, he studied the brands the cattle bore, the most prominent being the namesake of the company for which he was now working—a horizontal line followed by two capital Bs. Jet noted the brands that would be relatively easy to alter. Savvy brand readers could detect reworked brands, but Tom was one of the best. He was one of the few expert rustlers with branding knowledge and could fool the inspectors most of the time. Earmarking, though, could prove troublesome to even the best rustler. Tom had often told Jet that unbranded calves with slick or unmarked ears were the preferred prey. Jet shook his head, annoyed that he was again thinking like a crook. Three years had taught him a lot of bad habits.

Toward the end of the day, Ed rode up to the cattle the men were holding. "Let's bed them down here for the night and have some supper. We'll finish separating the dry stock from the cows and calves tomorrow. They should be paired up by then. Hal, take some men in the morning and sort out the long-haired and dim-branded cattle. We need to be able to read those brands." He shook his head. "By the looks of it, a lot of cattle that aren't ours have drifted onto the range. The reps can claim their cattle and return them to their home ranges after we identify those brands we can't read."

With the wranglers' help, Pepper had set up his chuck wagon in the new location. A tent had been put up and the stove was taken out of the cart once again. The rope corral for about one hundred horses had been attached to the bed wagon and secured with stakes. The smell of frying meat made Jet's mouth water. By casual observance, Jet could see that a supper of steak, baked beans, and canned tomatoes laced with canned corn was almost ready. He wondered if it was covered with pepper too. He hoped not.

Jet ate the surprisingly good meal, secretly wishing he could crawl into bed afterward and sleep for the night. But he knew he should volunteer to keep watch from sundown until eight o'clock just to show he was an all-around good fellow. But that would not be the end of his nightly duties; since he was a new hand, he would surely have to assume one of the night guards.

"Jet, you want to stand the fourth guard with me tonight?" Bert limped over and asked.

"Oh, sure, that sounds good. Guess I'll help with the herding after supper, too." At least while he was working, he didn't have to answer a bunch of questions—not that the boys were particularly nosy. He knew cowboy etiquette discouraged prying into other people's affairs. That went for outlaws, too. Jet joined Ed, the wagon boss, and some of the reps for the after-supper watch. The wagon boss and the reps wouldn't do any more night duty.

Although the herd had been given space to spread out, it took awhile for them to settle down after being separated from their calves during the roundup. By eight o'clock, when the first guard came on, they had quieted some. Jet rode into camp about a quarter to eight. Most of the men were beginning to bed down for the night, and he turned in, too.

He heard nothing, not even the howling coyotes or the bawling cattle, until someone woke him for the fourth guard. This guard began around two and would last until daybreak when the day herders would take over. Jet reached for his hat, tugged on his boots, retrieved his night horse from the picket line, and went out to join Bert and the herd.

The two men waved to each other and walked their horses in opposite directions around the herd. Jet wasn't much of a singer, but he heard Bert quietly serenading the cattle in his low, gentle voice. Jet looked up to appreciate the star-filled sky. He uttered a grateful sigh; tonight would be quiet. A storm would cause havoc with cattle, and he didn't relish a stampede.

"Hey, Jet, you got the time on you?" Bert asked in barely a whisper when they were about to pass each other on their opposite courses.

"No, I left my timepiece back at camp in my war bag. We quit at daybreak anyway."

"Yeah, guess so. Have you ever told time by the Big Dipper and the North Star?"

"Oh, I've tried a time or two, but I'm not very good at it."

Bert lifted his head to the heavens and squinted his eyes in concentration. "Well, they're both easy to find." He pointed. "There's the North Star and the Big Dipper. Now, I've been herding enough this time of the year, I can about tell you by the Dipper's pointer stars, it's three o'clock."

Jet flashed him a look of astonishment. Bert was a man of surprises. He could sing and tell time by the stars. "Not long until dawn, I 'spec," he muttered.

Jet's duty was about finished, but he caught himself trying to nod off; somehow he managed to sit the saddle until sunrise. As part of his job, he quietly rode into camp and woke Pepper to begin breakfast. "Hold the pepper on my eggs, would you?" he added.

While Pepper rattled the pots and pans, Jet bedded down for a few extra minutes of sleep, only to be awakened by the cook's call. "Roll out, or I'll throw it out."

Responding to his brief command, the men scrambled to bundle their bedrolls, tucked their war bags containing their personal items into the roll, tied them, and dropped them off by the bed wagon before lining up for a breakfast of eggs, biscuits, syrup, and hot coffee.

Ed approached Jet while he was rubbing his bleary eyes. "What job do you think you're fitted for?"

Jet thought a moment, not sure of what he should choose. He could do them all. "I'm a good roper."

"Heel or head?"

"Usually I aim for the heels, but if it's a small calf, I aim for the head."

"Good. We could use a fast roper. Give it a try," Ed said, satisfied.

After breakfast, Hal asked Jet to join the group working the cattle with unreadable brands. This time, Jet asked the horse wrangler for a good cutting horse. He looked the horses over, pleased with what he saw. He discovered that six extra horses had been provided for his use. He called out to the horse wrangler, "Which one's a good roping horse?"

"This here's a good one. Has a lot of cow sense. Be careful; he reads the cow's movements before a man can."

"Thanks, I'll remember that." Jet saddled the horse.

They began with the dry stock, consisting of steers, bulls, unbred cows, and unreadable brands. Once the unreadable brands were cut from the stock, Hal and his men went to work, roping the animals and taking them down, much the way it was done at branding. Then they clipped the long hair to get at the brand, determining which range owned the animal.

In the meantime, two horse wranglers scouted the creek bottoms to find wood for the branding fire. They bundled dry wood, secured the bundles into piles with a rope, and dragged them with their horses to a place Ed had selected for the branding site. Then they built a roaring fire for heating the irons. By the time the crew sorted the cows with the unbranded calves, the irons were red hot.

Jet assumed his roping position. Careful not to rile the bunched cattle, he swung his rope and caught an unbranded calf by the hind legs and dragged the bawling and struggling creature to the branding fire. Jet paid special attention to the brand of the fretting mother cow by its side. Once the calf reached the fire, Jet called out that brand. One wrestler flipped the calf over and put it down on the ground. He caught the top hind leg, pulled it back, and braced his foot against the other back leg. A second wrestler put his weight on the foreleg and pinned the animal. A man with a branding iron burned the sign into its hide. Another man skilled with a sharp knife castrated the bull calves while another vaccinated for black leg. By the time they were finished, Jet or another roper had dragged in another calf.

The afternoon air was gristly with clouds of dust and smoke, the stench of burnt hair, and the bawling of cattle. By evening, the cowhands looked for a stream or water hole in which to wash the putrid stench from their clothes and skin. Meanwhile, the representatives from the ranges close to the roundup site cut out their cattle and turned them toward their home range after one final inspection of brands.

Jet sighed in relief when branding ended for the day. He had fit in perfectly with the rest of the hands. They had only evaluated him on his performance, not caring anything about his past. An honest day's work was something he hadn't done for a while. He liked the feel of it.

The next morning, Jet awoke massaging his sore roping arm. He had proved he could keep up with the so-called best ropers of the crew. He rubbed his arm again, thinking he would ask Pepper for liniment if it wasn't better by evening. Jet fastened on chaps to protect his legs from the briars and shrubs that would surely tear at his legs as he rode through the canyons and ravines on yet another day of roundup. He found himself looking forward to another of Pepper's meals. Flapjacks, syrup, and bacon greeted the hungry crew.

At breakfast, Jet learned that the Bar Double B took the center of the roundup territory, about a five-mile radius. Some of the company's representatives were already headed southeast to help with other roundups and to bring back some of their stray cattle.

––––––

The next two days involved more branding and more roundups. The cleanup began on the fifth day. The cowboys separated the stray stock from each bunch. The wagon bosses, including Ed, inspected the cattle one last time, and then the various remaining representatives took the stray cattle back to their respective ranges.

Jet had planned on leaving from the ranch headquarters, but Ed addressed him on his way out. "How would you like to be a rep for Bar Double B outfit?"

"Me?"

"Yeah, you. I've been watching the way you handle cattle, and I like what I see. You seem to have a keen eye for reading brands, and that's the number-one requirement for a good rep. You said you haven't worked for an outfit lately?"

Jet hesitated, pondering his answer. "I drift from one job to another. Guess I don't stay in one place too long."

"If you're willing, I'd like you and Hal to depart tomorrow. Are you familiar with the country south of here?"

"Can't say I am. Most of my time's been spent in Wyoming and the Black Hills." *Oops,* Jet thought. *I shouldn't have mentioned the Black Hills.* He hoped he didn't look guilty.

"Hal knows the country where you're going."

Jet fidgeted, wondering if he should stay or move on. If he were out on his own, he might run into Tom. Jet was supposed to be scouting another rustling job. "I suppose I could help out."

"Good. And when you return, there will be a job waiting for you at the ranch headquarters. Even though the roundup will be over, there's still work to do."

"What kind of work?"

"I need line riders to hold the cattle on the range during the summer months. Cattle don't tend to stray much until the winter months, but they still need tending to. There's fence to fix and haying that needs to be done."

"Thanks, I'll give it some thought." Jet wasn't looking for a job, but he reasoned he had an entire month to come up with a rustling plan. "Say, Boss, could I take one of them good cutting horses from the remuda?"

"Yeah, help yourself. I had the wrangler sort you out a string of horses to take with you, and Pepper packed you up some grub for the ride. Stop by and pick it up before you leave." Ed left with a wave.

Jet chose the sorting horse he wanted and transferred his gear. He used several of the horses in the string to carry the food supply and other necessities for working a bunch of cattle over the next week or two. When Hal joined him, the two men headed to the south. Jet's only concern was Tom.

———————

After he and Hal had finished the southern roundups, Jet settled into the Bar Double B ranch routine. It was a Sunday morning, and his bunkmates were still sleeping. Their fits of snoring had settled into soft wheezes. Since returning from his rep job, Jet had been helping with line riding. Today was his day off, and he planned to enjoy it by doing absolutely nothing. It felt good to be above the suspicion of the law, and he knew he had won the respect and trust of his bunkmates. Blissfully, he turned over in his bed and fell back into quiet slumber. It seemed as though only a minute had passed before he felt someone shaking him. He shrugged off the intruder to his dream world and buried himself deeper into the covers.

Splat! Something wet hit his face and he scrambled to the surface, swinging his arms as though emerging from a water hole.

"Jet, calm down. It's just a little water." Hal stood over him. "It's time to get up and get ready for church."

"Church?" Jet couldn't remember the last time he had gone to church. "Nah, I'm just going to hang around here." By now, he was groggily sitting up in his bed, hands slightly raised, prepared for another attack.

"They got a free lunch after church. Pepper's off on Sundays, you know. Besides, the boss is a religious man. Maybe you want to stay on his good side," Hal advised.

"You mean to tell me all his hired hands go to church?" Jet pulled on his trousers and stood alongside his bunk, water dripping from his hair.

"Yep, except those who have to work."

"That's hard to believe."

"Well, it's true. Now come and eat some breakfast. Bert cooked up a mess of pancakes and eggs." Hal pulled a chair to a rickety table on the other side of the bunkhouse. He and

Jet filled their plates along with the rest of the crew.

"So, where's this church?"

Bert, pouring the last of the pancake batter on the griddle, answered, "About an hour or so from here—on the reservation."

"The reservation?"

"That's what I said. There's a mission church there. And some nice-looking Indian gals go there, too." Bert winked.

"I ain't looking for a gal or religion either," Jet said with a disgusted edge to his voice.

"Oh, it won't hurt you none," Hal said.

After the dishes were cleared away from the table, washed, and put in a makeshift cupboard, Jet took his turn at the washstand. He had taken his Saturday night bath in the washhouse the night before, but he hadn't shaved. He pulled his shaving equipment from the war bag. With a little water and his shaving brush, he lathered up his soap in a shaving cup. He then slathered the foamy soap all over his stubbly beard with the brush. Testing his straight razor and finding it dull, he whipped it back and forth on the razor strap that was hanging on a nail beside the washstand. He peered into the cracked mirror; his dark eyes looked back at him, almost lost in the white froth. He sighed and began to scrape off his whiskers, being careful not to take any skin along with each swipe.

At last, the men were tidied up as best they knew how. Proud of the layers of dirt they had scrubbed away and ribbing each other about looking good, they sauntered out to the corral to saddle their horses for the ride to the mission. Ed was waiting for them at the corrals. As they rode across the prairie, Jet chuckled at what Tom and his gang of boys might say if they knew Jet was on his way to church. He rolled a cigarette and lit it, drawing in its calming effect.

Ed turned his head and looked back. "No smoking on the Lord's day."

Jet frowned and snuffed out his smoke on the saddle horn. *This is going to be one long day*, he thought.

About an hour later, the mission loomed ahead. Several outbuildings surrounded a church in need of paint. The church bell rang out, its comforting sound drawing the men like a magnet. Suddenly, memory jabbed like a pin at Jet's conscience. Yes, he remembered now. He used to like hearing the church bells as a boy growing up in Kansas. What had happened to change those simpler, happier days?

When the men approached the church, they dismounted and tied their horses to the hitching rail. One by one, they removed their hats and hung their heads, looking quite sheepish as they followed Ed through the church doors. Jet eyed the back pews, but Ed kept walking until he selected a central vacant pew, which the slicked up men easily filled.

Jet navigated the order of the worship service without too much trouble, and even surprised himself with his familiarity of the hymns. *Funny what one remembers*, he thought.

The pastor spoke on salvation and read Scripture. " 'For whosoever shall call upon the name of the Lord shall be saved.' "

Jet reckoned he was beyond help, so he stopped listening and let his mind wander. He knew he couldn't stay at the ranch indefinitely, although he had thought about it. He liked not worrying about getting caught and sent to prison. No, he had to get back to Fort Pierre. Tom would be looking for him, even though Jet had a notion not to show up. There was no such thing as walking out on Tom; he would just hunt Jet down.

At the conclusion of the final hymn, Jet lowered his head, rotated his hat in his hand, and walked outside with Ed and the fellows.

"Brought a new man with me this time, Pastor. This here's Jet. He's been with us a few weeks." Ed clasped his hand on Jet's shoulder, which surprised Jet. He had never worked for a boss that seemed to care about his employees.

"I know you!" the pastor exclaimed. "We met on the stagecoach awhile ago. Surprised to see you this far east of Deadwood."

"So this is where your church is?" Jet mumbled.

"Make sure you stay for lunch before you leave," Elijah said to the men, his gaze lingering on Jet.

Hal, Bert, and a few others sidled up to a few of the young native women during lunch, leaving Jet to himself. Not interested in forming any commitments, he took his plate of sandwiches and cake and ensconced himself within the shade of a young tree. Being alone never bothered Jet. He watched the crowd as he finished his meal, tipped his hat over his eyes, and slumbered while conversation and laughter faded to a murmur in the background.

The next thing Jet knew, Hal was tapping him on the shoulder, waking him up to depart. He launched himself to his feet, readjusted his hat, dusted off his backside, and walked toward a group of ladies to thank them for the lunch. He tipped his hat to Evangeline and the other mission ladies. "Appreciate the lunch," he said.

Evangeline immediately recognized him. "Jet, I thought that might be you, but I never expected to see you here. You look different. We're so glad you joined us, and we hope to see you again."

"I probably won't be around much longer," Jet muttered. During the ride back to the ranch, Jet kept mulling over in his mind whether he should stay or return to Fort Pierre. He finally decided he had to return to Fort Pierre. Tom would be waiting for him there. When they reached the ranch headquarters and unsaddled their horses, Jet approached Ed. "Say, Boss, if you're not really needing me, I'd like to push on."

Ed removed the saddle from his horse and placed it on the ground. "I'd rather you not leave. You've been good help, but I knew you were just passing through. Let's put the saddles away, and you can come to the house with me and we'll settle up."

Jet had never been in the low log building of the ranch headquarters before. He was surprised when he entered. He expected more in the way of decor, but Ed enjoyed the same comforts and discomforts as his men. Jet would have liked to have known more about this unusual man, but didn't ask any questions. He accepted the wages Ed counted out and turned to leave.

"If you are in the area again, stop in and I'll give you a job."

"Thanks. I appreciate that." The men shook hands and he left. Jet knew he was riding away from a life he would have liked, but it just wasn't in the cards for him. Tom would be waiting, and he just had to show up.

———————

Jet was lying on the hotel bed, which was only slightly softer than his bunkhouse bed, when he heard a loud knock on his door. He jumped up and jerked the door open to find the same, scrubby Tom standing there.

"I see you took my suggestion and cleaned up," Jet said wryly.

"Did you think I would?" Tom jeered as he entered the small hotel room furnished with the bare essentials. Looking around and not finding what he was looking for, he growled. "I'm powerful thirsty. How about going somewhere for a drink?"

"Not a good idea. We shouldn't be seen anywhere together. I'm surprised you haven't been caught as careless as you are."

"What's the matter? You ashamed of me?"

"Yeah, that I am, but that's not the main reason. I just don't want to look suspicious."

"You worry too much. Guess I'll get one later. What you got lined up?"

"Nothing."

"Nothing? What you been doing for a month?"

"Working, but I haven't found an easy mark."

"Well, I have!"

"Where?"

"South of here. The boys are waiting on us."

"Why...why don't you go on without me."

"What's the matter? You sick?"

"I'd like to sit this one out."

"You can't do that. We're depending on you."

"What are you going to do if I decide to stay put?"

"Now don't try to double cross me or sneak out of town." Tom scowled. "What happened to you since you left us? You getting soft?"

"Nothing. Just been thinking."

"Too much thinking, I'd say. Remember, I have ways to get even. I'll see you this evening about two miles upstream from the mouth of the Bad River. Be there." Tom left, slamming the door.

Jet had never crossed Tom before, although he had witnessed his temper a time or two when someone had. There wasn't much time to make a decision. It was now or never. He didn't believe in killing, but Tom wouldn't think twice if he deemed it necessary. Jet was positive that Tom was watching the hotel to make sure he didn't run. After mulling over the options, Jet walked downstairs to the hotel's lobby and approached the clerk.

"Howdy, Mr. Jet. Are you planning on checking out?"

"Yeah, in a way I am. Do you remember that scruffy, short man that asked about me and came up to my room?"

"Why, yes I do," the clerk said in his squeaky, timid voice. "I was wondering what that fellow wanted with you."

"He's a no-good sort, and I think he wants to do me harm. I have something extra for you if you can figure out how to get me out of here unseen." Jet flashed a bill in front of his face, and the clerk's eyes widened under the wire spectacles.

He squeaked, "Let me think." He rubbed his chin and furrowed his brow for a time. "I know. I'm expecting a delivery from the meat market shortly. He comes to the back door. You could slip into the wagon box, and that will get you as far as the meat market. Then you will have to figure out the rest yourself."

"Is that the best you can do?"

The clerk shrunk back. "Unless you have a better idea."

Actually, Jet didn't have a better idea. He hoped the clerk's plan would work, or he might end up a dead man. All afternoon, Jet paced back and forth in the hotel, carefully parting the curtains to look out the windows for Tom. Shortly before the delivery wagon pulled up to the back door in the late afternoon, Jet happened to see Tom staggering out of a saloon across the street.

Ah, that's good for me. His senses will be dulled. That gives me a big advantage. Jet grinned at the thought.

Tom had settled in on a bench across the street, his head bobbing from time to time. Jet's nerves were in shambles by the time the deliveryman arrived. As soon as he came in the back door, the clerk and Jet filled him in on their plan.

The big burly deliveryman sized Jet up. "I don't know you from Adam; maybe you're a crook on the run."

Jet handed him a few bills as an incentive to help him out. They had agreed that the clerk would go out the front door as a diversion while Jet sneaked out the back and slid into the wagon unnoticed. Luckily, the deliveryman was large enough to screen Jet as he climbed into the wagon.

At just the right moment, the men put their plan into effect. Jet slithered into the wagon without any trouble and the deliveryman discreetly covered him up and drove off. Tom was nowhere in sight when the deliveryman drove up to his place of business.

"It's okay to come out now. In fact, I think that man you were trying to avoid passed out on the bench," the deliveryman informed him.

"Thanks much," Jet said, dropping a few more coins in the man's hand. He headed over to the stable to see if the black horse was still for sale. Jet scowled as he paid the livery man more than he had originally paid. Luckily, Ed had paid him well before he had left. He didn't have to think too much about where to go. He reined his horse to the north and hoped Ed would take him back.

––––––

The next morning, Jet rode up to the ranch headquarters, dismounted, and looped the reins over the rail. Ed came out of the ranch house just as Jet placed his boot on the first step.

"I thought I heard someone ride up. What you doing back so soon?"

"Change of plans. If my job's still open, I would like it back." Jet pushed his hat above his forehead.

Ed looked at him quizzically. "Well, sure. I haven't had time to hire anyone else. Is something wrong?"

"No, no. Everything's fine."

"If you say so, but you look like you're running from someone. I'm not one to judge, but if you have something to say, I'm listening. Come inside awhile. I'll get you a cup of coffee."

Jet hesitated before following. He wasn't about to bare his soul. Ed certainly wouldn't approve of what he had been involved in. Ed poured Jet a cup of coffee and motioned for him to sit.

"I don't mean to pry, but if it is something that endangers my men or this ranch, I need to know."

Jet sipped his coffee slowly, giving him time to think about what to say. "Oh, I got into a disagreement with a man over a card game. He's kind of an ornery cuss, so I thought it best to leave town." Jet's conscience stabbed him again.

"Where were you?"

"In Fort Pierre."

"Do you think he'd bother coming after you?"

"No, I don't think so. There's really no need to worry."

"I hope you're right. I don't need any trouble. You know the routine around here. There's corrals that need fixing. Hal hasn't left yet for the day. Go find him, and he'll tell you what to do."

Jet drained the last of his coffee. "Thanks, Boss. I really appreciate what you're doing for me."

Hal looked up when he heard Jet's boots jingle. "I thought that was your black horse. You missed us?" Hal slapped him on the back.

"I guess you could say that. The boss says there's corrals that need fixing."

"Yeah, we'll ride over to the summer range. Have you had breakfast?"

Jet's stomach growled in reply. "Just coffee."

"Check out the bunkhouse. I'm sure you can find a biscuit or two. It's going be a long day without anything to eat."

Jet found a few hard biscuits and several leftover flapjacks, which he devoured voraciously. He hadn't eaten for an entire day because he had taken no supplies when he lit out north. He wasn't sure that returning to the ranch was one of his best ideas, but he wasn't sure what else he could've done, unless he were to have taken a train east. But what would he do there? He liked the West and wanted to stay.

"There you are," Hal said when Jet came out of the bunkhouse. "I thought maybe you decided to take a nap, too, while you were at it."

"I'm ready. Found some biscuits and flapjacks. That will have to do until supper tonight."

"Good. Let's get going."

Jet pondered over the lies he had just told. He shouldn't have taken advantage of Ed that way, and he hoped with all his might that Tom wouldn't come looking for him. Was he endangering Ed and his men? No, that wouldn't happen. Tom would give up and go his way.

CHAPTER 10

A young telegraph clerk came rushing into the Birdcage Saloon on gangling legs, flexing like rubber stilts. "Kat! Kat, I have a telegram for you," he yelled, waving the piece of paper.

Kat turned from wiping beer scum off a table, the rag still in her hand. "Telegrams only mean one thing—bad news." She thanked the boy, who silently implored her for a tip, and deposited a couple coins in his hand. With trembling hands, she tossed the rag aside and read the message. Jennie approached her, concern lining her face. Kat couldn't take her eyes off the telegram. "I can't believe this. My sister's had an accident. Broke both legs, run over by a carriage. She says she can't take care of her little girl properly and needs my help."

"Oh, that's terrible!" Jennie gasped. "You have to leave again?"

"I can't leave my business, and she knows that. She wants me to keep her little girl until she recovers."

"Keep a little girl here? How old is she?"

"She's five. Of course this isn't the best place to take care of her! What am I going to do?"

"There's no one else who can help out?"

"Annabelle doesn't trust anyone else. She writes that she'll send her favorite quilt with her to comfort her, I suppose. During our last visit, Miranda dragged that worn quilt everywhere we went. " Kat sighed and sat at the table. "Someday, I'd like a little girl of my own, but the way my life's going, it's never going to happen."

"You're not that old yet. Don't give up hope. I wish I could help out, but I don't live the life of a saint either."

"A saint! Now that's an idea! I got an invitation about a month ago from an old friend to visit her at a mission on a reservation near Pierre. I could meet Miranda in Pierre and take my friend up on her invitation. The women there could help me out. Besides, what could be a better place than a mission? Could you take care of this place for a few weeks?"

"I guess we can. Just make sure you come back."

"Oh, I have to come back. We'll stay at the mission for a while, and then I'll bring her back to Deadwood for the remainder of the time. I'll try to find someone to watch her when I'm working."

"You could put an ad in the newspaper," Jennie suggested.

"That's not a bad idea. Where is a piece of paper?" Kat left the table and rummaged behind the bar looking for a pen, ink, and paper. "I'll write Minnie and send it today, along with a telegram to Annabelle. Oh, I wonder if I'll have time to answer an ad if I put one in today." She moaned. "Looks like I'm going away again."

———

The hot sun glared off the iron rails, sending up tremors of heat while Kat beat an invisible path back and forth across the Pierre depot's board floor. On each round, she peered out of the depot's open door, searching for the approaching train. *What am I doing?* she thought to herself. *I'm a saloon keeper. I know nothing about taking care of children. I hope Miranda doesn't get homesick and cries her eyes out.* Her heart quivered. What would she do if she did? It wasn't like she could take her back home to Cleveland. Kat reminded herself she was a grown woman, tough and resilient. She had dealt with all kinds of people, including drunks and ornery men in her Deadwood saloon. Surely, she could take care of a little girl. How hard could it be?

A half hour passed before the train rolled into the depot, puffing out an acrid odor and sounding its arrival with a bell. Kat scrambled outside and joined the throng milling around the depot. Soon, a little girl with a flushed face and strawberry blonde curls peeking out from under a brown bonnet appeared with a female escort.

"Miranda!" Kat waved at the girl, edging closer to the coach. "Miranda, do you remember me?" Kat asked as she knelt down in front of her. Miranda dropped her head and nodded. Kat glanced up at the woman who brought her out of the coach. "How was she?"

"Miranda was frightened for a while," the woman said with a warm smile, placing her hand on Miranda's shoulder.

"But she is a brave girl. We became good friends during the trip."

"Thanks so much for caring for her," Kat said.

"You are most welcome." The woman bowed slightly. I'll leave you two so you can become reacquainted. Oh, here's Miranda's quilt. I packed it up and put it in this bag before we got off the train." The woman handed the plain, black bag to Kat. "Good-bye, Miranda. Maybe we will see each other again sometime."

Kat stooped down to Miranda's level and softened her voice. "As soon as we pick up your bags, we'll go to a nice hotel I found. We'll spend the night here and take a boat ride tomorrow to visit a friend of mine. Would that be okay?"

"When can I see my mama?" Miranda began to wail.

"Oh, Miranda. I know you will miss your mama for a time, but she needs to rest and get strong. I promise I will take care of you until she gets well enough."

"But when can I see her?" Tears welled up in her bright, brown eyes. Miranda tugged at the black bag Kat was holding.

"How about I give you your quilt when we get to the hotel? Miranda, don't cry. It'll be okay. I'm taking you to a fun place. I promise. Do you like animals?" Miranda nodded through her tears. Kat gave her handkerchief to Miranda. She crumpled it up without an attempt to wipe her tear-stained face. "Here, let me help you." Kat pried the hanky from Miranda's grip and dried her tears. "I'm sure the mission has animals like horses, maybe dogs, and cats—"

"I like cats," she said, her little freckled face brightening some.

"Good. Now let's get your luggage and hail a hack driver to take us to the hotel. Are you hungry?" Miranda nodded. Kat inhaled deeply, silently congratulating herself for slogging through the first crisis.

Since hack drivers were plentiful in Pierre, it didn't take long for Kat to find one to deliver them to the hotel where Kat checked in, found their room, and unpacked a few clothes.

"Tomorrow, we'll ride on a riverboat. Would you like that?"

"I suppose."

"Now, let's attend to your hungry stomach. There's a dining room in this hotel. Let's see what they have to eat." Kat took hold of the girl's hand and walked down several flights of stairs to the dining room, papered with a green scroll pattern that lent a cool backdrop to the dark table and chairs.

"This room is rather pretty, don't you think?"

Miranda shrugged.

"What would you like to eat?"

"I don't know."

"We'll see what they have when the waitress brings a menu." Kat exhaled her anxiety and placed a linen napkin on her lap. Soon, a waitress wearing a black dress and a hat that looked like an upside-down, black bowl with ruffles, came over to their table. "Will you be ordering for two this evening?"

"Yes, I will. Do you have a menu we could see?"

"Sorry, ma'am. We have only one selection. Tonight, it is roast beef with all the trimmings."

"All right, bring us two orders. Coffee for me, and milk for the young lady."

"Will that be all?"

"For now, yes." Kat leaned across the table. "You do drink milk, don't you?" Miranda nodded. "Would you like to tell me about your trip?" Miranda shook her head. "You must have seen something interesting you could tell me about," Kat insisted.

"I was scared. I didn't want to look out the window."

Oh, great. She isn't going to like the boat ride either, Kat thought.

Soon, the waitress brought their order and placed it in front of them. Miranda moved her fork through the food, making rivers in the gravy. Kat knitted her brows and tapped her red fingernails on the table.

"I thought you were hungry."

"My mom doesn't make this kind of gravy."

"Well, just pick out the meat then. Here, I'll help you." Kat forked out the meat for her and moved it to the edge of her plate.

"Why are your fingernails red?"

Kat held up her hand and admired her perfectly manicured nails. "I put fingernail polish on them."

"Mama doesn't."

"Would you like me to paint your nails someday?"

Miranda wrinkled her nose and shook her head. She picked up her fork, ate a few morsels of meat, drank a few gulps of milk, and pushed away her glass of milk and plate.

Kat shoved the glass of milk back to her. "Could you at least drink your milk?"

"It's too warm." Miranda pushed it back, spilling some of it on the table. The waitress rushed over to wipe the puddle of spilled milk.

"You're such a patient mother."

A mother? Hardly, Kat thought. She relaxed her tightening jaw. *Maybe motherhood wasn't such a good idea after all.*

Miranda frowned and narrowed her eyes. "She said you were my mama. You're not my mama."

Kat motioned with her hands to quiet the child's voice. "She doesn't know that I'm your aunt." Kat dropped her fork. She wasn't hungry anymore. She firmly took hold of Miranda's hand and whipped her out of the dining room. Once they arrived back at their room, Kat tossed her handbag on the bed. "Would you like a bath before you turn in for the night? You must be exhausted." Miranda stared at the floor. "Your mother probably would like you to have one." She did her best to remove the edge from her voice.

"You're not my mother."

Kat gritted her teeth. "I know I'm not, but your mother can't take care of you now. She asked me to watch you for a while."

Miranda stood rigidly, glaring at Kat. "If Mama says so."

Kat drew Miranda's bath water and left her alone. "Call me if you need anything. I'll help you wash your hair. I'll just be here in the next room." Kat settled in a chair and propped up her feet when she heard a wail from the bathroom. "I'm coming!" She bailed out the chair and barged through the door. "What is it?" Water and soap cascaded down Miranda's face, threatening to slide right into her gaping mouth. Kat snatched the towel from the floor and wiped away the soap from her niece's stinging eyes. In spite of her constant howls, Kat managed to rinse Miranda's hair, scoop her up in a towel, and dry her off. Miranda wailed even more loudly while Kat helped her with her pajamas.

"I want my mama!"

"You'll see her in a few weeks. I promise. But, now it's bedtime. Won't it be fun to snooze together in the same bed?" Miranda glared at her as if Kat had suggested they eat a cold can of spinach. Kat shrank back, reminding herself this little challenge was her sister's child. Without another word, except for saying good night, she tucked her in. There was no good night kiss. "I'll be right here." Miranda curled up with her faded quilt and sniffled under the covers. Kat laid her head back on the upholstered chair. *Six weeks with a finicky, crying child. How will I survive?* she wondered.

––––––

"Minnie, we want you and Jeremiah to stay," Evangeline pleaded. She and Minnie were preparing the evening meal.

"Do you really?" Minnie replied. "We don't want to impose. Elijah's in charge of the mission now, and Jeremiah doesn't want to get in the way."

"Elijah doesn't feel that way. Stay as long as you want."

"That's so kind of you," Minnie said, cutting up meat for the stew pot. "I'll talk to Jeremiah and see what he says. You know I love it here. I feel so much more useful here than back in Iowa. Oh, there's some church work to do there, but it's very different."

"I'm glad you'll consider staying. I need someone to talk to besides Elijah." She turned to Minnie, smiling. "I hate to bother him all the time. He has so much on his mind."

"I like to visit with you, too. No matter how good men are, they just don't seem to understand us sometime."

Evangeline nodded. "Sara wants to go away to school this fall. She does well in her studies, so I don't want to hinder her from going. Then again, I'll miss her so much."

"Does she want to become a teacher?"

"Yes, she does."

"If that's the case, she could go to the Santee school, just like Elijah did," Minnie said.

"I suppose she could. I was thinking more like a school in the East."

"But is that necessary? You know how attached she is to you and Elijah."

"I know it would be hard on us all, but it'd be just for a while. I had a thought the other day that might help ease the loneliness for all of us when Sara leaves," Evangeline told Minnie.

Minnie finished up a pan of rolls and had just popped them into the oven when Cassandra walked in. "Evangeline is about to tell us about an idea of hers," Minnie said to Cassandra.

"Oh, and what is it?"

"Remember when we made the Jacob's Ladder quilt?"

"Certainly! How could I forget such an important project like that? We did have a good time, didn't we?" Cassandra said.

"I often thought of those afternoons we spent by the cozy fire with the Lakota women sewing and listening while Jeremiah read Scripture to us. By the way, where is the quilt we made that winter?"

"I'm not really sure. We've had several missionaries come and go, and I think one of the women may have taken the quilt with her," Cassandra said.

"You let her?" Evangeline was shocked. She secretly wondered how Cassandra could be so careless with the quilt that held so much meaning and so many memories of the ladies' time together.

"I didn't know the quilt was missing and that someone had taken it." Cassandra crossed her arms over her chest.

"That's a shame. There are memories in that quilt. Besides, I thought it was rather pretty. I suppose it couldn't be helped, but I sure don't like to think of it as missing. I'll just look forward to another quilt."

"You would like to do that again?" Cassandra asked.

"I would. I know we won't have the time we used to, since some of the students stay here all week long—even on the weekends. Our workload is heavier than ever. Not that I'm complaining."

"We wouldn't be able to invite many Lakota women, either. It's just too far for them to come. Two of our quilters still live at Swift Bear's old camp."

"But we could include some of the older girl students," Evangeline suggested.

"What patterns do you want to work on?" Cassandra asked.

"I know I may not be here in the fall, so I probably should keep quiet. But I'm thinking you should sew quilts using simple designs," Minnie said. "You could just tie them with yarn instead of quilting them."

"That's a good idea," Cassandra said. "We simply don't have the time or the help to quilt anymore. And I don't think we have to have a different pattern for each quilt."

"I agree," said Minnie, wiping her hands on the dishtowel. She searched through the sewing cupboard and brought out a pattern book. "Let's settle on, let's say, about three different patterns and make as many quilts in the time we have." Minnie laughed at herself. "Here I am planning quilt projects and I don't even know if I'll be here."

Cassandra leaned in to look over Minnie's shoulder. "What do you have in there that might work?"

"Hmm, how about a Pinwheel? That's an easy one." Minnie turned a few more pages. "Flying Geese and Nine Patch. Even beginning sewers can handle these."

"What do you think, Evangeline?" Cassandra asked.

Evangeline furrowed her brow in thought. "I understand what you are saying, and it does make sense, but I was thinking of doing another biblical pattern. Besides, I think the girls who are advanced in sewing will find those easy patterns tedious. They can still sew the patterns you suggested, but let's do another unique one."

Cassandra titled her head in question. "Do you have something special in mind?"

"One of the students' favorite stories is about Joseph and the coat of many colors his father Jacob gave him. The special coat causes Joseph's brothers to grow more jealous of him and eventually they sell him into slavery."

Minnie went back to the cupboard and brought out a large envelope of patterns. She arranged them on the table. "Actually, the Coat of Many Colors quilt isn't that difficult. It just requires a lot of cutting and piecing. Bright colors would be best. No problem there." She glanced at Evangeline. "Thankfully, Evangeline brought back some bright fabric while she was on her honeymoon."

"And we have the bundle of material I brought from the Missionary Society," Evangeline added.

"Oh, now I really do want to stay," Minnie said. "I just love quilting with you ladies."

"With you here, Minnie, we could reach our goal and then some. Either way, let's see how many quilts we can make for the boarding school students, including a special biblical quilt," Cassandra said. "Certainly, our students will appreciate a warm quilt of their very own."

Evangeline hadn't intended to entice Minnie to remain at the mission, but she was delighted that her dear friend would consider staying. Evangeline needed her.

––––––

"I haven't been up to see Swift Bear's grave in the church cemetery," Evangeline told Elijah one morning as they were walking back from the church. "It just isn't the same with him and Angeline gone."

"I know. I miss them, too."

"Do you have time to visit the cemetery with me today? I'd like to see who's buried there."

"I have some time this morning. Most of the graves don't have markers, but I suppose I could tell you who's there if you want to know."

"I'd like that. Let me get my shawl and hat and I'll be ready to go. It's always so windy at the top of the hill."

Elijah waited for her while she went into the house. She saw him through the window waving to Minnie and

Cassandra, who were shaking rugs and sweeping the porch. He shouted over to them, "Evangeline and I are going on a walk to the cemetery!"

"See you later. Stop in for coffee when you get back," Cassandra answered.

Evangeline joined Elijah outside and reached for his hand. "It's a lovely morning for a walk."

"I agree. The wind hasn't come up yet. And listen to the meadowlarks singing."

"They're such cheery birds. Makes a heart burst with thankfulness."

"It does at that." They both assumed an easy gait, although Evangeline had to step it up to keep in stride with Elijah. "When did the mission start using this cemetery plot? I only visited it once—when we buried Red Bird."

"Shortly before you came. Jeremiah had a difficult time convincing the older Lakota to put their dead underground. Before, they placed the bodies on scaffolds or in trees, believing their spirits would be closer to the Great Spirit. Finally, Jeremiah talked them into putting the bodies in boxes like coffins, but they still wouldn't bury them in the ground. The Lakota just placed them where they wanted. But now that the Lakota are Christians and realize the soul will go to heaven, they bury their dead like the white people." They climbed the little hill northwest of the mission. When they reached the top, Elijah let go of Evangeline's hand. "Here we are." Evangeline looked at the humble, wooden markers the wind had twisted out of the ground. "If you'll come over here, I'll show you the final resting place of Swift Bear."

She moved closer to him and once again reached for his hand. "I'm glad you wrote down Swift Bear's stories when you did. All of them would have been lost."

"I am, too. At first, I wasn't so sure it was the right thing to do, but now I know it was."

"If it wasn't for Swift Bear and his belief that his people should learn the white way, the mission would have never succeeded. I wish I had flowers to put on their graves."

Elijah moved a few paces to the right. "Over here is Red Bird. Her husband isn't beside her. He was probably wrapped in a blanket and placed on a scaffold years before."

Evangeline knelt at Red Bird's grave. "I can hardly read what the marker says. It's worn off by the weather."

Elijah bent down for a closer look. "You're right. The marker should be replaced."

Evangeline stood and looked around about her, frowning. "It's so barren up here. The cemetery needs flowers, trees, and some kind of blooming plants."

"Evangeline, you should know by now how hard it is to get anything to grow out here."

"I know. But we could at least try. Oh, look! Are those baby graves?"

"We had an outbreak of influenza a few years back."

"I can't imagine losing a precious baby. It just makes my heart break."

"Maybe we should go. You're in a strange mood today. I don't want you to become sad again."

"No, I want to look around a little more." Evangeline scrutinized every marker, commenting on the ones she knew from the mission, and then she looked toward the river breaks. "We should dig up some of those young cedars that grow practically wild near the river and plant some up here to add beauty and break the wind."

Elijah shrugged. "I guess we could do that. Just hope it rains. I wouldn't want to lug water up here."

"And do you know what else we need here?"

"Besides trees and better markers?"

"I'm thinking of irises. They're easy to grow and take little care. They only bloom in the spring, but a cemetery full of them—what a sight that would be!"

"Where are you going to get them?"

"I'll ask around Pierre the next time I go there. Someone will want to thin their iris bed, or maybe our Episcopalian neighbors have some."

"You could do that. Look, Evangeline." Elijah pointed toward the mission. "Minnie's company has arrived."

"I wish Sara were here to meet them, too."

"She'll be back from Sol and Lily's in a few days," Elijah reminded her.

Evangeline turned toward the trail winding into the mission. A woman and a young girl were in a buggy. "Yes, that must be them. Let's go meet them."

By the time they hiked down to the bottom of the hill, Minnie's guests were already inside the mission.

————

Kat had barely stepped from the buggy when Minnie rushed out of the kitchen. "My, I would've known you anywhere. You haven't changed all that much," Minnie gushed. "I'm so glad you came for a visit."

"Thanks for taking us in for a while." Kat turned from Miranda and whispered to Minnie, "Miranda is going to need me close by for a time. She doesn't seem to be adjusting well."

Minnie nodded. "I understand." She smiled at Miranda. "And this must be your niece. Welcome, young lady. I hope we can make you both comfortable during your stay." Minnie led them into the kitchen. "This is Cassandra, our head seamstress and Elijah's mother."

Kat slightly bowed her head. "Pleased to meet you."

"Now, what can I get for you, Miranda? A cookie?"

Miranda grinned.

"I guess I'll have to learn how to bake cookies," Kat said. "This is the most excitement I've seen from her since she arrived on the train."

Minnie chuckled as she handed Miranda a sugar cookie. "Don't worry. Between us, I think we can keep her entertained and happy." She winked at the child. "Oh, here comes Elijah and Evangeline! I forgot that you know them already, Kat." She laughed at her mistake. "You met them on the stagecoach."

"Yes, I did. Hello again," Kat said as Evangeline and Elijah entered the room. "This is my niece, Miranda. Say hello to Pastor Elijah and Evangeline."

Miranda looked up at them, shoved the rest of the cookie into her mouth, and looked at Minnie for another. Cassandra frowned at the child's impolite behavior.

Evangeline stifled a laugh. "Miranda, would you like to see the new kittens in the stable?"

Miranda nodded and followed Elijah and Evangeline outside. Cassandra excused herself, mumbling something about cleaning the church.

Now that they were alone, Kat and Minnie settled in for a visit. "Would you like a cup of tea or coffee?" Minnie offered. "I'm sure you must be thirsty from your travels."

"Thanks, Minnie. Tea would be nice."

Minnie poured hot water from the teakettle over tea leaves to steep. "Kat, tell me what you've been doing these past years."

"I've started a business. Probably not one you'd approve of, but it puts food on the table and pays the bills."

Minnie strained the tea leaves from the brew and poured the fragrant mint tea into cups. "Tell me anyway."

"I own a saloon." Kat sipped her tea slowly, allowing herself to relax for the first time since she'd read the letter from her sister.

"I see."

"That's why I'm here. I didn't want to take Miranda to Deadwood just yet. I'm not sure how to care for her there."

"We're glad to have you."

"As you have probably noticed, Miranda is a spoiled child. I'm not sure how to handle her."

"None of us here are experts on rearing children. I never had one of my own. Abe and I decided the freighting life was no good for children. The years went by so fast...and soon I was too old and Abe was gone."

"I know how you feel, Minnie. I'm about to lose my chance at raising a family, too. I have never met a man I wanted to spend the rest of my life with."

"A good man is hard to find. I found two and consider myself lucky. Even though Jeremiah and I aren't experienced in child rearing, there are enough of us here to figure out how to care for Miranda."

"Thanks. I don't know how to repay you for all you've done for me."

"It was nothing, but I worried about you when you left us in Deadwood."

"It was rough for a few years. I worked as a card dealer. My mother raised me with a few principles, so I couldn't stoop to being one of those...soiled doves."

Minnie poured more tea. "I'm glad to hear that. I knew a few in my day. They weren't happy."

Kat picked up a sugar cookie from a simple, white plate. "Eventually, the owner of the saloon where I worked offered me a deal on his business and a small house. I had been saving practically every penny I earned, so I agreed to buy it. I've been up to my neck in debt ever since. My business specializes in fine alcohol and the best card games in town."

"It sounds like you enjoy your work," Minnie said.

"I'm good at what I do. I know how to make money and have a knack for attracting customers. But I have been restless lately. I don't know if this is what I want to do with the rest of my life."

Suddenly, Miranda bolted into the kitchen, a kitten under each arm. "Look what I found."

"Oh, my!" Kat gasped. She reached and rescued the kittens from strangulation. "Be careful how you hold them." Kat demonstrated by cradling a kitten in her arm. "See how nice they are," she said as she stroked its soft, white fur.

Evangeline laughed. "We've found something to keep her occupied for quite a while." Evangeline stooped to talk to Miranda. "You'll love Sara. I'm sure she'll have a few ideas to keep you busy."

Kat hoped Sara would come soon. Miranda had been more demanding than her saloon customers. What she needed was a good night's sleep without any interruptions.

––––––

Evangeline had just opened the chicken house to let the hens out when she met Elijah in the yard. "Come and see what I brought you from the Episcopal mission," he said. Evangeline strolled over to the buckboard and peered in the back where Elijah pointed.

"Oh, the irises I wanted for the cemetery! Thank you, but why didn't you tell me about them last night? I can't wait to plant them."

"You just said it. I was afraid we would have been planting by moonlight."

She playfully slapped him on the shoulder. "I wouldn't have done that."

"I'm not so sure," he said, holding his arm as if in pain. "I'll drive up to the cemetery and unload the plants and a barrel of water before breakfast. Then you can plant them whenever you wish."

Evangeline hurried through breakfast. Minnie and Cassandra offered to do the cleanup so Evangeline could do her planting before it became too hot. She tied on a hat and found a spade and a pail before climbing the hill. The air was still and the birds sang beautifully as she walked the distance to the graveyard. When she reached the top of the hill, she rested a moment, calculating where the irises would look the best. She decided she would plant some near Swift Bear's and Red Bird's graves. The rest she would space out. She knew they would eventually multiply and fill the cemetery.

From the hilltop, she could see the surrounding countryside. *How peaceful it is here,* she thought as she dug the holes with her spade. She poured water into the deep indentations. Then she knelt down, situated the irises, and pulled in the soil around them.

How nice a stone marker would look on Swift Bear's and Red Bird's graves, she thought. This was something she could do for them that no one else would think of doing. The next time she went to Pierre she would visit the undertakers and see about ordering something appropriate for them.

Suddenly, she remembered ordering the granite upright stone inscribed with the name of her husband. She had added a weeping willow emblem, a symbol of her sorrow. But what had bothered her most about that marker was the word "cenotaph" etched into the granite. The innocuous word simply meant the grave was empty. She knew in her heart that his soul was with God, but his missing body, lost at sea, had often given her nightmares. Oh, how she had mourned his passing—an entire year of depression. How long would James remain in her memory? No, she couldn't forget him; his face, his blond curly hair, and that crooked smile still seemed fresh to her. Sometimes she felt that these thoughts dishonored Elijah, but she also knew her new husband was compassionate and understanding.

When she finished planting the irises, she sat and enjoyed the cool breezes fanning her face. She thought of the headstones that should be added to the cemetery. While musing in this quiet place, she heard the commotion of horses and a wagon coming up the trail to the cemetery. Elijah was driving, and Jeremiah was sitting beside him. She stood, curious about their errand.

"We brought you something else to plant," Elijah shouted.

She walked over to the wagon. Inside, small cedar trees had been freshly dug from the ground. "You remembered," she said to Elijah.

"Of course I did. Jeremiah helped me dig these by the river." Both men jumped from the wagon and lifted out several of the cedars. "Now tell us where you want them."

"Let me think a minute. How about making an avenue of trees? A row here to edge a pathway, and then another row on the opposing side. When they grow up, they'll make a shady lane. Can you bring more?"

"Oh, yes. There's plenty of seedlings by the river. The only problem is watering them until they get a good start," Jeremiah said. While Jeremiah was digging holes for the cedars, Evangeline told Elijah of her plans for headstones.

"You want headstones for Swift Bear, Angeline, and Red Bird?"

"Would that be all right with you?"

"I don't see why not. But maybe some of the other families will feel left out."

"I know, but perhaps in time I can add a few more. I think it's important to remember all of them."

"Don't look now, but I see your favorite young lady coming up the hill."

"Sara? I'm so glad she's back."

Sara was nearly out of breath when she reached Evangeline and Elijah. She threw her arms around Evangeline.

"How was your stay with Lily and the babies?" Evangeline asked, releasing her hold.

"I'm hungry. There wasn't much in the house to eat. I didn't want them to go any hungrier because I ate their food."

Evangeline stroked her hair. "That was considerate of you."

"Their grandmother even went out and gathered wild rose seeds. She brought them into the house and boiled them and then thickened the funny looking stuff with flour and ate them. I think my grandmother did that once."

"I take it you didn't ask for a sample?"

Sara wrinkled her nose. "No. I remembered I didn't like it."

"The government probably cut their rations again, or else the Indian agent is keeping some of the Indians' share for himself. Elijah, I can't bear to see people go hungry. What are we going to do?"

"I can write the Indian Commissioner again and tell him how the Lakota are suffering. If he has a heart, maybe he can do something."

"I wouldn't count on it," she retorted. "We'll go through our supplies and see what we can send them. Now then, young lady, let's get you to the kitchen and feed you." Evangeline and Elijah joined hands with Sara as they walked back to the mission. Despite the food shortage, Sara told them how she had enjoyed caring for the little ones.

"You're a natural with children. How lucky they were to have you help out. What can I fix for you, Sara?" Evangeline asked when they entered the kitchen.

"Anything, as long as it's real food."

"How about a sandwich until I can make something else for supper?"

"That'll work for me. Oh, I just about forgot. Sol wanted me to ask if you'd buy wood from him for the fall. He plans to cut wood by the river and deliver it to people in order to make money."

Elijah scrunched his lips in thought. "I suppose he needs the money to buy food for his family at the trader's store. I don't know if we'll have extra money to buy wood."

Evangeline placed the sandwich on the table in front of Sara. "Tell Sol we will buy several loads from him. It takes a lot of wood to heat all these buildings, and, Elijah, you simply don't have the time to cut all that wood."

Sara took the sandwich off the plate. "I'm going to see Cassandra. Maybe she has some cookies for me," she said and left the house.

"Evangeline, why did you tell Sara we would buy wood from Sol?"

"I know you don't want me to use my money to help out, but it isn't for our use; it's for our work here. I have money from James's estate. Where else would I spend it, except for the mission? This is our home, our life's work. We are never leaving, are we?"

"I don't want to leave, but I can't see into the future. Nothing is ever certain in this world. It's not that I won't let you use your money. I'm not sure the mission has a future. Maybe we have served our purpose and it's finished."

"Oh, don't say that. What would we do? I can't believe we're not still needed here. True, the day school is no longer feasible, but perhaps we should expand the boarding school idea."

"You know how Jeremiah was against boarding schools," Elijah reminded her.

"I remember, but that was because the students were treated badly at some of them. Can you imagine beating students into submission? We're kind to them. Don't you think they'd stay because they wanted to, not because they had to?"

"It depends on their families. If the parents think it's important, they'll send them."

"Even though the government has withdrawn funding, I have enough money to build a dormitory for the children and a house for us—if you let me."

"I'll have to think about this, Evangeline. It's a big step."

––––––––

After a few weeks at the mission, Kat became antsy. At first, she thought she would like the peace and solitude, but she found she became bored with the daily routine. Miranda, however, was enjoying herself. She dragged the kittens around the mission and rode with Sara on the horses, took walks, and gathered the eggs. Her preoccupation with the outdoors lessened her self-centeredness. Even Cassandra became able to tolerate the little girl. Kat watched Minnie and Cassandra spend the entirety of each day cooking, washing, and cleaning. Kat helped with the cooking occasionally, but she wasn't very good at it.

"Tomorrow is Sunday," Minnie reminded her. "We always provide the congregation with a lunch after the service. Everyone travels long distances to church, so we feed them."

"How many people are you talking about?" Kat drummed her fingernails on the kitchen table.

"About thirty or so. Some of the cowboys come, too. Ed, who manages a big ranch around here, brings most of his crew. He told me once that requiring his men to attend church made for better harmony among them, less fights." Minnie searched the cupboard for ingredients. "We'll need you to help us bake cakes." Minnie thumbed through the cookbook and stopped at a page smudged with frequent use. She plucked an apron from a peg on the wall and handed it to Kat. "Put this on. The recipe is in this book, and the ingredients are in the cupboard. If you don't understand, just ask." Minnie turned abruptly to another task.

"I'll try, but I'm not the best cook." Kat placed the opening of the apron over her head and then tied it in the back. Admiring its handiwork, she asked, "I suppose someone here made this?"

"Cassandra did. Of course, we all sew." Minnie punched down a batch of bread dough and covered it with a towel. "Do you sew?"

"No, I never learned." Kat laughed. "I could teach you how to play a game of faro, though."

"I suppose you could." Minnie looked to see if anyone was within earshot. "Actually," she whispered, cupping her hands to her mouth, "I already know how."

"Yes, I'll bet you do," Kat said with a grin. "Don't worry; your secret is safe with me."

"If you'd stay awhile, we could teach you to sew," Minnie offered.

"I don't really need to know how. I buy my dresses and aprons." Kat didn't have too much trouble following the recipe. She poured the batter into a greased pan and popped it into the oven. Soon, the applesauce cake delivered a sweet, tantalizing scent. "Don't you ever get tired of cooking and cleaning?"

Minnie quickly turned the handle of the flour sifter, tumbling the dry ingredients for another cake. "I don't let myself think about it. I feel like I'm doing this for someone."

"So all you get is satisfaction?"

"It's not so much what I get as what I can give to others."

What do I give to others? Jobs—now that's important, Kat mused. *A safe place to gamble, to drink, to socialize.* She shrugged her shoulders.

"It's very good of you to take care of Miranda," Minnie said, changing the subject.

"I really didn't have any choice. She's a handful, though," said Kat, shaking her head. "We should be going back to Deadwood in a couple of weeks. We're probably in your way."

"I don't think of it that way. Stay as long as you like. Will you come to church tomorrow?"

"I'm not much of a churchgoer."

"There's no pressure. Just come and listen to Elijah preach, and fellowship with us."

"I suppose it wouldn't hurt anything. Do you suppose Elijah will mind?"

Minnie looked at her and smiled. "He'll be glad you came."

CHAPTER 11

Kat couldn't decide what to wear to church on Sunday. She hadn't packed anything plain or pious. Most of her ensembles were too low cut or too flamboyant. Finally, she settled on her red dress. She thought of asking Minnie about borrowing a black shawl to tone it down a notch. She frowned at the small mirror in her room. *Don't these people believe in mirrors?* She applied her makeup and secured a black hat on her red hair.

Miranda had dressed earlier and had already walked with Sara to the church. Kat left for the service alone and stopped by Minnie's quarters to borrow her shawl. Minnie took one look at the fire red dress and graciously handed her the wrap.

"Jeremiah's at the church, so let's walk together. Afterward, you can come back to the kitchen with me to get the coffee, sandwiches, and cake." Once they entered the church, Minnie whispered to Kat, "Jeremiah's going to help with the service, so let's sit together. Where would you like to sit?"

Kat surveyed the interior of the church and pursed her lips with approval. She was rather surprised at the quality of furnishings, expecting something rather plain.

"I prefer the back pews," she told Minnie. While Minnie sat in a meditative spirit, Kat took the opportunity to glance around. Evangeline walked in with Miranda and Sara. *Such a pretty woman,* Kat thought as she watched Evangeline. *And she has money, too. I wonder why she prefers this desolate mission to Boston?*

Cassandra slid in beside Minnie. Kat smiled, although she secretively thought Cassandra was a funny sort.

Just before the service was to begin, a group of cowboys came in. Kat had seen plenty of cowboys in her saloon, but she did a double take. One of the men looked like Jet. *But it can't be,* she thought. Soon his back was toward her, and she couldn't see his face anymore. During the service, she fixed her gaze on the tall cowboy sitting three rows ahead of her. *What would Jet be doing in church, dressed like that?* Kat's thoughts kept wandering so much that she hardly listened to what Elijah said. She tried to catch another glimpse of him as he walked out, but Minnie interrupted her just as he walked by. Kat practically sprinted after Minnie and Cassandra, glancing back at the cowboys a time or two. She watched them sit on the ground and felt relieved to have another chance at spotting Jet.

The women gathered the cake and boxed sandwiches and returned to the church yard. Kat scanned the crowd and saw the man who looked like Jet sitting with some of the others. *I'm going to find out if that's him,* she told herself. Kat wasn't shy with men; she dealt with them all the time in her saloon. She called out to Minnie, "I'll start with the cowboys."

Minnie nodded that she'd heard Kat.

Taking sandwiches first, Kat served the cowboys, saving Jet for last. When he looked up and saw her standing over him, he gaped in surprise.

"You're Jet, aren't you?" she asked while handing him the sandwiches.

He took a sandwich, his stare not leaving her face. "Yeah, that's me."

"Your clothes kind of threw me off, but there are not too many men your height or with your distinctive hair."

"Guess not," he said, averting his gaze toward the sandwich.

"I'll be back with cake," Kat told the cowboys. "Jet, I'd like to talk to you before you leave," she said to him quietly.

"You would?"

"Come and find me. I'll be around somewhere." Kat left to eat her lunch with the mission ladies. She took a sandwich and a piece of her applesauce cake and sat beside Evangeline. "Evangeline, do you know that's Jet from our stage ride?" She nodded toward him.

"Oh, yes, we know. I forgot to tell you. Isn't it a coincidence that we'd see him again?"

"Has he been here before?"

"Several times."

"Don't you think it's odd he's here and not in Deadwood? You do remember he said he was a tailor?"

"Yes, now that you mention it. I guess I do remember. I've never questioned him, though. I didn't become acquainted with him that much when we were on the coach, and I thought it was none of my business."

Kat was going to make it her business. It just didn't add up. She kept watch on Jet, and when he left the group, she intercepted him. Jet flinched as she approached him. "I looked for you at the tailor shops in Deadwood, but no one had heard of you or knew of anyone that matched your description."

"Why were you looking for me?"

"Just curious. Maybe I didn't believe what you told us." She sternly looked him over.

"What did I tell you?"

"That you are a tailor."

"And what if I'm not?"

"I've been around long enough to know when a man is hiding something. I see it all the time."

"So I'm not a tailor. I just said that so people wouldn't think I was a drifter. Is that a crime?"

"I thought so! You look better in the duds you're wearing than you did in that crummy suit and goofy hat."

He laughed. "You didn't like my suit?"

"No. You looked ridiculous. Why did you wear it, anyway?"

"I...I needed to look respectable for a job when I got to Deadwood."

"Well, did you?"

"Did I what?"

"Find a job."

"No, I guess they didn't like my suit either."

This time Kat laughed. Not only was Jet a tall and handsome cowboy but he also had a sense of humor. "I gather you work on a ranch somewhere?"

"Yeah, I found a job at the Bar Double B. Now it's my turn to ask you questions." He pointed to a spot on the shady side of the church. "Let's sit over there. Tell me what are you doing so far from Deadwood."

She smiled. "It is rather strange that we'd meet at church." She took a deep breath and began her story. "Minnie and I met each other years ago on my way to Deadwood. She was on the trail with her freighter husband, Abe. I was just a teenager traveling with another freighter. I couldn't afford stage fare. I was supposed to help with the freight to pay my way, but he didn't feed me very well, so I asked Minnie for a handout."

"What were you doing all by yourself?"

"I got into a fight with my daddy. He wanted me to marry a man I didn't like, so I left home. I heard about gold in the Black Hills. It sounded like a good place to go. Well, anyway, after I got through beating you at cards on that stage, I left my compact on the seat. There's a picture inside of my sister and me. Evangeline found it and showed it to Minnie when Evangeline came back to the mission. Minnie recognized me in that picture, and we have been corresponding ever since."

"Incredible. So you're here to get it?"

"No. They sent it to me. My sister, Annabelle, lives in Cleveland and had an accident, both legs broken. She wrote me asking if I could take care of her little girl, Miranda, while she heals. So I thought maybe now was a good time to visit the mission."

"I see. How long do you plan on staying here?"

"At least a couple more weeks."

Jet glanced up to see Ed gathering his men. "I see that my crew's about ready to leave."

"Do you come to church every Sunday?"

"Almost."

"Maybe I'll see you again?"

"Maybe." Jet drew himself to his feet and tipped his hat.

Kat watched the tall, lean man walk away. He hadn't answered all her questions. *Who is he, really?* she wondered. In the next two Sundays, she would have to get the answers.

————

"Of all the nerve," Elijah exclaimed, holding a letter from the Indian commissioner.

"What is it?" Evangeline asked as she snapped fresh sheets to make their bed.

"Listen to what the commissioner wrote in response to my letter concerning the reduced rations to the Lakota people. 'There is no need of distress under a provident use of what is given them.' I'd like to see if he could live on what is rationed."

"Elijah!"

"I'm sorry, but I get so frustrated with Indian policies. Those who make the decisions are in Washington, miles and miles from here. What do they know about our problems?"

"I know. I feel the same way at times. What are we going to do?"

"I've been thinking of our conversation about money. You would be able to buy materials and even food. Perhaps I am wrong in denying you the opportunity to help."

"Have you had a change of heart?"

"I have been discussing this issue with Jeremiah. I hope you don't mind."

"No. It's something that needs to be discussed with another pastor, and Jeremiah has the right kind of experience."

"He agrees that day schools no longer serve the purpose they once had. He does have objections to boarding schools, but knows he can trust us to run one with compassion and worthy goals."

"And, may I remind you that there are many wealthy women in the East who have contributed money to build facilities for schools, such as dormitories and churches. I wouldn't be the first or the last."

"I do know of them. If it is your wish, I won't deny you your generosity," he said with a sigh.

Evangeline threw her arms around him, kissing him fervently. "I'm so glad you've changed your mind. How do we begin?"

"I've asked Minnie and Jeremiah to come to the church so we can begin planning. If we get started soon, perhaps we can have something built by the beginning of the school session."

Evangeline smiled. "Once we are able to accommodate students, we can make sure they are fed well, taking some of the burden off their families. And we will make sure they are able to return home often. That's important to me."

"And to me, too. Are you ready to go on over to the church? I think Minnie and Jeremiah are there."

Evangeline draped her shawl over her shoulders and walked hand in hand with Elijah to the church. As soon as she saw Minnie, she smiled and gushed with excitement. "Isn't this going to be wonderful? A school with a large dormitory to house many students!"

Minnie nodded, but Jeremiah cautioned, "Before we get too carried away, we'll have to find out if we have enough parents who will send their children to school. Elijah, you have established a good reputation at your day school. The families trust you. I'm sure there will be no problem, but we'd better find out anyway." He unrolled a large piece of paper and began to sketch out a few plans. All four intently watched him draw a plan for a new dormitory that would accommodate thirty students.

"With the dozen students who now room here, plus the thirty extra accommodations, we could serve more than forty students," Elijah calculated.

Jeremiah looked up at him. "Are you and Evangeline going to be able to handle forty students day and night and on weekends?"

Elijah shrugged and looked up at Evangeline. "In time, Sara will be able to help," she said.

"What are you going to do in the meantime? Cassandra needs to slow down. She won't be able to keep up with the washing, cleaning, and cooking," Minnie reminded them.

Elijah stroked his chin. "I suppose we'll have to find someone to help out."

"Minnie and I have been talking. We've tried Iowa for about six years now. As you know, we have no children or serious family ties. We miss the mission. True, we have aged, but we have a little life in us yet." He laughed and reached for Minnie's hand. "If you'll have us, we'd like to stay and help out. Although, I still recommend you find a young teacher, and maybe a cook. Forty students will take a lot of energy."

"Of course we want you to stay!" Evangeline placed her hands together as if in prayer and held the tips of her fingers to her lips. "Our prayers have been answered." She beamed with happiness. "I'll contact Alice at the Missionary Society and see who she can find to assist us here." As the sketch neared completion, Evangeline said, "I know my father will help us with this project if we need him."

Elijah squinted and scratched his head in thought. "We can get the supplies delivered to Pierre, and from there they can be brought to us by boat. I'll have to meet with someone in Pierre to help us design this building."

"What about a house for you two?" Jeremiah asked as he leaned back in his chair.

Evangeline looked at Elijah for an answer. He sat silently for a moment. "I...I shouldn't deny you a home either, Evangeline. What do you suggest?"

"I would like a house to share just with you. Perhaps we can design something that isn't too extravagant. What can you draw up for us, Jeremiah?"

"Tell me what you would like and I'll see if I can come up with something that Elijah can take to Pierre with him." After listening to Evangeline's wishes, Jeremiah designed a one-story dwelling with two bedrooms, a kitchen, and a living area accented with a large fireplace. A porch wrapped around two sides of the house.

Evangeline beamed at the home that unfolded before them. "I love it," she said to Elijah. I'll plant flowers on this side of the house, and we can put rocking chairs out on the porch. *And maybe we'll have children who will play on the porch while we watch daylight slip away,* she thought. So far, she hadn't conceived and was starting to worry. She loved working by Elijah's side for the sake of the mission, but she so wanted a family of her own.

––––––

The week passed a little too slowly for Kat. She was looking forward to Sunday and hoped Jet would show up again. Nearly every day she found herself thinking about his long, lanky frame and black, wavy hair. She had planned on leaving for Deadwood after two or three weeks, but now she was in no hurry to get back. Sara had taken charge of Miranda, leaving Kat time for herself and her thoughts. She wanted to stay at the mission longer, but she had to make herself useful to earn their room and board. The next time she saw Minnie, she asked if they could remain at the mission.

"Sure you can. You have been a great help."

"I have?" Kat asked in surprise.

"Anyone who helps with the cooking and gardening is greatly appreciated," Minnie said as she washed the green beans they had picked from the garden earlier. She pushed over a pile of beans toward Kat to snap.

"I could do more for you if you would tell me what you need."

"Soon, the men will begin building a dormitory for thirty more students. Now I know you're not a carpenter, but I think we women can help with painting and making curtains and bedding for the new rooms—in addition to the regular cooking, washing, and cleaning, of course."

"I can't sew, remember?"

"Oh, you can learn to sew a straight seam. There's nothing to it."

"I'd like to sew something to wear. I don't know what I was thinking when I packed. Nothing I brought is right for this mission." She laughed.

Minnie rinsed off the snapped beans, covered them with water, and added salt. "You have never been to a mission before. You had no idea. I'm sure we can whip you up something from material we have around here, although I'm going to have to make a trip to Pierre for material for the curtains and such."

"Is there time to sew up a skirt and blouse before Sunday?"

"I think so. Cassandra can lay out the pattern and you can cut it out. Now, let me have a look in the cupboard and see what we have left."

While the beans were boiling and the meat was roasting, Minnie rummaged through the lengths of fabric in the sewing cupboard. Cassandra came into the kitchen carrying a basket of eggs.

"What are you looking for, Minnie?"

"Kat would like a plain skirt and blouse to wear here at the mission. Ah, here is some brown." She pulled out a length of material. This would make a skirt. And here's a yellow print. Would this work?" She held it up for Kat to see. "It goes great with your red hair."

"It works for me." Kat preferred her red dress, but she had to blend in with her surroundings. She wondered which dress Jet would like.

"Let me find a pattern in this box," Cassandra offered. "This one should fit you, but I may have to adjust it some.

Cassandra folded the brown fabric in half lengthwise and placed the pattern pieces on the fold. Handing Kat the pins, she showed her how to pin the pattern to the material. "When you're done, I'll check it before you cut."

Kat nodded and went to work. At lunchtime, she took a break and helped set the table and dish up the food. Conversation centered on plans for the new dormitory and Evangeline's new house. Elijah had been to Pierre to consult with a builder. The materials had been ordered for the mission additions, and help had been hired. Elijah and Jeremiah were planning on doing much of the work, but the two of them alone wouldn't be enough.

"We plan to help as much as we can," Minnie said. The other women nodded in agreement.

After helping with the lunch cleanup, Cassandra examined the pattern layout and gave the approval for cutting. When Kat finished cutting and unpinned the pieces, she waited to see what she should do next. Cassandra threaded the needle of the sewing machine and placed a scrap of material under the needle. "Are you ready for your first sewing lesson, Kat?"

"You mean now?"

"No time like the present. Sit down in front of the sewing machine and I'll tell you what to do." Kat moved to the chair Cassandra was holding for her. "Place your hands like so." She demonstrated. "You will have to guide the material, like this. Lower the feeder foot with this lever and keep your hand clear of the needle. Position your feet on the treadle. Place one foot slightly ahead of the other, and pump the pedal with your feet. Now take your right hand and move the wheel toward you."

Kat thought she did what Cassandra had told her, but the thread snapped right out of the needle. "Oh, what did I do now?"

"Nothing that every beginner doesn't do. You backpedaled. It takes a little practice to master the foot action. It needs to be a smooth, continuous action." Seeing that the thread came completely out of the threading eyelets, Cassandra suggested that Kat learn how to thread the needle. After almost an hour of trial and error, Kat began to master the machine. Cassandra let her sew the straight seams of her skirt.

"I can't believe I'm actually sewing," Kat remarked.

"You can sew all the simple seams. I'll put on the band, and then I'll show you how to hem. The blouse is quite a bit more difficult with setting in the sleeves, sewing on the cuffs and collar, and making buttonholes, but there are some straight seams you may sew."

It took several days for the women to finish the garments. Kat was amazed at what Cassandra could accomplish with a piece of fabric, thread, and a sewing machine. Kat tried on the new creation for several fittings.

"The colors go nicely with your red hair," Cassandra said.

"Thank you," Kat said, looking at herself in the only full-length mirror at the mission and marveling at Cassandra's uncharacteristic compliment. "Now if only I had a hat to complete this outfit."

"Minnie might have something you could borrow."

————

When Sunday arrived, Kat borrowed a straw hat from

Minnie. She pinned it in place and toned down her makeup to match the plain appearance, hoping that Jet would still recognize her and approve. Ed and his men arrived early for Sunday morning worship. Kat nodded a greeting to Jet as he entered the church, relieved that he had come. Her heart fluttered when she saw him and her pulse quickened when she thought of speaking to him after the service. Admonishing herself for behaving like a schoolgirl, she did her best to concentrate on Elijah's sermon. But as soon as the service was over, Jet left the church and she zipped out of the pew to catch him.

"You're staying for lunch, aren't you?" she asked when she found him outside the church.

"Yeah, the boss thinks we need to socialize. Some of the men like to make eyes at the Indian maidens." He laughed.

"Does that go for you, too?"

"Nah, I'm not looking for any commitments."

"Your friends probably aren't, either. They're just lonely for female company."

"Maybe so, but experience tells me whenever you get involved with a woman, you get burned."

"I see. I didn't know you were so cynical."

"Cynical?" Jet asked.

"You don't trust us."

"That's what I mean," he said.

"I don't trust what you tell me either," Kat spat back.

"What do you mean?"

"You're not a tailor," she said, "and I don't think you're just a ranch hand either."

"Is that so?" He laughed again. "Well, who am I, then?"

"You're not going to tell me, are you?"

"You aren't a missionary, either, although you look like one today."

Kat softened. "Do you like my outfit?"

"Sure looks different from last Sunday."

"So you don't approve?"

"I didn't say that. My, you're a cagey woman."

Kat laughed. "We aren't getting anywhere with this conversation. I don't suppose you'd want to sit and eat with me?"

"I don't know. If you stop with the third degree, I might."

"I don't know what we'd talk about, since neither of us will tell the truth."

"We could talk about the weather."

"We could. I'll go help the women and then I'll meet you under that tree." She pointed to the one he sat under last Sunday. She hurried to serve the sandwiches and cake. Usually, Ed and his men didn't stay long after they finished eating, which left her little time to spend with the mysterious cowboy. There was something about him that drew her like a moth to light. She might get burned, but she was willing to take that chance. It had been forever since she had felt anything for a man. Underneath his evasiveness, she felt there was someone she could trust.

––––––

The following Sunday, Jet had made arrangements to meet Kat before the church service. She watched for him from the window and saw him ride in alone. She restrained herself from appearing anxious and flying out the door. Instead, she paced herself as she walked to the church where he tied up his horse.

"How was your week?" she asked him, hoping he didn't notice the excitement in her voice.

"Busy as usual, but I like the work. The boss is a good man." He turned to her and smiled. "Do you want to sit together today?"

Kat placed her hand lightly to her throat. "Yes, I'd like that."

Jet laughed. "I don't usually meet my women at church."

"The same goes for me, too. How many women are we talking about?" she chided. "Am I one of them?"

"I reckon you are if that's alright with you."

"I thought you didn't like women," she reminded him.

"You don't let anything alone, do you?"

Kat smiled, reached up, and took his arm. "Let's take a walk."

"Is that your way of saying yes?"

"It is, but I don't know for how long. I'll eventually have to return to Deadwood. I have a business to run, and I've been away far too long as it is."

"What kind of business?"

"I own a saloon. Does that surprise you?"

"No, that explains your attitude." He looked down at her and smirked. "You have to be tough to run a saloon."

"I guess you're right."

"My job won't last forever, either. I haven't asked the boss if he'll need me for the winter. I suppose I'll have to move on after a while." Jet looked out toward the horizon where cattle were grazing. His voice drifted, "I'd like to own a ranch and cattle someday. Have me a bunch of horses. What about you? Do you like it here?"

"It's a little desolate for my taste. I miss being able to get out and see people. And, I like to buy what I want instead of making everything I need."

"Like the clothes you're wearing?"

"Is it that noticeable?" she asked, slightly offended.

"Looks a lot different from the first few times I saw you."

"I just didn't want to stand out like the saloon girl I am."

Jet hung his head in sudden shyness. "You look nice. I didn't mean anything by what I said. I see church is about ready to start. Shall we go?" Jet chose a pew several rows behind his boss and the men. Kat knew why he did that. The men in his outfit would certainly razz him. How he must have endured some kidding when he chose to ride to the church alone this morning. Oh, well. He could take care of himself. She settled in beside him, absorbing his closeness.

Kat's mind drifted to Jet's comment about owning a ranch. Could she live like this forever? Give up her fancy clothes, her makeup, all her pretty things—to cook, clean, sew, and manage a chicken coop? She shuddered at the thought. Cows and horses? They weren't her favorites, either. But she had to admit, she wasn't content with owning a saloon. What did she want, anyway?

Minnie pulled Kat aside after the service. "No need to help us serve today. You need that extra time with Jet."

"No, that's okay. I'll help. It's the least I can do."

"You need to spend time with your man."

"My man? He's not my man."

"Don't tell me that. I can see the sparks between you."

Kat batted her hand at her old friend. "Minnie, you shouldn't be talking that way. You're a pastor's wife."

Minnie blushed. "Now go, and we'll take care of things."

Kat spotted Jet with his bunkmates. They were laughing

at something. She didn't want to barge in on them, so she did her best to draw his attention. When she thought he glanced her way, she waved as unobtrusively as she could, and then stomped her foot when he didn't catch the hint.

A nagging thought occurred to her. *Was he avoiding her for the sake of his friends?* She waited patiently for another opportunity, but he didn't look her way again. Fuming, she turned and stomped to the kitchen.

"What are you doing here?" Minnie wanted to know.

"I've changed my mind. I want to help serve."

"Okay, then. We can always use the help."

Kat picked up the tray of sandwiches, serving the women first and then circling back to Jet and his friends. She glared at Jet, but he didn't notice her distress.

"I'll meet you under the tree in a few minutes," he said.

After Kat served the cake, she filled her own plate with a sandwich and cake and joined Jet at their usual spot. "Didn't you notice me waving to you?"

"No, I didn't. What were you waving for?"

"I was trying to get your attention. Minnie said I didn't need to help them today. I was to go and spend the time with you."

"Sorry about that."

"I have a feeling you ignored me in front of your friends."

"Well, I...I have to guard my reputation. You know how fellers are. They'd razz me something fierce on our way back to the ranch."

"I thought so."

"Now, don't get so touchy."

"I'm not being touchy. I just don't like being ignored."

Jet threw down his sandwich and frowned. "Alright, I

ignored you. How about I make it up to you? Let's have our own private picnic after church next Sunday. I'm not much of a cook, but maybe I can convince Pepper to come up with something."

She hesitated, contemplating the silent treatment, but she just couldn't waste the few precious moments they had together. "I like that idea. I'll bring something, too. How about I talk to Elijah about borrowing the buggy? We could take a ride and find a nice picnic spot."

Jet reached beside him for his hat and slanted it low on his forehead. His dark eyes met hers. "I'll see you then."

Kat watched him ride away with the ranch hands and wondered why she was involving herself with a man she would surely have to leave.

CHAPTER 12

Heavy, black clouds oozed like an ink spill across the sky. Jet left the deserted bunkhouse and groped his way to the corrals. Something was causing a ruckus with the horses, and he was alone. Since the other men were still out with the cattle, he knew he should see what was causing the commotion. Maybe coyotes, or worse yet, wolves.

He approached the stock cautiously, his rifle poised for a quick response. The horses milled around the enclosure, whinnying and kicking up their heels. Jet walked around the perimeter of the corral but he did not see a wild animal causing the trouble. He spoke gently to horses, calling each by name. They seemed to respond to his voice. He relaxed and let the gun drop to his side and walked the edge of the corral once again. A noise startled him. He whirled around with his gun raised, only to meet another rifle pointed at his heart.

"Drop the gun," Tom ordered. "I told you that you wouldn't get away with double-crossing me." His sinister laugh rang through the darkness.

With his hands raised, Jet found his voice. He argued, "I didn't double-cross you. I just didn't show up."

"I waited for you, and you slipped out of town. Didn't you think I'd find you?"

"I told you, I'm done with rustling. I don't owe you nothing."

Two of Tom's other men stepped out of the shadows. One was Tom's son, Jed, and the other man Jet did not know. Both stood with their feet apart, pointing their guns in his direction.

"I think you do owe me. Are you forgetting I'm the one who saved your hide in the bar fight with them soldiers in Hayes City?"

"I didn't forget, but I've repaid you many times over by stealing cattle for you."

"I ain't got time to talk. You're the best wrangler I've ever had, and you're coming with us. Tie him on his horse, boys. We'd better get moving before somebody sees us."

Jet made a break, but the two men tackled and pistol-whipped him before hoisting him onto a horse.

———————

Jet didn't know how long he was out, but his head throbbed like a reverberating anvil. He could hear the crunch of gravel and supposed they were traveling on rocky ground to hide their trail.

Tracking them would be difficult, Jet thought. *But who would be interested enough to come after me, anyway?*

Remorse clouded his thoughts. He had attempted to turn his life around, but Tom was as bad as the devil himself, always in pursuit.

Jet wasn't sure where they were. The moon had broken through the clouds, illuminating their trail. After a time, they urged their horses into a series of river breaks until they came to a deep cleft between two hills where some sort of ramshackle shelter had been hastily assembled. When they stopped, Tom pulled Jet off the horse and left him on the ground for the remainder of the night. Jet drifted in and out of consciousness until the next morning. The sun beat on his face and woke him up. His head pounded mercilessly, but somehow he managed to maneuver himself into a sitting position. From this vantage point, he saw a wide river, not quite as wide as the Missouri. He smelled coffee boiling and hoped his captors would untie him and offer him some. Tom came near him and laughed, exposing his discolored teeth.

"Did you sleep well?" Tom kicked him in the legs. "Have you changed your mind about helping us?"

Jet nodded. He glared at the man with whom he had shared camp with many times, but he had never seen this dark side of him. He knew he was defeated.

"Good. I'm glad you came to your senses." Tom cut the ropes binding Jet's wrists and ankles and poured a cup of coffee while Jet rubbed circulation back into his extremities. Tom handed the cup to Jet and let him drink it all before continuing. "There's a bunch of cattle roaming these here river breaks. I don't think they'll miss a few here and there. We've been hiding out here, waiting and watching. Haven't seen a soul. We need you to help us drive a few more cattle down south to Nebraska near the railhead."

"And if I help you this time, will you let me go?"

"You think I'm stupid? We can't do that. You know too much."

Jet massaged the back of his neck. "But I've never said anything to anyone about our connection."

"I can never be sure." Tom pointed his finger in Jet's face. "Don't try running from us again. I will shoot you down. Can I count on you?"

"I have no other choice." But Jet knew there would be an opportunity for a break sometime, and he would take it.

Tom and his gang bided time playing cards and lazing around camp. Jet kept to himself, studying the group of men Tom had assembled. Most were from the old gang when Jet rode with them. None had been trustworthy, and Jet hadn't bothered to become friendly with any of them while he had been in their company. A few young boys had joined the gang since Jet had left.

Probably looking for excitement, Jet thought. *What money they made wouldn't be worth the danger if they were caught.* He shook his head at the wasted lives, including his own.

One of Tom's men rode into camp one afternoon reporting that a sizable bunch of cattle had strayed from the main herd.

"That's what we've been waiting for," Tom shouted to his men. "Let's drive them south."

The men eagerly jumped to their feet, tired of inactivity and ready for some dangerous fun. Jet reluctantly got to his feet, mounted his horse, and waited for instructions.

Tom was already in the saddle, excitement blazing in his eyes. "Drive them down into the ravines, so we don't look too obvious. Jet and I will bring up the drag."

The riders edged toward the cattle, coaxing them and bunching them toward a ravine. A quick count yielded fifty head. Tom grinned after he finished the count.

About an hour into the drive, one of the men shouted, "Riders coming from the west!"

Jet batted the dust with his hand for a better look. There were two riders, and they seemed to be picking up speed. His heart leaped into his throat. This was the first time in the three years with Tom that anyone had come upon them.

Tom drew his gun from his holster. He shouted to Jet, "You and me will make a stand against them. We can take them. I'm not letting the cattle go."

By now, Jet could see the glint of guns drawn in the approaching riders' hands. He thought they should just make a run for it. But Tom was the boss and he had a gun. Jet had to stay and die. Jet and Tom hastily dismounted behind an outcropping they would use for cover.

Tom began shooting, then abruptly turned to Jet and handed him a loaded gun. "They're aiming to kill us. But if you turn that gun on me, Jet, I'll kill you for sure."

Jet took the gun—a weapon he hardly ever used against men—and fired haphazardly. He wasn't about to kill a human being, not even Tom, but he didn't want to die, either. Panic paralyzed him.

"Where did you learn to shoot? Hit something, will you!" Tom hollered at him. "They're going to kill us!"

A few bullets ricocheted off the rocks. Jet dunked his head, but not fast enough. A bullet grazed his ear and the survival instinct kicked in. He began to take more careful aim. He wanted to live. But as hard as he tried, he couldn't make his aim count.

"I think I nicked one," Tom yelled with glee.

Blood trickled down Jet's face. A sharp pain tugged at his ear, but he reloaded and fired again. Another bullet zinged by him, and one thudded into Tom's body. He slumped down at Jet's feet. Jet threw down his gun, stooped, and rolled Tom over. He looked into Tom's open, unmoving eyes. The barrage of gunfire subsided, and Jet waited with his hands raised in surrender as the two men came toward him. Jet knew one of the large men, but he didn't say anything.

The range detective bent down over Tom. "This one's dead." He then turned to Jet, grabbed his arms and handcuffed him. "Who are you?"

"Jet Black."

"Jet!" Tex exclaimed. I thought you looked familiar, but I never expected to see you here, rustling cattle."

"You know this man?"

"We met once," Tex answered.

"I'm taking him in. I'll wire the law in Nebraska to be on the lookout for stolen cattle. Maybe we'll be able to arrest the others. Give me a hand with this body." Tex helped the range detective hoist Tom across his horse.

"I guess this is where we part company," Tex said to the range detective. "I aim to keep heading east."

"Best of luck to you. Taking out these rustlers might make this area a little safer. Grateful for your company." The range detective and Jet turned their horses to the setting sun. "Guess we'd better be off."

Tex shook his head toward Jet. "Never know about a fellow, do you?"

The day Jet had dreaded since hooking up with Tom had come. He was presumed guilty, even by Tex, before he could he tell his side of the story. He shuddered at what was about to happen to him. For the first time ever, Jet envied Tom. The scoundrel would not feel the noose around his neck or wither away in prison. And for the first time since he was abducted, he thought of Kat and her flaming red hair. She was a survivor—like him, until now. He would have liked to have known her better. They had spent just a short time together, though enough for him to become interested. Worst of all, she would think he had run out on her.

Jet kept quiet the entire trip back to Rapid City. There was no need to try and convince the range detective of his innocence. He doubted anyone would believe he had been abducted. He *was* guilty of crimes, and he didn't want to give himself away by saying too much. What could he do about his past?

CHAPTER 13

Evangeline cooled herself on the small porch while scrubbing new potatoes from the garden. The heat made her dizzy and nauseous, and Cassandra had suggested she rest in the shade. A cool breeze blew in from the north while she worked at her task. Vines that they had transplanted from the creek bottom wound their tendrils around the railing and support posts. Their glossy leaves reminded her of a refreshing glade. She sighed peacefully and pretended she was out of reach of this wretched sun and merciless prairie.

Feeding all the workers kept the women busy. The dormitory was taking shape and they expected the painting and other finishing touches to begin by the end of the summer. She waved to Miranda and Sara who were taking a mid-morning snack to the working men. She smiled, thinking of the close bond that had developed between the two girls.

After she finished filling the cooking pot with potatoes, she heard the horses whinnying in the corral. A lone rider was coming from the west. She stood and shaded her eyes with her hand to lessen the brightness of the sun. He rode at a slow trot, but she couldn't make out who it was. Thinking it might be someone from the ranch, she called to the kitchen, "Kat! Come and see who is riding in."

Kat came out on the porch and wiped her hands on her apron. Her eyes strained to see their visitor. "You know who that looks like to me?"

"Who?"

"He's built an awfully lot like Tex."

"Tex! What would he be doing out here?"

"He's a cattleman, and this is grazing country. Remember, he said he would look you and Elijah up sometime. Well, this is it."

"But I didn't think it would be this soon. You know, I think you're right," Evangeline said as the rider became more visible. Within a few minutes, he came into view. They watched as he rode up to the porch.

Tex hailed them. "Is this the Cheyenne River Mission?"

"Sure is," Kat said.

"Kat! I didn't expect to see you here."

"It's a long story. I'll tell you the details later."

Tex nodded, dismounted, and tied up his horse. "Evangeline, how good to see you again. I've been riding since morning. I need a break," he said as he tried to straighten his posture.

"Come and sit here on the porch where it's a little cooler," Evangeline said.

Kat turned toward the kitchen door. "Minnie made some lemonade. I'll get you a glass."

"I'd appreciate that. It's a hot one today. He removed his hat and wiped his forehead with his shirt sleeve.

"I assume you're here looking for pasture," Evangeline said.

"I think I found some not far from the reservation. There's grass and water and it will be close when the reservation opens for lease."

The kitchen screen door slammed and Kat came out onto the porch and handed Tex a glass of lemonade. "Where's Netty?"

"Thanks," he said, tipping the glass to his lips. "She's on her way back to Texas. I put her on the train on my way out here. Curt, my son, is at the ranch keeping watch on the herd. I suppose we'll be moving them in a few weeks."

Evangeline handed the pot of potatoes to Kat. "So we'll be neighbors?"

Tex glanced around the mission. "I guess so. I'll winter in Texas, but Curt and the hired hands will stay on. I see you're putting up a new building."

"A dormitory. We were a day school to begin with, but we decided to convert to a small boarding school. The Lakota families are more scattered now, so a day school doesn't work anymore. I can take you over to meet Elijah, Jeremiah, and the workers. You'll stay a few days, won't you?"

"I'll do that. Thanks for the invitation. My horse needs rest and so do I."

Evangeline walked with Tex to the new building. On the way, they stopped at the chicken house and Evangeline watered the hens. Elijah was surprised to see Tex and it wasn't long before they became immersed in building terminology. Evangeline left them to their discussion and returned to the kitchen.

"We'll have to set twelve places today," Cassandra said. "I do hope we can stretch this meal."

"Oh, I made extra. We'll make do." Minnie creamed the potatoes and canned peas before dishing up the roasted meat.

Jeremiah came in first, kissed Minnie on the cheek, and sat in his usual chair. "Just like old times. I like a table full of people."

Minnie smiled at his exuberance. "Could you scare up a few more chairs for us, please?"

"Certainly. I'll see what I can do." As soon as Jeremiah found enough chairs, everyone pulled up to the table. He said grace and the hungry crew dished up their food as they shared the day's events.

"It must be providence that we are coming together again," Elijah said, shaking his head in astonishment. "Jet is even in the country. He's been coming to church."

"Jet?" Tex appeared startled. "I forgot to tell you about meeting up with Jet on the trail."

Kat's eyes grew wide with interest. "You saw Jet? Where?"

"About a day's ride west of here, but…it wasn't a friendly meeting."

Kat put down her fork, unable to take another bite. "What do you mean?"

"Coming east on the trail, I hooked up with a range detective. He was scouting for rustlers. I rode with him a ways, and we came upon a suspicious cattle drive. One man started shooting at us. We shot back and killed him." Kat's lower lip trembled. "I believe Jet called the unlucky man Tom. Anyway, the drovers split in all directions when we came, so they had to be rustlers."

"I don't believe it. Are you sure it was Jet? Our Jet?" Elijah asked.

"It's the same Jet who was on the stage with us. He wasn't dressed like he was then. Looked like any ordinary cowboy."

"But that can't be." Kat insisted. "He's working for Ed Reynolds, manager of the Bar Double B ranch. Why, I saw him last Sunday in church. He's alright, isn't he?"

"The range detective took him into Rapid City."

"This is just awful," Kat moaned.

"I'm sorry to bring you bad news. I didn't think much about it at the time. I just accepted that Jet was a bad sort."

Elijah mused aloud. "He did keep to himself. But he was polite and did a good job, according to Ed."

"Did he ever tell you what he was doing in these parts?" Tex asked.

"We didn't ask," said Elijah, shaking his head. "It's hard to believe he's a cattle rustler."

Kat worried about Jet all night. She had prided herself on being a good judge of character. She wanted to find Jet and ask him what was going on, but that would require contacting Annabelle to see if Miranda could be sent back to Cleveland. Her thoughts whirled. She would wait until she could talk with Ed after church. She could even accept that Jet was a rustler but his grave situation sickened her. She hoped Ed would have some answers for her.

———

Sunday morning dragged on, and by the time church

was to start, Kat had worked herself into a bundle of nerves. She dressed and waited at the church for Ed and his men to ride in for the church service. *Oh, please, Ed, come to church today,* she silently pleaded. She fixed her eyes on the western horizon until finally they appeared. She knew better than to search for Jet, but when Ed rode up, she ran out to meet him.

"Jet's not with us," Ed said before he got off his horse.

"I know," she said. "Something terrible has happened."

"What is it?"

"Jet's been arrested for cattle thieving. Do you know anything about it?"

"All I know is when we came back to the ranch Monday night, Jet was gone. I've been bothered by his disappearance. He left all his belongings behind."

"Don't you think that's strange?"

"Yes, it's very strange. He had back pay coming to him."

"I have to find him. Will you help me?"

"What can I do?"

"I have to send a telegram to my sister in Cleveland. Is your ranch near a telegraph?"

"There's one at a relay station not far from the ranch."

"If I write out what to say, will you send it and wait for a reply?"

"I can do that."

"I would be so grateful. I'll give you the note after church." Kat considered not even attending the worship service. She doubted she would be able to concentrate, but finally decided that time would help to collect her thoughts. Immediately after the service, Kat jotted down the message and handed it to Ed.

"I'll send a man with the reply as soon as I can," Ed promised. "And when you find Jet, notify me immediately. I may be able to help."

"I will. Thank you."

That afternoon, Kat began packing in hopes that Annabelle had recovered enough to take Miranda back. Kat felt she was shirking her responsibility, but realized Jet meant more to her than she had thought. She expected a reply late that day. She paced her room, and when she grew tired of that, she walked around the mission. The air was cool, and the mourning doves cooed.

She almost gave up hope, but then she saw a rider. Recognizing him as one of Ed's men, she ran to meet him. She thanked him for bringing the reply and offered him a bunk for the night. He refused and retreated to the west. She quickly read the telegram, and to her delight, Annabelle had written that Miranda could return. She held the telegram against her chest, closed her eyes, and sighed with relief. Tomorrow, she and Miranda would make plans to leave the mission.

Kat informed everyone around the supper table of her plans. Jeremiah and Minnie offered to take Kat and Miranda to Pierre to meet the train.

"I need a break from the labor," Jeremiah laughed. "I can't seem to do what I used to. My old body just won't cooperate anymore." He massaged his knees.

Minnie patted his hand, and he knew that he was perfect in her eyes. "We need material for curtains and such. I'm looking forward to a jaunt—and a chance to shop." She chuckled.

"Thanks for welcoming Miranda and me to the mission.

We'll miss you."

"Just plan on coming back," Minnie said with a wink.

Kat looked directly at Sara and smiled. "Thanks, Sara, for your friendship with Miranda. You have made such a difference in her life. You'll make a wonderful teacher someday."

Sara beamed. "Thank you. Would it be too much to ask if I may go along, too? I'd like to choose the material for my school dresses." She looked first at Evangeline and then at Cassandra.

"Minnie, what do you think?" Evangeline asked.

"I think we could make room for you. What a holiday we'll have!"

Jeremiah smiled and rumpled his thinning, red hair. "Would you ladies be ready by morning?"

"I don't see why not. Kat, are you ready?" Minnie asked.

"Oh, yes, I'm most anxious."

"And Miranda, are you looking forward to seeing your mother?" Minnie added.

Miranda nodded.

―――――

After Miranda boarded the train to return home to her mother, Kat, Sara, and Minnie commenced shopping. Since Kat couldn't leave on the stage until later that night, she spent her time with Minnie and Sara shopping for fabric.

It feels good to return to civilization, Kat thought. She missed watching people go about their lives, and she certainly didn't mind shopping. But she wished she were on her way to Jet.

Cassandra had recorded the yardage needed for each of

Sara's dresses. Pierre provided a good selection of material, which Minnie and Sara perused with care. Kat forced herself to be interested, but her mind continually slipped back to Jet and the predicament he was in. She just couldn't bring herself to believe he was a rustler.

"I like them all," Sara wailed after several hours of shopping. "How can I possibly choose?"

Minnie shared her views on suitability and price. "There are just too many choices," she said. "But you're going to have to make a few decisions." They asked Kat's opinion.

"I think," Kat said, "you would look fetching in the navy blue. Stay away from the yellowish-green one."

Sara finally settled on her selections. Once they were measured and cut, Minnie searched for quilt materials. Kat had absolutely no experience with quilting, but she readily approved the bright colors. Choosing colors was one of her strengths.

Later in the day, they met Jeremiah, who had been purchasing supplies for the new dormitory.

"I found everything I needed and hauled packages up and down the stairs in our hotel room all day. I'm exhausted and ready to eat. I hope everything we bought will fit into the buckboard." He laughed, and his face lit up with a ruddy glow. "How did you ladies fare?"

"Oh, we had a grand time choosing material. Sara's going to look right smart in her new clothes." Minnie beamed at the young girl.

Sara smiled back. "Tomorrow, we'll look for new shoes and a new hat."

Jeremiah glanced at his pocket watch. "Shall we eat supper at the hotel? Kat should surely enjoy a good meal before she leaves on the evening stagecoach. Do you agree, Kat?"

"I'm not all that hungry, but I should eat something."

"That's fine with me," Minnie said.

When they were seated in the hotel dining room and had ordered their meal, Minnie turned her attention to Kat. "I know the waiting has to be hard on you. Have faith; everything will turn out for good."

"I'll try, but it's hard. I don't even know Jet that well, but I have this strong intuition that he's not a bad man. I believe he needs my help."

Jeremiah patted her hand. "I believe it, too."

"I don't know much about the law, but I feel that Jet's in great danger. From what I have learned while living in Deadwood, the authorities are beginning to bring in convictions for cattle theft. I just can't believe he would be involved in a crime like that. If it wasn't for Tex, I wouldn't have believed any of it."

Jeremiah nodded. "One never knows what motivates a person to do wrong things. He probably just got in with a bad crowd. He can turn his life around if he wants. Even if he serves time, he will eventually get out of prison. Just be prepared."

"I don't like to see you going through this ordeal alone. Is there someone who could be with you?" Minnie asked.

"I have friends in Deadwood if I need them," Kat said.

Minnie's eyes warmed at Kat's statement. "Please let us know what's happening."

"I appreciate your concern and your prayers. I'll write to you the first chance I get."

After supper, Jeremiah escorted Kat to the stage. She

thanked him profusely for everything and climbed aboard the coach.

The horses and stage couldn't move fast enough for Kat. She didn't feel a bit sociable and practically ignored the other two ladies and the man on the coach. This time, she didn't invite anyone to play cards with her. Instead, she played solitaire until it became too dark. Then she pretended to sleep. Her impatience nearly got the best of her, and to her surprise, she prayed a simple supplication for Jet's safety.

After two days on the stage, the first thing she did in Rapid City was hire a hack driver to take her to the jail. She was hopeful that Jet would be incarcerated there. Otherwise, she would have to inquire in Deadwood or Spearfish. She waited in the office until the jailer came from a side room and asked her what she wanted.

"I'm here to see Jet Black," she explained.

"He's here, but no visitors are allowed," the jailer said.

"What do you mean?"

"Are you his wife?"

"No, I'm a friend."

"Like I said. No visitors."

Kat raised her voice. "I'm not leaving here until I see him."

The jailor plopped down behind the desk, smirking. "Suit yourself."

Sensing the futility of her situation, she asked, "Has he seen a lawyer?"

"No, I don't think so."

"Well, has he seen anyone?"

"Nope."

"Listen here. This is inhumane. I'm here to see if he's alright. If you don't let me in to see him, I'm going to find someone who will."

"Hold on, lady." The jailer put up his hands. "Quit your yelling. If it's that important, I'll let you in, but only for a few minutes."

"Fine. Show me the way." She followed the slovenly jailer through a dank, dark passageway until they came to a block of cells.

"Someone to see you," the jailer announced to Jet.

"Was that you out there making all that commotion?" Jet asked her when he saw Kat standing outside his cell.

"Is that all you can say to me after I've come all this way?" she said, still in a huff.

He pushed himself off a cot and came to the bars. "I...I'm glad to see you. How did you find out I was here?"

"Tex came by the mission and told us, or I'd never have known about you. Are you a rustler?" she whispered.

Jet placed his hands on the bars and glanced around at the jailer, who was watching their every move.

"Keep your hands off them bars," the jailer yelled.

Jet released the bars. "I can't talk here. But believe me, I've never hurt a soul."

"I want to believe you," she said, resisting the notion to reach for him. "You look better than I expected. You haven't slept much, have you?"

"It's hard to sleep, knowing that I'll have to go to prison for who knows how long."

She pulled her cape tightly around herself and shivered. "How can I help?"

"I need a good lawyer. Oh, they'll appoint someone for me, but I have a feeling he'll be friends with the prosecutor and not really care what happens to me."

"I talked to Ed. I'm supposed to telegram him after I've seen you, but I don't know why."

"So he knows, too?"

"Yes, I told him."

"Was he angry?"

"No, I'd say he was more concerned."

Jet shook his head. "I've never had a boss like him before. I liked working for him." He struck the bars with his hand. The jailer flashed a warning look. "Darn my luck. The guard is signaling me to wrap up our talk."

"I don't like that guard," she said, frowning.

"I know. I heard."

Kat smirked. "Well, I got in here, didn't I?"

He smiled. "You did. And I am glad to see you."

"Good." She managed a smile. "I'll look around for a lawyer. I'm going to Deadwood tonight to check on my business, but I'll be back." She turned to leave, and then whisked by the jailer, slamming him into the wall as she passed.

––––––

Kat went to the Birdcage Saloon the day she arrived in Deadwood. She had already telegraphed Ed, and her nerves were still getting the best of her.

"We're so glad to see you," Jennie said. She ran for a hug when Kat entered the saloon.

Jake and Clem stood in line to hug her, too. "My, we have missed you. The place isn't the same without you," Jake said.

"It feels like I've been gone a million years." She glanced around the bar.

"We haven't changed a thing," Clem said.

"I see that. How's business been?"

"It's about the same. All the receipts are behind the counter where we always keep them," Jake said.

"I'll look at them later. I trust you and thank you all for running this place while I was caring for Miranda. I should be able to stay for a bit, however, I think I'll be making some trips to Rapid City," Kat said wearily.

Jennie looked concerned. "Tell us what's going on. You're plumb worn out."

Kat heaved a sigh. "Leave it to me to become infatuated with a cattle rustler."

"A cattle rustler! Where did you meet a cattle rustler?" Clem asked.

"At a mission."

"A mission! Come on, let's sit at the table. I have a feeling this is going to be good. Tell us more," Jennie encouraged.

Kat sat first and her three friends joined her. She had their full attention. "I didn't know he was a rustler at the time. In fact, he surprised us all. He was working for a cattle outfit when I saw him at the mission. However, I'd met him before on a stage, that time I lost my compact."

"You're losing me here." Jennie furrowed her brow.

"Yeah, what's this about a compact?" Jake asked.

"It's kind of complicated. His name is Jet, and when I met him on the stage returning from Cleveland, he was wearing this awful suit. He said he was a tailor in Deadwood, which I thought was odd because I had never seen him before and his suit was so crummy. After several days back in Deadwood,

I went looking for him. No one had even heard of him. And what would be the odds of him being at the mission I was visiting!" Her friends shook their heads. "He was wearing western clothes then. I have to admit he looked much better this time around."

"You always did like the cowboys," Clem laughed.

Kat frowned.

"But what was he doing at a mission?" Jake asked.

"Ed, his boss, encourages his hired hands to attend church. I know it sounds strange. After church that first Sunday I saw him, I confronted him about the suit and the tailor story. He sidestepped the issue and said he did it to find a job in Deadwood. Like a fool, I accepted his story. I took a liking to him as I think he did toward me. Who knows? Our relationship might have gone somewhere. But then I found out he was arrested for cattle theft."

Jennie leaned on her elbow. "What a story! Where he is now?"

"In the Rapid City jail."

"You must be brokenhearted," Jennie said.

"I've been to see him."

"You mean you haven't given up on him?"

"I truly believe he's not a bad person."

Jennie shook her head. "I don't see why you would want to get involved."

"He doesn't have anyone to help him out. There's just something about him. I'm going to try and find a good lawyer for him. In fact, I'm going to start looking today."

"Sounds like something you would do, Kat. You're always watching out for the other guy," Clem said.

"Thanks, Clem. I guess I have been like that since I was

little. Annabelle said I was always dragging some poor, lost animal home, or feeding some hungry child."

"I just hope this act of kindness doesn't get you in trouble this time," Jake advised. "I wish you luck, but he sounds like a lost cause to me."

"I hope you know what you're doing," Clem added.

Kat threw up her hands. "To me, it's worth the risk."

Their conversation ended when a few customers entered the saloon and Clem and Jake left the table to wait on them.

"By the way, how are Annabelle and Miranda?" Jennie asked when the fellows left.

"Annabelle was well enough for me to send Miranda back to Cleveland. And I'm happy to say that Miranda isn't quite the spoiled child she was when she first came to the mission. In fact, the mission was good for both of us."

"Your mission sounds like quite a place," Jennie said.

"You're right," Kat mused. "It's quite a place. I think I'll miss it, although it was hard to get used to at first."

"How do you mean?"

"It's quite desolate and so far from everything. And the weather can be challenging, to say the least."

Before the supper hour, the telegram boy came into the saloon with a telegram from Ed.

Kat hurriedly read it to herself. "Well, I don't believe it."

Jennie came over to her as soon as the boy left. "Believe what?"

"Ed, Jet's boss, is a lawyer. Now doesn't that beat all! I wonder how many other secrets he has."

"What's he say?" Jennie looked sideways at the telegram.

"He wants to represent Jet. He already contacted the district attorney in Rapid City and told him he's on his way.

Why didn't he tell me he was a lawyer before I left? It could have saved me worrying about finding one."

"So you'll be going to Rapid City again?"

"The way I figure it, Ed should be in Rapid City the day after tomorrow and I'm going to be there when he arrives."

————

Kat boarded the stage for Rapid City once again. She disliked shirking the responsibilities of her business, but her life seemed to be taking on new directions. Jet had become important to her and she felt she could trust her three employees with the saloon.

Her only thought now was to get to the jail and see that Jet was okay. She didn't know what kind of lawyer Ed would be, but she hoped he was a good one. When she walked into the jail, the same jailor who had given her trouble earlier was on duty.

"I'm here to see Jet," she stated with determination in her voice.

The jailor propped his feet upon the desk and folded his arms across his chest. "He's with a lawyer."

"I know the lawyer. Could you please tell them I'm here? They're expecting me."

The jailor looked at her with contempt, sprang off his chair, and went back to the cell. Soon, he sauntered back and motioned for her to join Jet and Ed in consultation. Kat followed, not bothering to thank the jailor for his begrudged courtesy. Her first glance fell on Jet. She took in his every physical detail. He looked thin and scared.

"Ed, I'm so glad you're here," she said, her voice quavering.

"Now don't' worry. I'm going to do the best I can, but we

can't sweep the truth under the rug."

"What do you mean?"

"Whatever is said between Jet and me is confidential."

"So that means you can't talk about his case in front of me."

Ed nodded.

"I can leave and let you two discuss the case against him. I just wanted to make sure that Jet was well and that you had arrived like you said."

Jet's eyes met hers for a brief moment. "Thanks for coming by, Kat."

She felt herself blushing—something she very seldom did. "I'll be back later. I plan on staying in town for a few days."

"Don't put yourself out for me," Jet said.

"I want to," she said, and left the jail. But before she walked out of the office, she made her point with the surly jailer. "I'll be back—several times, in fact."

––––––

Jet watched Kat disappear from sight before continuing his conversation with Ed.

"Like I said before, you need to tell me everything," Ed said. "Don't keep any secrets from me, or they may come back to haunt us."

"You know I appreciate your coming all this way to help me out, but I don't understand why you want to bother."

"Let's just say I have had a few rough spots in my life, and if it wasn't for people who cared, I might not be as well off as I am today. Besides, I don't feel like you're a bad person, but you have made some bad choices."

Jet nodded. His biggest mistake was hooking up with Tom. He tried to right that wrong, but he wasn't able to break free. Now, he'd have to pay for his bad choices.

"How long have you rustled cattle?" Jet didn't answer immediately. "It's important that you tell me the truth. There's always a squealer out there who will tell all."

"About three years." Jet lowered his head.

"So this is the first time you have been caught?"

Jet nodded.

"Any close calls?"

"A couple of times."

"Could anyone identify you?"

"No."

"Have you rustled horses?"

"Once."

"Where was that?"

"In the southern Black Hills."

"Most of the time you operated in the Black Hills. Is that right?"

"Yeah, that's right. It's easy to hide out there."

"Tom has always been the instigator of your forays?"

"Most of the time. I was supposed to plan one for him this time around."

Ed slowed down the barrage of questions. "I'm curious. Did you come to my ranch with the intention of rustling?"

"I...did. I'm not proud of it, though. It was getting too dangerous to continue in the Hills. The authorities were really cracking the law there. We split the money from the last venture in Deadwood and agreed to go our separate ways. I said I would look around the reservation area. Tom went down to the southern part of the state, but then I changed my mind. I wanted to end rustling and get away from Tom. I met him in Fort Pierre and told him that, but he wouldn't hear of me leaving. I sneaked out of town."

"Now we come to the part about you being abducted?" Ed asked.

"That's right. I had hoped he would never find me, but he did. Him and the gang forced me to go with them on another caper. I could have refused, but I'd be dead right now. I didn't want to shoot at those men. Tom gave me a gun and ordered me to shoot, or we would be killed, he said."

Ed sighed and rubbed his chin. "The way I see it, a judge and jury will have to hold you accountable for rustling and for shooting at the two men, but I think we can play on the court's sympathy that you wanted to reform. We need someone to testify that you were taken away from the ranch."

"The rest of Tom's men sure won't support my story. They'll say that I went along willingly."

"But the court has to be convinced without a shadow of a doubt that you're either innocent or guilty. Remember, you left the Bar Double B without your paycheck or any of your belongings. I can testify to that."

"Do you think that will be enough?"

"We'll have to wait and see on that one. But I'll do my best to convince them."

"Is there a chance I can get off?" Jet asked.

"I don't believe I can cause that to happen, but I'll bet we can get you a reduced sentence. I'm afraid you're going to have to pay for your transgressions."

Jet nodded. "Would you kind of watch out for Kat? I know she's tough and can take care of herself, but I'd feel better if you'd keep an eye on her."

––––––

The trial commenced on a cloudy day, threatening rain. Kat approached the courthouse with a heavy heart. She was sensible enough to know that Jet would not be acquitted. That would be simply too good to be true. Cattlemen and the general public considered cattle rustlers the lowest form of humanity to walk the earth. Lately, judges were handing out hefty sentences. Ed had his work cut out for him.

She thought about Pastor Elijah Fletcher and the mission church. She had rarely prayed in her life, but she said another prayer for Jet as she raced against the first droplets of rain. When she entered the courtroom, she slid into a seat near the back and brushed off the raindrops that had beaded on her tight, peacock blue jacket. It wasn't long before Jet came into the courtroom and sat at a table with Ed. She sat up straight in order to catch a glimpse of him. Ed and Jet bent their heads together, conferring for several minutes before the middle-aged judge pounded his gavel and brought the court to order. She had no idea what Ed had planned for Jet's defense, but she discovered that she was wringing her hands in anticipation.

When the prosecutor finished his opening statement, Kat felt terror surge through her. Was there hope for Jet? She had to believe there was, and she felt better when Ed faced the jury. Kat didn't know much about law, but she could see that Ed would concentrate on Jet's character and on his intention to resist a life of crime. She knew Ed could not call Jet to the stand to testify in his own defense, for he would surely incriminate himself upon cross-examination.

The prosecutor called the range detective as his first witness to establish the credibility of his case. The stocky range detective lumbered toward the witness stand.

After he was sworn in, the prosecutor asked, "What is it you do for a living?"

"I'm a range detective hired by the Stockman's Association."

"What are your duties?"

"To apprehend and arrest rustlers."

"Tell us what you saw on the day in question."

The range detective cleared his throat. "Well, I was riding along when I met up with Tex McMurray on the trail. We was visiting and came up on this small bunch of cattle and some herders. Since there's been a lot of rustling along the Cheyenne, I grabbed my rifle and rode closer to have a look. Then we heard gunfire, and a bullet whistled toward us. We got off our horses right quick and found cover and shot back."

"Are you positive that you and Tex did not fire first?"

"Yeah."

"How many men were shooting at you?"

"At first I heard one, then later two."

"How long did the shooting last?"

"Not long."

"What do you mean by, 'Not long?'" the prosecutor prompted.

"Maybe five minutes at most."

"When the barrage of gunfire ceased, what did you do?"

"We approached the men shooting. When we got there, we saw a man down and another man leaning over him."

"Did you identify the man who was shot?"

"No. I could not."

"Is the man who was leaning over the downed man in this courtroom?"

"He's over there." The range detective pointed at Jet.

"Did you arrest him?"

"Yeah, I cuffed him."

"What happened to the rest of the riders you had seen?"

"They left the herd. Scattered to the wind."

"Could you identify any of them?"

"No, they were too far away."

"Did you investigate the cattle?"

"I rode over to them. They were unbranded strays, for the most part. Only a few were carrying brands."

"As a law man with experience, how did you determine that these cattle were in the process of being stolen?"

"We were shot at for no reason and the cowboys scattered, leaving the herd. I checked out the owner of the brand on a few of those cattle and he told me they had been missing from his herd for some time," the range detective said.

The judge looked at Ed. "Your witness."

Ed approached the witness stand, a thoughtful expression on his face. "Did the man you arrested offer any resistance?"

"No, he held up his hands when we approached."

"Did he say anything to you? For example, did he explain why he was there?"

"He did. He said he wasn't part of the rustling and that he was forced to go along with it."

"Explain what you meant by hearing only one shot and then later two."

"Just like I said, it sounded like only one man was firing

at us, and later, we heard additional gunfire."

"Did the defendant have a rifle in his hand when you approached the two men?"

"No. It was lying on the ground, but it had been fired. I checked it when I got a chance."

"Did you recognize the man who was shot?"

"No, never saw him before."

"No more questions," Ed said.

Kat's heart raced. *I'll bet he's relieved that the prosecution could not connect Jet to any prior rustling,* she thought. *However, some secret witness could still ruin everything.*

The prosecution called Tex to the stand. Tex corroborated the range detective's account. Ed saw no need to cross-examine. With no other witnesses to testify for the prosecution, Ed called his first witness, Hal.

"Hal, explain to the jury what you do for a living."

"I'm the foreman for the Bar Double B Ranch."

"And how long have you held that position?"

"For about five years."

"Where were you when the defendant was allegedly abducted?"

"All the fellows and me were out on the range. Jet was left behind to keep an eye on things."

"When did you notice that the defendant was missing?"

"As soon as we got back. Jet wasn't in the bunkhouse, and his horse was missing."

"Why were you concerned that he was gone?"

"Because the bunkhouse door was left wide open, and a plate of food was barely touched."

"Did Jet seem to take any personal possessions with him?"

"No, his war bag was in the bunkhouse along with his handgun."

"Did you think that was unusual?"

"Objection! Leading the witness."

"Sustained," the judge ordered.

"What did you do when you discovered the defendant was gone?"

"I went to the ranch house and told, ah...you...he was gone."

"And what did I say?"

"We'd wait until morning and look for him then."

"Tell us what happened the next morning."

"We found several sets of hoofprints leading out. We followed them a ways, but lost the trail."

"Did it appear that he was riding with a group of men?"

The prosecutor stood quickly. "Objection, leading the witness."

"Overruled," the judge said. "Answer the question."

"Yeah, it did."

"No further questions at this time," said Ed.

"Your witness," the judge said.

The prosecution approached Hal. "Whose idea was it for the defendant to stay behind?"

"Ah...Jet volunteered."

"Did the defendant own a rifle?"

"Yeah, he did."

"Were you able to find the rifle at the ranch?"

"No."

"No further questions," the prosecutor said.

"You may step down," the judge told Hal.

Ed called Bert to the stand. After being sworn in, Ed

asked him to identify himself as well as his occupation.

"Did you work with the defendant quite often?"

"Yeah, I was one of them that asked Jet to come work for us when we was rounding up cattle. We was shorthanded that day."

"What kind of man would you describe the defendant to be?"

"Good sort of guy, good worker, honest, kind of keeps to himself."

"Has he caused any sort of trouble at the ranch?"

"No, not at all."

"Do you attend church on Sundays?"

"Objection, irrelevant."

"I'm trying to attest to his character," Ed argued.

"Overruled," the judge said. "Answer the question."

"We do."

"Does the defendant accompany you to church?"

"He does."

"No further questions."

"Your witness."

The prosecution stood at his table. "How long have you known the defendant?"

"Just a few months."

"You say he keeps to himself. Do you know anything about his past?"

"Objection!" Ed shouted. "He is not on trial for his past."

"Sustained."

Bert appeared confused.

"No more questions."

"You may step down," the judge ordered.

After determining that neither the defense nor the

prosecution had any more witnesses, the lawyers gave their summations. Ed attempted to plant doubt in each juror's mind that Jet rustled cattle in the Cheyenne River breaks. The prosecutor, on the other hand, reminded them that Jet was willingly rustling cattle and had fired on the range detective and Tex.

The jury left the courtroom to deliberate after the summations ended. Kat also left, hoping that fresh air would still her throbbing head. She was oblivious to the vibrant display of fall colors glistening from the fresh rain. She only heard the possible verdicts in her head. What would she do if the jury found Jet guilty? She had been walking for over an hour before she returned to see Ed outside the court house.

"Have they reached a verdict?" she asked him.

"They have. Court will reconvene in a half hour."

"Do you have any idea what the decision will be?"

"I don't think they'll let him off, but I'm hopeful the judge will be lenient." Ed gently took hold of her arm. "I know this isn't what you want to hear, but I want you to be prepared. Let's go inside."

The jury filed in a half hour later. Shortly thereafter, the judge asked the foreman to read the verdict. Kat stopped breathing as he read the statement. Her eyes were on Jet.

"We, the jury, find the defendant guilty."

Jet stood motionless, and then dropped his head. Kat's heart cried out to him.

The judge said, "In light of the evidence presented, I recommend a sentence of one year in the state penitentiary."

One year? Her heart sank. It would seem like an eternity, but on the other hand, in just one year they could be together. She remembered Ed's words about leniency.

After the courtroom cleared, she hurried over to Jet. But before she reached him, she suddenly realized they had never expressed their feelings for each other. She really didn't know how he felt about her. The thought restrained her from throwing her arms around him.

"Thanks for being here," Jet said to her.

"I'll write you."

"I would like that," he said before the guard led him away.

"A year isn't too bad," Ed reassured her. "The sentence could have been much longer. And, it's possible he could be let out early on good behavior. I doubt he will cause any trouble."

"Thanks for all you've done for him. Not too many people would have gone out of their way for him, but you did."

"I have faith in him, and I told him he could have his old job back when he gets out. May I buy you a cup of coffee before we part company?"

"I could use one."

When they had settled themselves into an eating establishment down the street, Ed ordered them two cups of coffee. "Try not to worry about Jet. Prison is no picnic, but he's a survivor."

"It'll be hard to think of him there. I don't know much about him, do you?" she asked, stirring cream into her coffee.

"He never said much to me, but that's not unusual for cowpunchers. Nearly all of them have a past they're running from."

"I guess I know that. I have seen plenty of them in my saloon. Some are a sad lot. I guess I've always had a soft spot for them."

"I had a feeling about him when he came to work for the ranch. I thought he might be casing out the ranch. He had admitted that while we were discussing his defense. Something changed his mind about going through with his plans. He did a day's work and was always honest with me, so I wanted to go that extra mile with him."

"The least I can do is write him letters. He has to have someone who cares on the outside. The penitentiary at Sioux Falls is too far away to visit. Do you know if he has any family somewhere?"

"He never told me of any."

"It's a terrible feeling to be alone." She shook her head. "I'm lucky, though. I have a sister and a niece." She offered her hand to Ed. "I must be going. I don't want to miss my stage. Thanks, and I hope we meet again."

"I'm sure we will. Let me know if there is anything else I can do."

———

Kat left the Birdcage Saloon to walk home for lunch. She felt flat and grumpy. It had been months since Jet was sent to prison, but she just couldn't get Jet out of her mind, especially the way he looked when they led him away after the verdict. As usual, she stopped at her mailbox on the way to her house. She was surprised to find a letter with Jet's scrawl across the envelope. Her heartbeat quickened as she tore into it and began reading. She went through the screen door to her kitchen and groped for a chair. She sat and read:

Dear Kat,

No doubt you're surprised to get a letter from me, in fact, I'm surprised to be writing one. Never was much of a letter writer but since you supported me thru thick and thin I thought I would tell you that I'm good considering where I'm at. This prison here has decided to build a stone wall all around the prison yard. And guess who gets to build it? You got it—the prisoners. They've been at this for a while. Once there was a wooden fence but they took it down.

The stone used for the wall comes from these parts, not far from the prison along the bluffs of the Big Sioux River. In fact, the stone is close to the surface of the ground. The warden loaded us up in a wagon and took us there the next day after I got here. Stone cutters came and cut blocks which we loaded in tram cars. They call it quartzite. It's pink and red and heavy. The prisoners tell me they had a good quarry business here at one time and used the stone in buildings around the town. I haven't seen this on my own as no one trusts that I'd come back! The work's hard but beats being cooped up in a cell all day. I worked all day with a short break for lunch.

Don't know what will happen when it really starts to snow. We've already been out through cold and rain. That rock is darn slick then. Some of the men suffer from dust from the stone cutting. They're couffin' and hackin' all over the place. So far I'm good. Maybe because I haven't been here that long.

Don't worry about me even though the food's terrible and the company's not much better. Here comes the guard! Means lights out.

Your friend,

Jet

She let the letter fall to the table. Clearly, he didn't write her everything. Her imagination went wild with abuses that he must be experiencing. Were the prisoners chained together when they were out working? He didn't write about that. Were the other prisoners mean to him? These were things she would not know. He would never tell her. She just had to be content knowing that he was well enough to write and that he was enjoying fresh air. If she were the praying kind, she would have asked for help.

CHAPTER 14

Tex and Tater rode toward Evangeline and Elijah, who were standing on the front porch admiring the last remnants of autumn.

"Why, it's Tex coming this way. I wonder what he's doing here." Evangeline waved.

"What brings you way out here?" Elijah asked when Tex reined his horse to a stop.

"We're on our way east, looking for some Hereford bulls. Thought maybe we could bunk here for the night."

"Sure, you're always welcome," Elijah said.

"This here's my cook and ranch hand, Tater."

"Pleased to meet you. Get down and come inside. Have you eaten?"

"We had some hardtack and jerked meat on the trail. Don't bother with us."

"We can at least visit some before you turn in. You can

sleep in the dormitory we're building." Elijah shook their hands. "No beds yet, but you'll be indoors."

"Much obliged."

Once inside, Evangeline brewed coffee and sliced some bread.

"We moved the cattle to a range closer to the reservation," Tex explained while buttering his bread. "No homesteaders there yet. We left Curt and the boys behind to keep an eye on the cattle."

"Where do you intend to find Hereford bulls?" Elijah asked.

"I heard there were some for sale around Pierre."

"Herefords are a good idea, but how are you going to use them on the open range? I would think you'd need some fences."

"Oh, we'll figure it out. I probably won't buy any, but I would just like to know where I can find some."

Evangeline sliced more bread, placed it on the table, and asked, "Are you returning to Texas for the winter?"

"I might go back for Christmas and stay awhile. Think I'll spend most of my time on the ranch. We'll have to get some outbuildings put up before the snow."

Sol came lumbering into the mission yard with a wagon, full of wood. He stopped by the mission door, jumped down from his wagon and knocked on the kitchen door. Elijah opened it and invited Sol inside.

"Need a cup of coffee, Sol? It's getting kind of nippy out there, isn't it?"

"Yeah, I thought I dressed warm enough, but I'm chilled to the bone. You see I brought some wood?"

"I do. I'd like you to meet Tex and his ranch hand and

cook, Tater." The men shook hands. "Evangeline and I met Tex on our way to Denver during our honeymoon. He just moved his cattle west of here from the Belle Fourche River."

"We have a big day ahead of us tomorrow and ought to turn in for the night. Thanks for the coffee and bread." Tex stood. "Just point us in the right direction."

"The building's open," Elijah said. "Just toss your bedroll anywhere. Come by for breakfast."

"We'll do that." Tex and Tater disappeared into the twilight.

Elijah looked out the window at the full load of wood that Sol had brought. "I suppose we can take two more loads of wood. The new building is going to take a lot more fuel, especially if it's a cold winter. I wish the railroad would get here soon so we can get coal for our stoves." Elijah poured more coffee.

"Thanks," Sol said.

Evangeline sliced another loaf of bread and placed it in front of Sol. "Here, I'll bet you're hungry, too." She made a mental note to bake more bread tomorrow.

"I could use a little something." Sol devoured two slices in no time.

"I haven't seen you in a while. How did your calf prospects turn out this year?"

Sol hesitated. "I don't know what to think of my situation. My calf numbers are way down, and I'm not making any gain. What's funny about all this is the cowman near us claims he has had many sets of twin calves. Now isn't that a little strange?"

"I should say so. Can you prove anything suspicious?"

"No, I can't. You know the whites say the Indians do

all the stealing, but I think the whites do their share, too. Another thing I'm not happy about is all the cattle put on our land by the whites who married Indian women."

"You think they're taking more than their share?"

"That's for sure. We don't get one dime from them. I'll bet that Tex fellow is biding his time for leasing to be made legal. If the government decides to lease our land, tribal ranching will end. We can't compete with the big cattle outfits running cattle all over the reservation."

"But they'll pay you for the leases, won't they?"

"Sure they will. But is that best for us?"

Evangeline could see the conflict between cattlemen like Tex and the people she and Elijah served. She wanted to be friends with them all, but would she and Elijah have to choose sides?

———

Two weeks before the fall school session, the women began painting the new dormitory. They had decided on an off-white color for the walls. Each morning, Evangeline awoke stiff and sore from the previous day's work, but she loved every minute of seeing the dormitory come to life. The building smelled so fresh and new and seemed so homey with its brightly colored curtains at the windows. She was so thankful she was able to fund the project, and she couldn't wait to see the children's faces when they came to school this fall.

"Too bad Kat isn't here to see some of her handiwork," Cassandra said as she continued to hang the curtains in the girls' rooms. The women had sewn straight curtains from various print fabrics.

"By the way, what have you heard from Kat lately?" Evangeline asked.

"As you already know, Jet's been sent off to prison for a year," said Minnie. "Kat wrote she's thinking of making Jet a quilt, even though she's never made one." Minnie laughed. "You know our Kat—she'll try anything once."

"Will she have some help?"

Minnie nodded. "She and her friend Jennie have recruited several women to help. Sounds like most of them don't know much about sewing, except for maybe one."

"I commend them anyway," Cassandra added. "The sewing she learned here will undoubtedly help."

"Minnie sorted through the pile of freshly ironed curtains. "I like the calico curtains for the girls. I think they're a little more feminine." She held one up to the window.

Cassandra threaded another curtain on a rod. "We'll still have time before the cold weather to complete our quilts."

"We'll definitely make that a part of their sewing project this fall. If they make their own quilts, they will be liable to take care of them," Minnie said, handing Cassandra the matching half of the curtain set.

Cassandra stood back to admire the bright window coverings against the creamy walls. "There, doesn't that look nice?"

"What about rugs?" Evangeline asked. "They take a lot of time and fabric to make."

"I believe we can do without them for now. Again, we'll just teach the girls to make them. If they're not made before spring, it won't matter that much."

After they finished hanging the girls' curtains on the

north side of the dormitory, they diverted their attention to the south end where the boys would room.

"I like the red and blue checkered curtains. They're my favorite," Minnie said. "They look good in the boys' rooms."

Evangeline frowned in worry. "I hope the beds and mattresses arrive before the children do."

"If nothing else, they can sleep on the floor," Cassandra said, practical as ever.

The women left the bedrooms after the curtains were hung and entered the dining area in the middle of the dormitory. Off this room was the new kitchen.

"This will be handy, although I will miss all the wonderful memories of the old kitchen. We had so many good meals and conversations." Minnie gazed at the new walls.

"We'll still use the building, but for sewing and extra rooms," Cassandra said. "Is it possible to get a few more machines?"

"I've already ordered five more sewing machines," Evangeline told them.

"Wonderful! I can't wait to see them."

Evangeline stood with her hand on her hips, surveying the space. "We talked about moving in the old stove, but I think a new one would be in order, something larger than we have now."

Minnie smiled. "A bigger oven?"

"I think we could manage that and a larger cooking surface. We'll be cooking for many more hungry mouths, three meals a day, often seven days a week. Later, let's look through the Montgomery Ward catalog and see what they have."

"My, I hope we're up to the task of running a boarding school," Cassandra said.

"Don't worry. If we need to, we'll recruit help. It depends on the students. I am hoping some of the former students return; they would be a great help." Evangeline smiled at Cassandra and Minnie. "You ladies have worked so hard, and I would like you to slow down."

Minnie shrugged. "Don't worry about us. What about tables?"

"I talked to Elijah about that," Evangeline said. "He and the boys will build us new ones in carpentry class. Perhaps they could make chairs as well. If not, I'll order some. In the meantime, I think the old ones can be moved in here."

"You've thought of everything," Cassandra said.

"I'm sure I have forgotten something. Elijah and I have spent many nights discussing the boarding school. I just hope it will work the way we have planned. Now, what about your living quarters, Minnie?" Evangeline asked. "Since you're going to be living in the dormitory and watching over the children with Jeremiah this winter, I think you should choose your own color for the walls and curtains."

"Let's take a look at the space once again, and then I'll have to think about it."

A large room on the ground level just off the kitchen had been built especially for the dormitory supervisors. In addition to a bed and bureau, there was enough room for a living area with chairs and a fireplace, which still needed to be completed.

"Oh, this is so cozy. You'll never get rid of us," Minnie said delightedly.

Evangeline laughed. "That's the idea. We never want you to go."

Just then, Elijah and Jeremiah walked into the room where the women were laughing.

"How's it going, ladies?" Jeremiah said, his face all aglow.

Minnie beamed. "Just look at this, Jeremiah. Won't it be wonderful to live here for the winter? We can still be useful and close to our friends." She turned to Evangeline. "Thank you, thank you for including us in your plans. We feel so honored."

"I don't think we could have done this without you," Evangeline said.

Elijah nodded.

"We didn't coerce you to stay, did we? I mean, we didn't make you think you had to? We didn't mean to interfere with your retirement," Evangeline added.

"Not at all," Jeremiah said with a shrug. "I don't think I can ever retire. Service is in my blood. I come from a line of missionaries and ministers. In 1834, my grandfather forged ahead into the Minnesota wilderness with his wife when the natives were especially uncivilized and dangerous."

"I shudder to think of the women accompanying their menfolk to such a desolate and dangerous place. What courage they must have had," Minnie said. "When Jeremiah told me of his family, I marveled at them all. And to think, they even reared children in such a place. But the sad part is that some of the sweet children didn't survive."

Jeremiah smiled at his wife's compassion. "Their courage and faith put me to shame. By the time I arrived here, other missionaries had already come before me. So, I really wasn't blazing any new trails. The missionaries had already put together dictionaries and Bibles in the native language. And, I didn't have to worry about losing my scalp. It's easier now."

"And your father?" Evangeline asked.

"The missionaries moved west with the Word. My father became a missionary in eastern South Dakota. He told me of growing up in the wilderness and how hard his parents worked to convert the Indians. At times they became so frustrated with progress, but they persevered. Father had it more difficult than I did. But watching his dedication inspired me to continue his work."

"You're an inspiration, Jeremiah," Elijah said.

––––––

"Oh, look!" Evangeline exclaimed as she peered out the kitchen window. "Here comes Cassandra with Sara. They're carrying an armful of dresses, the ones she made for Sara, I suppose."

"It warms my heart to see Mother has found joy in Sara," Elijah said.

"Perhaps Sara is the daughter Cassandra always wanted." Evangeline left the window to meet them at the door.

Sara flounced through the door, her face beaming. "Do you have time to see the dresses we made? I'll try them on for you."

Evangeline nodded and Sara disappeared into her bedroom. "Have a seat, Cassandra," she offered.

Shortly after the women made themselves comfortable, Sara returned, clothed in a tan dress with a fitted bodice and a flowing skirt. Evangeline studied the extra care Cassandra had given to sewing it. Her skill was evident in the details— piping, embroidery, and other finishing touches. The garment fit Sara's developing figure perfectly and was most flattering of her youth.

Evangeline couldn't help but smile with pride and pleasure as Sara modeled each creation for them. Sara was shy and withdrawn when they had first met. It took much coaxing, but finally Evangeline was able to win her confidence.

"Which is your favorite?" Sara asked Evangeline when she had finished modeling the last dress.

"You look fabulous in them all. How could I possibly choose?"

"Cassandra, what do you think?" Sara asked, twirling around in a skirt and jacket of lavender and gray.

"I agree with Evangeline. They are all rather suitable for you." Cassandra's remark didn't dim Sara's smile. She was used to Cassandra and her difficulty complimenting anyone. Cassandra probably had received few compliments in her life and had never learned to give them.

"Thank you for sewing with Sara. I could have tried, but the outcome would have been so different. I shudder to think." Evangeline laughed.

"I was happy to do it. I lose myself in sewing. That's how I survived the orphanage."

"It does still haunt you, then?"

"Oh, yes, though not as badly as it once did. I am so thankful for this mission. It has given me a purpose, and I feel so secure here."

"I feel the same way. I don't know if I ever thanked you for coming to Boston and asking me to come back here."

"No thanks needed." Cassandra glanced down at her hands in her lap.

"It must have been incredibly difficult to give up your security here and come back to Boston where you were so unhappy," Evangeline pressed.

"I'll admit, it was, but it was something I had to do for Elijah. I had to set aside my fears."

Sara returned promptly from the bedroom with the dresses gathered up in her arms.

A sad expression suddenly spread across Evangeline's face. "I guess you're ready for school?" She caressed the new dresses.

"I am, and I'm so excited," Sara replied, not noticing Evangeline's mood change. She bent down and softly kissed Cassandra on the cheek. "Thanks for sewing these."

Taken aback by the show of affection, Cassandra mumbled, "You're welcome." After Sara left with her dresses, Cassandra said to Evangeline, "I fear we will be behind in our quilt making. At the rate we're going, we aren't going to have enough before the cold sets in. We simply don't have the time."

"I probably could order some blankets."

"I know, but a handmade quilt is so special. I have an idea that might work."

"What is it?" Evangeline asked. "I'm open to suggestions."

"How about we have a quilting bee on a Saturday? The students would have their parents come and get them on a Saturday, but instead of going home immediately that day, everyone would stay to quilt. And, maybe some of the native women would even sew up a few quilt tops before then."

"I think that's a great idea. Let's do it."

———————

Thankfully, Alice, an agent in the Missionary Society in Boston, had recruited help from the society for the Cheyenne River Mission. An older widow, accompanied by a woman in her twenties, arrived a week before the school session. Neither had served as a missionary before. They boarded in the extra rooms in the dormitory.

"I hope Bea can keep up with the cooking," Cassandra said to Evangeline one day in the kitchen.

"She looks to be healthy enough, and she has a sunny disposition, much like Minnie."

"How old do you think she is?"

"In her early sixties," Evangeline guessed. "I don't think she would have come out here if she didn't feel up to it. Besides, we can help her out. And Ethel's youth and exuberance will be a breath of fresh air around here. She reminds me of Jessie."

"Poor girl. Jessie's life was cut short. I should have been more cordial toward her."

"Don't live in the past, Cassandra."

"I try to remember that. I suppose I worry too much. It's just that I have enough to keep up with, the sewing classes as well as the sewing required around here."

"And we appreciate you very much. Leave the worrying to me."

The days were still hot and oppressive when parents brought their children to school. Elijah and Jeremiah had scouted the countryside for potential students. Almost everyone knew of Elijah and Jeremiah and trusted they would take care of their children when they were away from home. By the end of their solicitous travels, they had recruited more than twenty students.

Many of these students had attended the day school, but a few came from families who were struggling to make ends meet. Enrolling their children in boarding school would take some of the economic pressure off their family.

The mission staff welcomed children of various ages and showed them to their rooms, now complete with beds, mattresses, and fresh sheets. Two students would occupy each room. Crudely fashioned washstands held pitchers of water, a bowl, and fresh towels.

Bea and Minnie had prepared a meal for everyone and served it in the new dining room. They did their best to make the students welcome. Since not everyone arrived at the same time, the women served the meal all day long. Jeremiah and Elijah talked with each family, assuring them their children would be treated with kindness and that they could return home on weekends as well as holidays. They also emphasized they should stay in school the entire week. When the parents were sure their children were settled, they left for home in their wagons.

At the end of the day, Bea, Minnie, and Evangeline sat on the open porch, exhausted.

"We had better get used to this," said Minnie. "This is the way our life will be for some time."

Bea stretched out her legs and sighed. "I hope we don't run out of food. They all ate like they hadn't eaten for days!"

"But isn't it wonderful to see some of our old students returning? The new ones are so timid and unsure. Have you been around Indian children before?" Minnie asked Bea.

"Not too many. I worked as a cook at a private school out East. I enjoy children."

"Good, I'm glad to hear that. You will find yourself becoming attached to the children here, too. They are standoffish at first, but when they learn to trust you, they'll come around," Evangeline assured her.

Cassandra joined the women on the porch after checking on the boarders. "It's hot on the upper level. We have the windows wide open, but there isn't much of a breeze tonight. I found some of them stretched out on the floor."

Evangeline wrinkled her brow in concern. "Most of them are used to sleeping outside on hot nights. I suppose the floor feels cooler than a bed."

Minnie yawned and added, "Oh, the hot weather will break in a few weeks. We'll just have to endure it for a short time."

"I have heard that sometimes Indian children run away from boarding schools. Will we have that problem here?" Bea asked.

The mission women glanced at Evangeline to hear her answer. "We certainly hope not. I think if we are too strict about when they can go home, they will. Perfect attendance isn't important to them. Some of the families might even be lax in getting their children to school."

"It's always been that way, even when we operated the day school," Minnie said. "Sometimes a student could be gone all week long. Of course, their absence interrupts their studies and puts them behind. But we do the best we can."

Evangeline hoped their best effort would be good enough. The boarding school was a new journey for all of them. Would they be able to keep up the workload? More importantly, would their students be happy here?

––––––––

Elijah hitched a team of horses to the buckboard so that Evangeline could drive over to Swift Bear's old camp and fetch several of the older ladies who still lived there and bring them to the first quilting session of the year.

"I don't think you should be driving the wagon alone. You're not that experienced yet," Elijah said. "What if the horses spook and you get thrown out?"

"Would you feel better if someone went with me?" she asked, a little miffed at his lack of confidence in her.

"I would go, but I have duties here to attend to. Mother can go with you. I'll ask her to. Wait here, and I'll be right back."

Evangeline rolled her eyes and impatiently remained by the stable until Elijah returned with Cassandra.

Cassandra appeared as disconcerted as Evangeline when she climbed into the wagon and sat beside her. "Do you want me to drive the horses?"

"No, I have to learn sometime. Having you by my side will comfort Elijah. Thanks for coming along. Were you busy?"

"I'm always busy, but whatever I was doing can wait. Minnie can take over until I get back."

On the trip over, Evangeline held the reins tensely. She reminisced about the fellowship they had shared in the sewing circle seven years ago with Red Bird, Angeline, Josephine, Alvina, other Lakota women, and the older students.

"Did you continue the quilting sessions after I left?" Evangeline inquired of Cassandra.

"Not with the biblical themes. Most of the older ladies had become quite accomplished with their quilting and didn't need me. They took to the star design, mostly. We made simple patchwork designs with the female students. They took those quilts home with them after they finished."

"I am looking forward to another sewing circle. While I lived in Boston, I stopped quilting for the most part, although I attempted to make a Storm at Sea with Gertrude."

"Gertrude? Have you mentioned her to me before?"

"I don't think so. She was an elderly lady who lived near our horse farm on the coast near Boston. I befriended her for a time. She was a little strange, though. Her husband had died at sea, and she made the Storm at Sea quilt pattern."

"That's not strange. The Storm at Sea is a pretty pattern."

"That's all she made though. The exact same quilt pattern was all over her house. It made me dizzy. The quilt had the illusion of movement. Poor woman; I think she would have gone quite mad if she had continued to live there."

"What happened to her?"

"Luckily, the lighthouse keeper befriended her and even asked her to marry him. They moved to Boston. I hope she's happy now."

"I hope she is, too."

"Anyway, I think I forgot everything I learned about quilting."

"Oh, I'm sure you have remembered enough."

When they arrived at the practically deserted camp, Evangeline said, "I can't believe how this camp has changed. It used to be so lively. Children scampered about with their dogs, and people roasted meat on the fire. It doesn't even look like anyone's here."

At that very moment, Alvina and Josephine, bent with age, shuffled out of their cabins. They were carrying their sewing baskets with their favorite needles and scissors. Evangeline and Cassandra helped the women into the buckboard. They sat silently until they arrived back at the mission and joined the students who were already assembled in the sewing room. Evangeline studied the practice block Minnie had made for this week's lesson and placed it on the table for all to see.

"Ladies, Evangeline has suggested we make another biblical quilt pattern," Cassandra told them. "We thought it would be wonderful to make a quilt for each boarding school student. We have assigned the younger girls easy quilt patterns. Since we have become a boarding school, we have little time for sewing and quilting. But, we are going to try and make the Coat of Many Colors quilt with the help of the older girls." She held up the sample quilt block Minnie had made. "As you can see, it is made of brightly colored triangles and squares." Then Cassandra explained her idea of a quilting bee to be held on a Saturday. The ladies and students agreed it was a good idea.

"With the boarding school quilts completed, I hope it will give us time to devote to the one biblical quilt. When that is finished, we will hang it in the new dormitory," Evangeline said.

Cassandra nodded. "Good idea. You can use the block Minnie has made as a guide to select a color scheme. When you have decided, I suggest you assemble the center star first, and then put in the corner pieces. There's a lot of cutting and sewing, but I know we'll be rewarded in the end."

The women sorted through the prints and solids for the right combination of color and texture. They finally selected a color scheme, including as many colors as they could. After all, they were creating Joseph's coat.

Evangeline smiled as she watched the women hard at work on the quilting project. She thought of Red Bird, who had been so patient to teach her about quilting, and she wondered if Gertrude was working on a new quilt pattern. Surely her husband would have encouraged her to make something other than the Storm at Sea. And to think, even Kat was sewing a quilt! Evangeline loved these cozy afternoons, and she was sure other women everywhere did, too.

———

Evangeline helped Cassandra put her quilting bee plan into action one Saturday before Thanksgiving. The day was cold but no snow had fallen yet. The day before, the ladies had oiled the machines and made sure the tensions were just right. They rewound the bobbins and threaded each machine.

The Lakota women rallied around the idea of making quilts for the students for the winter. Most of the mothers and grandmothers of the boarding school students took advantage of the outing. Not only would they be sewing, but the occasion presented an opportunity to socialize with one another. Cassandra had suggested that only patchwork and crazy quilts were to be made. Star quilts would be too time-consuming. Several of the Lakota women brought quilt tops they had stitched at home.

Minnie, Bea, and Lily had prepared a big breakfast for the participants, who arrived at different times throughout the morning. After breakfast, Cassandra and Lily organized the groups of women and students to specific tasks. Some began tying completed quilt tops, others pieced and sewed, and the remainder finished the tied quilts with binding.

Friendly chatter permeated the entire mission. Elijah and Jeremiah hustled to the church to escape the frenzy.

"We're skipping lunch today, but we'll be back here at suppertime," Minnie reminded them.

Lily, Minnie, and Cassandra volunteered to supervise the various quilting activities. Minnie oversaw those tying the quilts, Cassandra instructed the women who were piecing, and Lily helped with binding the quilts. Evangeline floated from one station to another. Bea and Ethel remained in the kitchen to prepare the supper.

Minnie had brought out worn blankets to use as batting. She instructed her work group to layer the quilt back, the blanket, and the finished quilt top on the table and to pin the layers together.

"We're going to cut the back material so it is larger than the quilt top, since Lily's group is going to bring the extra material up over the batting and quilt top to form the binding." Minnie issued the tying instructions before they began. "Take each stitch four and a half inches apart—that's about the width of your fist. Keep going until you run out of yarn. Then cut midway between the stitches and tie in a double knot. And begin again."

"Like this?" one of the students asked.

"Just like that," Minnie confirmed. "I do have batting for when we use all of the old blankets, but we'll have to take our stitches closer together. Oh, and don't place the ties close to the edge because the binding will go there. Another thing— make sure your needle goes through all three layers."

When the tying was completed, Evangeline transferred the quilt to Lily's group for binding. She instructed her group to trim the batting to the size of the quilt top, then to bring the extra quilt backing up over the quilt top and stitch it down.

"Use a pencil and mark a cutting line one and a half inches beyond the edge of the quilt on the backing. Then cut the backing on that line. Square off the corners," she said.

The younger students had been sewing Flying Geese, Pinwheel, and Nine-Patch patterns in their sewing classes. Cassandra had her group count and finish up the blocks needed for a particular design and sew them together into a quilt top.

"If we have time, we'll attempt a string quilt too," said Cassandra.

"What's a string quilt?" one of the women asked.

"It's simply sewing strips of material onto a foundation square. The strips don't have to be cut to a certain size. Those quilts are very easy to make and a good use for scraps," Cassandra explained.

The quilters sewed through lunch and into the late afternoon. When the machines stopped whirling, the quilters assessed their accomplishments for the day. Twelve quilts were completed and five more were nearly finished. Cassandra and Minnie unfolded each one for all to see. There were Flying Geese quilts made of only triangles, Pinwheel quilts of varying colors, and Nine-Patch quilts as unique as the placement of colors, and two string quilt tops.

Each student who had participated chose the quilt they wanted and wrapped themselves up in them.

A smile spread across Cassandra's face. "I believe the quilting bee turned out well."

Evangeline sighed with relief. "Yes, it did. What a great idea, Cassandra. We're closer to our goal."

"Several of the Lakota women said they would finish the other quilt tops they didn't get to. That will certainly help us out," Cassandra added.

"I think we deserve a fine meal and some relaxation," Evangeline said. "Smelling the beef roasting in the oven all afternoon has piqued my appetite. Let's go see what Bea and Ethel have cooked up for us."

Evangeline led the way to the kitchen where Elijah and Jeremiah had already gathered. Elijah profusely thanked everyone for their assistance with the quilting project and said grace before the crowd dished up the roast beef, potatoes, gravy, and all the fixings.

"You ladies are a marvel," Jeremiah remarked. "It appears everyone had a good time and accomplished what they set out to do."

CHAPTER 15

The heavy clouds threatened snow flurries before Evangeline and Elijah finished moving into their new home. They had enjoyed a grand Thanksgiving dinner prepared by Bea, Cassandra, and Minnie. Sara returned home from Santee, and a few of the students remained at the boarding school.

The house was a simple frame dwelling with a large kitchen, living area, and two bedrooms. Evangeline had the funds to make it larger and more ornate, but she reminded herself that she was there to serve, not to create a show place in which to live.

She was convinced that she could wait to move until spring, but secretly she hoped she could be in her own house for the winter, especially now that she and Elijah were expecting a baby by spring! She appreciated the men who had worked until dark every night for the past two months to complete their house.

Elijah and Evangeline had very little to move from the cabin they had shared after they were married. She had no idea how Elijah had found the time to make their bedstead for the new house from small cottonwood logs, as well as a bureau and blanket chest. She had ordered an elastic felt mattress instead of relying on a straw-stuffed one. She had no desire to endure that discomfort if she could avoid it. Elijah helped her place it on the bed. She shook out the linens she had brought from their cabin and watched them float down on the bed. She tucked in the edges tightly. She snapped the star quilt that the congregation had made for them as a wedding gift and covered the bedstead, admiring its beauty. The red and white in the quilt brightened the room considerably. She folded the Job's Tears quilt that Cassandra and Sara made for her as a homecoming present. She draped it across her blanket chest at the foot of the bed, gently smoothing it with her hands.

Dark boards covered the floors, and a fireplace built from local rocks warmed the large kitchen. She had placed two rocking chairs on either side of it, which had been wedding gifts from her parents. She looked forward to sitting by the fire with Elijah on cold nights, reading, talking about their days, and rocking the baby.

She hadn't told Elijah about the baby yet. She wanted to be sure. How relieved she was that she could conceive. While she was married to James, she was barren, and she had no idea if it was because of her or James. And now... well, she just couldn't believe it. What a miracle!

Grateful that she could prepare meals in her own home, she began supper. True, she would miss the company of the others, but they would still share meals occasionally. Evangeline worked the handle on the pump, which was bolted down by her dry sink. It drew water from a cistern under the house. With only a few movements of her arm, water streamed forth, filling a cooking pot. She used the water sparingly, knowing the resource at her fingertips was scarce.

Her kitchen window faced the church, so she could see Elijah's comings and goings. Elijah had suggested the idea to have her sink and pump near the window so she could see outside while she was cooking or washing dishes.

He is so thoughtful, she mused to herself as she continued the meal preparation. They had become so much closer through their marriage. She was thrilled at the intimacy they had discovered. She peeled potatoes and tossed them into the boiling water. She had already placed venison in the oven to roast; its fragrance filled the kitchen.

When Elijah entered the kitchen, a whoosh of cold air accompanied him. He deposited a load of logs into the wood box and rubbed his hands together, complaining of the cold. After kissing his wife, he said, "Ah, it smells good in here. I don't ever remember having a cozy home of my own. All I remember is living at one mission or another in an extra room somewhere. There, I seemed to be sharing with someone continually. Not that I minded that much, but I like a space to call my own—our own."

Her eyes gleamed. "I love our home, too. Thanks for making it happen."

Elijah stood by the fireplace he had built with his own hands. "Does it seem to draw well?" he looked the flue over with a critical eye while holding his hands to the warmth.

"Oh, I think so. I didn't seem to have any trouble starting it, and there's very little smoke." She smiled at him.

Elijah warmed himself by the fire. "I...I've been thinking about visiting Standing Rock. Ed and a few of his men have a contract to deliver beeves to the reservation. I asked him if I could go along and help him drive the cattle north."

"Oh. Are you thinking your father will be there for the winter?"

"I am hoping he will. Would you mind if I left for a while? Jeremiah will be here to watch over all of you."

"You know I dislike being away from you, but I understand your concern for your father. Go if you must. But please be careful." She turned to him with pleading eyes.

"Would tomorrow morning be too soon?"

She laughed. "You have already discussed this with Jeremiah, haven't you?"

"I confess. I did. Since the students will be off for an extended Thanksgiving break, I thought this might be a good time to leave."

"I just worry about you. But, I'll be more content knowing someone like Ed is with you."

"The chuck wagon will be going with us. And we'll have tents, too, if the weather gets too cold."

"What are you going to tell your mother?"

"I don't like lying to her. I will say I'm going to help Ed. I hope she believes that, because it's mostly true. I just don't think she should know about Father yet. I'm sure she thinks he will never come back, or perhaps that he is dead. No sense riling her up if we don't have to."

Evangeline grabbed a pot holder, carefully eased the meat out of the oven, and began slicing the venison roast.

"Wash up, Elijah. We're about ready to eat."

After he pumped water and washed, he sat at the table. Evangeline set the rest of the supper in front of him, and then took her place. They bowed for grace and dished up the steaming food.

Evangeline continued on with their conversation while she helped herself to the potatoes. "Cassandra has had many disappointments in her life."

Elijah nodded. "I haven't gotten over the news that she grew up in an orphanage. The worst part is she never told anyone, not even me."

"That came as a major surprise for me, too, although it helped to explain her bitterness."

"All along, I thought it was because my father left us, and the life in the East she sacrificed to be at the mission."

"I suppose it all contributed to her attitude. I wish we could do more to make her happy."

"Her faith has been growing, and I think she has found peace, although sometimes it's hard to tell."

A grandchild might brighten her days, Evangeline thought. Still, she wanted to be sure before lifting everyone's spirits. Besides, Elijah would not leave her behind if he knew.

After supper, she washed the dishes and sat in her rocking chair beside the fire with Elijah. While Elijah read, she admired the snap and pop of the fire and the cozy, warm rays it provided. She closed her eyes in peaceful reflection, thankful for her blessings.

———————

The next morning, as Elijah was fastening his chaps, Evangeline entered the kitchen. She stopped short to watch.

"Elijah, you look so different! You don't look like a preacher anymore."

"And how is a preacher supposed to look?"

"Like you usually do." She said as she walked around him, scrutinizing his new appearance. His tall, straight frame was flattered by the vest, trousers, shirt, and neckerchief. "Where did you get these clothes?"

"Ed gave them to me the last time he came to church," he said as he pulled on a pair of boots and wedged a wide-brim hat on his head.

"And you hid them from me?"

"I wasn't sure it was a good idea."

She laughed. "Oh, Elijah, I love your concern for my feelings." She hugged him.

"Now, don't worry." Elijah kissed her. When he was about to release her, she pulled him closer. "I'll be all right." He bundled up in a warm coat and went to saddle his horse. When he came back to the house, he stuffed the saddlebags with extra clothes and food Evangeline had insisted he take along. She stepped out on the porch and waved him out of sight.

Elijah felt a pang of sadness for leaving his wife behind. He hadn't realized how important she was to him until just a few months ago. They had married because they cared for each other and the mission, but their relationship was blossoming. Was it love? Anyway, he had to find his father. He possessed a nagging urge to leave. Something was nudging him.

The countryside was settling in for its winter rest. Elijah appreciated the change of seasons, which was much more predictable than other areas of life. All in all, he had much to be thankful for. The mission was holding on, and now he had found his father. What more could he want?

The grass had browned, and the sky had turned steel gray. The wind blew hard and cold as he rode. Soon, he spotted the dust stirred up by the steers and rode toward them.

When Hal saw him, he motioned for him to ride flank. The steers appeared to be trailing quite well, and he lapsed into thought. Trailing cattle wasn't new to him; he had done this as a young boy when he had helped the Indian ranchers. He had always wanted to join a trail drive in Texas and bring cattle all the way to Montana, but Cassandra wouldn't hear of it. That dream faded for good when he chose to become an instructor at the mission.

In a few hours, the chuck wagon drove ahead to prepare the noon meal. Elijah's stomach began to rumble, and he looked forward to warming his feet by a fire. Pepper had an interesting reputation with the meals he dished up, and Elijah looked forward to experiencing one.

Within a few hours, the drive slowed. The steers were allowed to graze while the crew ate lunch.

"We'll let them graze a few hours before we continue to our night camp," Ed told them. He asked Elijah to say a blessing before the crew began to chow down on steak, fried potatoes, and beans.

Hot food helped to thaw the cold that had fringed Elijah's body. He sat close to the fire, enjoying its warmth.

After they broke camp, the cowpunchers rounded up the steers and the drive pushed on until it began to snow lightly. The chuck wagon rumbled on ahead once again to find a good camp site. This time, when they arrived at camp, the milling cattle were held in a bunch by a small crew and the rest of the outfit pitched tents for the night. Pepper miraculously produced soup and biscuits for supper. The men ate heartily, and those not on duty retreated to their tents for the night to play cards or catch up on sleep.

"I'll take a watch," Elijah volunteered.

"No, you won't. We've got it covered," Ed told him, pouring them each another cup of coffee. Both sat under cover near the stove, watching the inclement weather roll in.

"What brought you out to this part of the country, anyway?" Elijah asked.

"I'm originally from Kansas," Ed said, settling back against his bedroll. "As a boy, I saw the cattle herds being driven north. After a time, I got the wandering fever and lit out for Texas when I was about twenty. It seemed like an adventure I didn't want to miss."

"What was it like out there on the trail? I always had a secret desire to do that. I never did, though."

"Those early years were hard ones. The cowpunchers who worked those trails were tough and rough. It took about eleven men to trail a herd of cattle. And of those eleven, over half were hard living. The younger ones were the worst. It seemed like they always had something to prove. When we got to a town, those younger ones drank the bars dry and spent their money on wild women. I grew up with some principles by then, so most of time I never joined the ones who didn't know when to quit. Although, I have to admit, I did my share of tipping whiskey. A throat becomes parched after trailing those ornery critters for days on end."

"How many years did you trail cattle?"

"Oh, about three seasons. And then I went to the East to study law."

"Law?"

"I had a knack for book learning. I passed the bar and practiced law for a time in Kansas. But, I grew tired of that. An opportunity to manage a ranch arose, and I took it." Ed threw the coffee grounds from the bottom of his cup into the fire. "The days of the long drives are over. The railroad took care of that, but I still can ride the range land for a little while longer."

"And that too will end, won't it?"

"Yeah, the days of the open range are numbered. I enjoy every day I can."

"I marvel at how you can get your men to church about every Sunday."

Ed grinned. "I do, too. I find that I have less problems with fighting and drinking. However, gambling is another matter. The nights get mighty long at the ranch, especially in winter. The fellows usually play a friendly game."

Elijah threw another log on the fire and stretched out his legs toward its warmth. "I came along to look for my father."

"I figured you had another motive."

"I finally found him after he deserted me and my mother when I was young."

"Where was he?" Ed asked.

"In Denver, performing in a Wild West show. I'm hoping he's wintering up north on the reservation."

"I imagine it was tough without a father, but you have done quite well without him, in my opinion."

"Never thought of it that way." Elijah had to admit he had

accomplished much without a father, but he had Jeremiah to urge him along the right path. He didn't need approval from his father anymore, but still he wanted him in his life.

––––––

The next morning, the sun emerged and melted what little snow was on the ground. After a hearty breakfast of flapjacks and bacon, the men dismantled the tents and stored them in the wagon. Then they rounded up the four hundred steers and strung them out for the trip north.

On the third day, the weary, bedraggled crew arrived at the beef issue destination. Elijah had never been to this particular one before, but he had been to others. Indians had haphazardly erected their white tepees for the big event. Horses and canvassed wagons stood nearby, waiting to haul the butchered meat home. Children sat on the wagon tongues, playing with their dogs and visiting, but when they saw the steers being driven in, they jumped up to watch.

To Elijah, the buildings and corrals looked similar to others he had seen. Corrals for the beef issue were constructed of milled lumber. A slaughter house stood nearby, as well as a headquarters and two residences, one for the boss farmer and another for a matron who administered medicines to the Indian families. The boss farmer, who taught the Indians about farming, issued beef, and distributed other rations, came out of his house to meet the contractor.

Ed offered his hand to the boss farmer, introducing himself. "And this is Elijah Fletcher."

"Pleased to meet you. I'm Theodore Lancaster, the boss farmer here."

"I brought you four hundred steers, one bunch for this issue and enough for two more."

Theodore looked the herd over approvingly. "They look pretty good. Not too skinny. Tell your men to drive about one hundred and twenty into that corral."

"In the corral?"

"We don't let the cattle out on the prairie for the Indians to shoot anymore. They used to enjoy getting their beef that way. It reminded them of their old buffalo hunts, but a couple of their men got caught in the cross fire one year. For safety purposes, we shoot the cattle in the corral now."

Elijah nodded. He had witnessed such an event. The cattle were let out one by one, and mounted Indian males chased them out on the prairie to shoot them. Such displays caused great excitement among the crowds.

Ed shouted the orders to the cowpunchers who sorted out the right number of steers and drove them into the corral. Day herders took the remainder of the herd away from the corral to graze on the surrounding grass. Another bunch of steers would be issued in ten or eleven days.

"As you can see, many anxious families are waiting to butcher their beef. I'll get my men out here to get this started." Theodore left for a moment and returned with four men carrying rifles.

Soon, the sound of gunfire pelted the air and several steers thudded into the dust. Horse teams dragged the lifeless carcasses, one by one, out of the corral and onto the prairie where the families began the skinning and dressing. Men and women worked side by side, hacking flesh, blood, and bone. After the men had gutted the critters, the women took the paunches and the entrails to a nearby stream to wash them.

Ed watched the butchering process with interest. "You would think with the modern cooking pots that they have now, they wouldn't bother to save the steers' stomachs."

"They do make a peculiar cooking pot. I suppose you have seen them suspended from four poles, two on either side," Elijah said.

Ed nodded.

"I guess the old ways die hard. I'm going to walk around and mingle with them. Maybe some of them know my father. You're not leaving right away?"

"No, we'll camp a ways from here and ride back in the morning."

"I'll see you in camp, then." Elijah left Ed and walked through the mass of dead steers and the Lakota who were intent on the task before them. The sight of so much blood and the stench of death nauseated him. Most of the Lakota paid him little heed as he looked around for someone he might know. He stopped and visited now and then, but didn't tarry too long in any one place. Someone yelled out his name, and he turned to see his father, wearing a heavy jacket and standing with a bloody knife in his hand. He had just finished skinning a steer.

"Elijah, what are you doing here?"

"I rode along with the beef contractor with the intention of finding you before winter set in."

Ben hobbled over to Elijah.

"What happened to you? You're limping. And your hand, it's bleeding."

"Oh, I cut myself while skinning." He untied the kerchief from his neck and wrapped it around his hand.

"And your leg?"

"A horse threw me while I was performing in one of the shows. My leg hasn't been healing right after the break. Don't know if I can perform anymore."

"Where are you living now?"

"I'm holding up at the Cheyenne Agency. I came here to butcher my share of meat. Food isn't too plentiful on the reservation. While I performed at the Wild West shows, I ate anything I wanted." He shook his head. "Here, on the reservation, rations can sometimes be short. Hard to get used to seeing people hungry."

"They'll be well fed tonight. I'm lucky to have found you. I was going to ride up to Standing Rock where I thought you would be this time of the year."

"People there would have known where to tell you to find me."

"Why not come back to the mission with me? We usually have enough to eat. And, we have a room for you. We built a dormitory for the students. Not all the rooms are filled yet."

"I don't know if I can do that. I'm sure Cassandra has no interest in seeing me."

"Why don't I talk to her? I'll tell her I found you and let her warm up to the idea of seeing you again."

"That's up to you."

"Would you come back if she didn't object?"

"It's too much to hope that she would want me back, or even allow me to come back to the mission." Ben unwrapped the handkerchief from his hand, examined the cut, and rewrapped it.

"From what you said, I think you want to return."

"Maybe. It's too much to ask."

"So you're not planning to join the Wild West show next year?"

"If that's all there is left for me. I'll give it a try again if my leg heals enough."

"I had planned to spend a few days looking for you, but since I found you, I might as well return with Ed and the men. I promise I will talk to Cassandra on your behalf. I know I won't convince her right away, so give me several months. Where can I find you again?"

"I'll be at the agency all winter. You can reach me there by mail."

Elijah glanced at Ben's hand wrapped in the kerchief. "I'll walk over to the house with you. You need to have that hand taken care of."

"It'll be all right," Ben protested.

"Just the same, I think we'll have the matron look at it."

A few women with sick, young children entered the door of the small house ahead of them. A tiny, middle-aged woman met them in the doorway. She smiled and ushered them into her cottage where she tended to medical needs. While Elijah and Ben waited, the wiry woman dispensed medications to a few young children and counseled some parents on healthcare issues. Then she came over to Elijah and Ben.

"I see that you have cut yourself," she said to Ben.

"Oh, it's nothing, but my son said I needed to come here."

She escorted Ben to a washbasin and filled it with water. She then removed the kerchief and washed the wound. "It doesn't look too deep, but I'll put salve on it and bandage it for you. Keep it clean and it should heal in a few days," she said as she finished bandaging the laceration.

When they left the building, Elijah spoke one last time to his father. "I'll write to you and let you know what Cassandra has to say."

Elijah watched as Ben limped toward his wagon and realized how fast his father was aging. *He does need someone to care for him,* he thought. *I may not need him, but does he need me?*

After the butchering, the crowds of people began to disperse. The families loaded the meat into their wagons. They'd enjoy a good supper tonight. The women would then spend days preserving the remainder of the beef by slicing it into thin strips and drying them in the sun. Many Lakota were also picking up other rations at the beef issue station. Several carried out coffee, salt, bacon, navy beans, rice, flour, baking powder, and laundry soap. They loaded the rations into their wagons. With a joyful heart, Elijah watched them as they drove their filled wagons home.

––––––

While Elijah returned home from the trail drive, he mulled over how he would tell Cassandra about Ben. He decided there was no easy way. He hoped she would be able to withstand the shock. He rode his horse into the stable, unsaddled him, and trudged across a new layer of snow to his house. Evangeline wasn't there, so he strode over to the dormitory and found her working on lessons for the next week.

"Oh, Elijah, I'm so glad you're back. Did you miss me?" she teased, flinging her arms around him.

"Of course, I did. I'm glad to be home, too." He nuzzled

her hair with his face.

"I didn't expect you home for several more days. Did you find him?" Evangeline whispered.

"I did. Can you believe he was at the beef issue?"

"Really?"

"I need to talk to Mother alone. Do you know where she is?"

"She's sewing a quilt."

"I have to get this over with, and I'm not looking forward to what she'll have to say."

"You're going to tell her about Ben?"

"Ben is ailing with a bad leg. He doesn't know if he will continue with the Wild West show. And he looks old, Evangeline. He needs someone to care for him."

"So, I take it you have forgiven him."

Elijah lowered his head. "I have to. He's my father. I believe he would come back if Mother would let him."

"You are going to ask her now?"

"Yes."

"I don't know that she has it in her heart to forgive," Evangeline said. "I'm not sure I could, either."

"I'll remember that." Elijah glanced around to see that no one was looking, planted a kiss on her cheek, and left. He walked to the old mission building and entered the former kitchen, which had been converted into a large sewing room. The new sewing machines Evangeline had purchased smelled of fresh oil. They stood idle, except for one. Cassandra was bent over it, sewing a patchwork block together.

"I'm back."

She looked up from her sewing. "Oh, Elijah! I'm pleased

to see you're safe. How did the drive go?"

"It went fine. I helped out a little, although I'm no cowpuncher. I do admire their skills."

"Remember when you were dead set on going to Texas to trail cattle north?"

"Yeah, that was silly of me. You knew best what I should do with my life. I...I saw someone at the beef issue. Someone you know." He knew he should thank his mother for her dedication to him, but he felt too embarrassed to tell her.

Cassandra returned to sewing the squares together as she talked. "I can't imagine who that would be." Elijah hesitated, hardly able to make the words leave his lips. Cassandra stopped sewing and looked up at him. "Well, who was it?"

"I saw...my father."

Cassandra turned pale and her hands began to tremble. "Ben?"

Elijah nodded.

"He's alive? I can't believe he's alive. How—how could you even talk to him after what he has done to us?"

"But Mother, he's alive." *How could she be so heartless?* he thought.

"I honestly don't know how I feel about that." She tried to still her trembling hands.

"I can't believe you're saying that. I've been looking for him for some time, and I finally found him. I didn't tell you this, but Evangeline and I saw him when we went to Denver. Remember us telling you of a Wild West show there? We saw him in the show and spoke to him afterward. He's been performing with them for about twelve years."

"I am certain that I do not care. He is beyond my

concern." She flashed him an irritated glance.

Elijah ignored her remarks. "We talked to him then, but I thought it was best not to tell you. But this last time I visited with him, he was limping and doesn't know if he can be in the shows anymore. He's old and lonely."

"And I haven't been lonely all these years? He's the one who left."

"I'm not defending what he did. Whatever came between you and him is none of my business, but I think he would come back if you would let him."

"I don't know how you can ask that of me. I'm supposed to forgive him just like that?" She snapped her fingers for emphasis.

"Just think about it. I know it is a shock, but I said I would ask."

Cassandra stopped sewing. "My answer is no."

––––––

Several weeks later, when Evangeline was sure she was pregnant, she planned how she would tell Elijah the good news. Even though she was exceedingly happy about it, she couldn't help but remember James. Since she was unable to conceive while she was married to him, she realized that she may have been able to have a baby all along, but something with James may have prevented it. A sense of melancholy overwhelmed her. Poor James had been deprived of being a father.

Just the sight of Elijah working around their home brought levity to her heart, and her sadness dissipated. *I can't wait any longer,* she thought. *I have to tell him.* She put on a fresh pot of coffee and went outside.

"I've made coffee. Want to come on in and have some?"

"This is a nice surprise. Sure, I can take a break and warm up a little. Any fresh cookies to go with it?"

"Well, no. But I have some good news for you."

Elijah took her hand and they entered the kitchen together. "I'm always ready for good news. What is it?"

"I hope you're as thrilled as I am."

He waited for her to pour his coffee. "Well, what is it?"

"You're going to be surprised," she teased.

"Do you want me to guess?"

"No. Are you ready?"

"Yes."

"We're going to have a baby."

Elijah sat motionlessly for a moment. "Evangeline, that's wonderful, but I...I thought you couldn't have children."

"I thought so, too, but I think it wasn't because of me," she said, blushing.

Elijah thought about her statement and said, "Oh, I see."

"Are you happy?"

"Of course I'm happy," he said. He reached over and hugged her. "Can you imagine what Sara will say? And my mother? We should tell our families before we break the news to Jeremiah and Minnie."

"And my parents! I'll have to write them soon. Mama will surely come for a visit once the baby is born."

"Shall I call Cassandra over here and tell her now? I see she's outside, not far from the house. Let me go and get her." Elijah left the kitchen while Evangeline waited, pacing the floor.

"So what is all this mystery?" Cassandra asked as soon as she saw Evangeline. "Elijah wouldn't even give me a hint."

Evangeline blurted out the news, and Cassandra clasped her hands together. "Oh, I have wanted to be a grandmother for such a long time." She broke into a rare smile. "Are you feeling well, Evangeline?"

"I'm better than I was to begin with. But I do get tired, and I have no appetite."

"It will pass with time, but you are probably going to have to cut down on the work you do around here," Cassandra said. "Elijah, I think you should consider hiring someone to help with the cleaning and such."

"It's too late to bring somebody from the East," Elijah answered in panic.

"How about Lily? They need the money," Evangeline said. "And I'm sure she could leave the children with someone when she comes to work. We wouldn't need her every day."

"I like the idea. I'll talk to her when I see them in church. You should probably see a doctor, too." Elijah said.

"But it's so far away."

"Maybe, but I think it would be for the best."

"Let's wait a few months, and then we'll talk about it."

"Now that Bea and Ethel are here, I think we should be able to get away for a few days," Elijah added.

"I'm excited to help with the layette. Just tell me what I should start sewing," Cassandra said.

"Gosh, I don't really know what I need, other than diapers, blankets, and some sort of sleepwear. After the baby arrives, we'll know if we'll need dresses."

"Let's put our heads together. I'm sure we can come up with some ideas. Have you told everyone else about the baby?"

"Now that we have told you, we'll tell them tomorrow

sometime."

"It will be wonderful to have a little one around here." Cassandra beamed at the thought.

"Stay for supper, Cassandra, and then we can talk more about the baby," Evangeline said.

"I would like that, thank you. Now that we are about finished with curtains and linens for the dormitory, I'll have time to dedicate to sewing for my grandchild."

Elijah reached for his hat. "I have some work to finish at the church. I'll let you ladies do the planning, and I'll be back for supper."

"We'll see you then." Evangeline kissed him sweetly on the cheek.

"Was Elijah a good baby?" Evangeline asked curiously as she watched the future father walk toward the church.

"He was a fairly good baby. He had colic, but after that he wasn't any trouble. I would have liked to have had another child, but I wasn't able to for some reason. A little girl would have been nice." Cassandra sighed.

Cassandra left immediately after supper, and Evangeline sat to write letters about the baby to her mother and to Sara. She would have liked to have told them the news in person. She reassured Sara that she should be finished with school before the baby would be born.

Having sealed the letters in their envelopes, she took a piece of paper and began a list of things she would need. She hadn't been around babies very much, so she didn't know exactly what she needed. Diapers were at the top of her list. Cassandra could help her with them. Then there were blankets, quilts...

She suddenly realized she must make a baby quilt! It

was strange that Cassandra didn't mention quilts earlier. *Perhaps she had a surprise in mind,* Evangeline thought. But she wanted to make her own baby quilt, sewing mother's love with every stitch. The Nine-Patch design came to mind. If done in pastels and white, it would work well for an infant quilt. And maybe she could hand stitch it. She imagined herself sitting by the fire with Elijah in the evenings.

––––––

It wasn't long until she received responses from both Sara and Maud. Sara wrote:

I'll be in school during all the preparations. I'm disappointed that I'll miss out on the excitement, and I won't be there to help you and make the layette. I've been thinking about what I can do that would be special. I'll make something for the baby while I'm away. Maybe I'll learn to knit or even crochet. I imagine someone at Santee can teach me. How about a pair of baby booties? But what color? Oh, I can't wait. This is all too exciting!

Maud also answered immediately:

Dear Evangeline,
Your father and I are ecstatic about the forthcoming birth of our grandchild. I am troubled that you won't let me buy the layette, but I insist on purchasing the christening dress, cap, and shoes. How quaint that Cassandra is sewing for the new arrival.
I also insist that you come home to Boston to have the baby. I can't imagine delivering in such a primitive place.

I have kept all your baby furniture. Wouldn't it be fun to use the white wicker pieces again? We could also hire a baby nurse to help out so you don't wear yourself out. I had one when you were born. I don't know what I'd have done without her—

Maud rambled on about decorating a nursery, hosting a baby shower, and a myriad of other topics. Evangeline shook her head as she read the letter. She had no intention of leaving the mission to have her baby, although secretly she wished there was a doctor nearby. She wasn't naive about complications during pregnancy and birth. And her mother was right—this was a primitive land.

CHAPTER 16

By the end of December, the students had settled into their studies and routine at the boarding school. Evangeline was thankful that everything was running smoothly. Evangeline's pregnancy caused her to become very weary at the end of the day, even though the mission had added Bea and Ethel to the staff. Ethel assisted Evangeline in the classroom. She performed quite well, and Evangeline hoped Ethel could take over after Christmas. Evangeline knew another teacher would be helpful, but she was saving that spot for Sara when she came back from Santee. In the meantime, Evangeline would do her best to fill in.

No one had been idle at the mission since it opened. Lily came by three times a week to help pick up loose ends. Bea and Minnie spent hours in the kitchen preparing meals and teaching the girls to cook and bake. They laughed and visited together, seeming to get along quite well. Cassandra spent most of her time teaching sewing in the old mission building. Sewing was something she loved to do, although she had helped Minnie in the kitchen when the mission operated as a day school. Jeremiah and Elijah shared the workload with the boys. Jeremiah was holding up well, and Elijah thrived on challenge.

On the morning of their sewing circle, Evangeline stopped by the sewing room before she went to eat her lunch in the kitchen.

"My, it looks as if it was a busy day!" she said as she entered. The place was empty except for Cassandra, who was stitching quilt blocks together. The students had left for lunch. "Minnie asked me to come over and see if you needed help preparing for the sewing circle this afternoon. She said she's going to be tied up in the kitchen."

"I know. I hardly ever see her anymore," Cassandra said grimly. "I almost have this block done. Then I'll come to lunch."

"I'll wait for you, and we can walk over together."

"If you want to. You could cut out the templates while you wait."

Evangeline picked up a pair of scissors and cut out the templates Cassandra had drawn on scraps of cardboard. As she sat cutting the shapes, Evangeline realized she seldom saw Minnie and Cassandra together. It used to be that they were always together working on some project.

"Do you miss not being in the kitchen with Minnie like you used to?"

Cassandra stiffened a little before she spoke. "Some, but Minnie seems preoccupied these days."

"You mean she's preoccupied with Bea?"

Cassandra shrugged. "They do seem to have a lot to talk about."

Evangeline wondered if Cassandra would talk to Minnie about Ben if given the chance. Evangeline wanted Cassandra to confide in her, but knew that was too much to ask. Their relationship had improved since Cassandra had come to Boston and talked her into coming back to the mission. However, Cassandra still was difficult to approach about emotional topics.

"Have you heard from Sara lately?" Cassandra asked as she cut a length of thread.

"No, I haven't. But in a few weeks, she will be home for Christmas. We all miss her."

"I certainly do. And she's a great help in the sewing room."

"You've taught her everything she knows about sewing."

"She has a talent for it." Cassandra put down the block. "This block requires precision, but I'm ready for lunch." By the time Cassandra and Evangeline arrived to eat their lunch, most of the children had finished and were on the playground. "Oh, I forgot to tell you," Cassandra said. "Elijah has sent two older boys to the camp to bring the women back for the sewing circle. He doesn't want you driving around in a wagon anymore."

Evangeline laughed. "I'm sure he doesn't."

After lunch, the women cleaned the kitchen before walking over to the sewing room.

"What if we put aside our other quilt projects and plan a baby quilt?" Cassandra suggested to the group of women who had gathered.

"I've already thought about it," said Evangeline. "I'm

planning on hand stitching a Nine-Patch quilt in the evenings, but thanks for asking."

"Maybe we can help you put it together and quilt it," Minnie said. She was clearly disappointed.

Evangeline contemplated the time needed to hand stitch an entire baby quilt between now and the arrival of the baby. "Perhaps I would like that. I have to admit that quilting is my least favorite part of making a quilt."

Once they entered the sewing room, Cassandra gained the sewing group's attention. "For now, let's continue with the Coat of Many Colors. It's coming along nicely. Any questions about your blocks?"

The women and students shook their heads and commenced where they had left off from the previous week. For the next two hours, block after block took shape with as much precision as their nimble hands could employ.

Minnie clipped the thread on her last piece and left the sewing machine. "Bea and I had better start supper. My, time sure flies while sewing."

Evangeline had pressed the last seam of her quilt block. "I'll walk over to the kitchen with you." Cassandra and Lily stayed behind to clean up. Evangeline remained near the kitchen, hoping to get a moment alone with Minnie. Bea had gone to the henhouse to gather eggs, which left just a few minutes for Evangeline to talk to Minnie alone.

"Minnie, I've been wanting to speak to you, but it's so difficult with so many people around."

She looked up from the dishes she was washing. "I know. Progress is good, but I miss our little chats. What is it? Something wrong?"

Evangeline pulled a dishcloth from the rack. "It's Cassandra. She's been withdrawn lately. Have you noticed?"

"Oh? I guess I haven't." Minnie stopped scrubbing a pan for a second. "Oh, dear, is that the problem?"

"I know you've been close."

"We have, but I guess I haven't been paying attention to her lately. It seems I'm always too busy. You know, it was easy to develop a friendship when we shared a cabin together, but since I have been married and moved away, we just haven't fallen into that comfortable routine like we once had."

"I can see why, but she's alone most of the time. And she just might be a little jealous of Bea."

"Jealous? I never thought of Cassandra being jealous."

"You were her only friend when she was the most bitter. No one else wanted much to do with her. I never knew how you could even tolerate her, but you did."

"I felt sorry for her. Now I see why she acted the way she did. But you know the new baby will perk her up for sure. I'll make an effort to include her in what we're doing. Thanks for telling me."

"You're such a good person, Minnie. I hesitated to tell you."

"It's quite all right. We can share anything. Remember that."

In January, Sol, Lily, and the children moved what they needed to the mission for the winter. Sol would help with the chores, maintain the facilities, cut wood, stoke the fires, and make periodic trips back to their ranch to check on his livestock. Lily would clean and fill in where she was needed.

Since both Sol and Lily had attended the mission school when they were young, the couple fit into the staff quite nicely. Jeremiah and Elijah had taught Sol many practical skills, and Cassandra had taught Lily to sew and cook. Lily joined the sewing circle on Wednesday afternoons. Since the sewing room was adjacent to their living quarters, her children could nap while she sewed.

One evening after supper, Elijah was sitting by the fire and Evangeline was working on her baby quilt when Sol knocked on the door.

"Sol, what brings you out after a hard day's work? You should be resting," Elijah said from the comfort of his chair.

"I have an idea to talk over with you."

"Come, sit, and tell us what's on your mind."

Sol removed his hat, rested it on his knee, and turned it around in his hands several times. "What would you think if we put on a rodeo this coming summer for the boys at the mission? I notice they get kind of bored. You know, I have some rodeo stock at my place that we could use."

Elijah pursed his lips. "A rodeo? That might be a good idea, but my first concern is for the boys' safety. I'll have to give it some thought. If I think we can do it, I'd have to see what the parents say about it. Perhaps I can talk with them after a church service."

"I'll need some help putting it together. I know you're too busy."

Elijah stroked his chin. "Someone experienced in such an event would be helpful, I suppose."

"Yeah, that would help."

Elijah thought a moment. "I know of someone, but I would have to ask if he's interested."

"We'd need an arena, corrals, and such."

"That's a tall order. Do you think the boys would build it if we gave them the materials? We could make it a class project."

"That's a good idea. It would be something they'd be interested in."

"Would you head it?"

"Sure, I like rodeos."

"Evangeline and I will talk about it."

"Sounds fair to me," Sol said as he stood.

After Sol closed the door behind him with a dull thud, Evangeline exclaimed, "A rodeo?"

"He's right about the boys having too much time on their hands after school, even after chores. Having regular rodeos could draw more people to our mission and keep them here."

"What if someone gets hurt? There are no doctors for miles."

"I know. That bothers me, too, not only for the rodeo participants but for the children here—for you and our child."

"Are you thinking what I'm thinking?" Evangeline smiled, arching her eyebrows.

"Yes. We need a doctor to serve the mission. Someone not interested in how much money he can make, but how he can serve a worthy cause."

"Exactly! I'll write Alice at the Missionary Society. She can help us out."

"Good. The sooner the better. Now, what about the rodeo idea? I don't know if we have enough money. You'd have to fund it, I suppose." He frowned.

"Certainly, what can a few boards cost? You told Sol you had someone in mind to help him. I'm curious. Who are you thinking of?"

"Ben."

"Your father? Do you think he would?"

"Rodeos are much like Wild West shows. He'd be perfect for the job. Now, all I have to do is find him."

"Have you thought about what Cassandra will say?"

"I have to think of the mission first. She'll come around in time."

"Good luck. She's coming over this evening. Are you going to approach her then?"

"No time like the present."

––––––

Cassandra rapped at the door, carrying a few items for the baby's layette.

"Come in," Evangeline said, taking the little clothes from her arms. "Thanks, Cassandra, for making these adorable little day gowns. What beautiful embroidery you have done on each. Here's a puppy, and oh, this one has a kitty. How cute!"

"It was my pleasure. Before long, we'll have a little one to cuddle."

"Sit down and stay awhile," Evangeline invited, feeling a little guilty about setting her up for a shock.

Cassandra inspected the quilt blocks Evangeline had cut

on the table. "How's it coming with the quilt?"

"Oh, I think it'll be fine. Since I have no idea whether it will be a boy or a girl, I'm going to combine pink, blue, and green."

Cassandra nodded. "It'll be special."

"Mother, I have something important to tell you," Elijah said, interrupting the talk about the baby.

Cassandra frowned. "I have a feeling it's about Ben again. You just won't let the subject drop, will you?"

Elijah ignored her comment and pressed on. "Sol was by earlier, and he'd like to organize a few rodeos at the mission. I was thinking of asking Ben to help out. What would you think of the idea?"

Cassandra heaved a sigh. "I wouldn't think you would need to ask, but I suppose you won't be satisfied until I see him." She shrugged. "Do what you think is best. I'll have to face him sometime. Just don't have any childish notion that we'll get back together!" she snapped.

"I have no notions about that."

"He is your father, and I have no right to come between you. Besides, he will be the grandfather of your child. Does he know about the baby?"

"He doesn't know. I'm not even sure he'll come back to the mission, but I'm going to find him and ask."

"Very well." She glanced at the mantle clock. "I see it's time that I retire. Another busy day tomorrow. You will tell me if Ben is coming? Just so I'm prepared."

"I will."

Evangeline followed Cassandra to the door, speaking in a low tone. "I hope you're not upset. I truly appreciate the clothes you made for the baby. I know you had to stay up late to do this."

"It doesn't matter. You have no idea how much I look forward to this baby." Cassandra turned and brusquely left.

———————

The aroma of simmering chicken accented with bay leaf, celery, and onion drew Evangeline to the kitchen. She found Minnie busy deboning two cooked stewing hens. Cassandra picked up the drying noodles that covered the kitchen table and placed them in two huge pots of boiling water on the stove.

"Are we expecting guests?" she asked, calculating that there was enough soup to feed many more than their usual company.

Minnie tossed an equal amount of vegetables into each pot and then returned to cutting the remainder of the cooked chicken into pieces. "Chicken soup is what the doctor ordered for the outbreak of flu in this dorm."

"Along with this concoction," Bea added. Evangeline peered into a slimy mass Bea was stirring.

"What is it?" Evangeline said, wrinkling her nose.

Bea laughed. "Something to take for coughing. And there's plenty of coughing around here," she said wearily. "I hardly slept a wink last night."

"What's in it?" She bent over the pot again, trying to deduce the ingredients.

"Last night we set flaxseed to soaking. This morning, I boiled up licorice root and raisins, then added the soaked flaxseed. The directions say to cook it for a half hour." Bea glanced at the clock. "In fact, it should be ready for straining. Could you get the strainer for me?" Evangeline pulled the strainer out of the cupboard and handed it to Bea. Bea poured the concoction through the sieve, then added lemon and sugar. She double-checked the recipe, running her finger along each line. "There you have it," she announced.

Evangeline raised her eyebrows and delicately sniffed it. "But does it help?"

"Here comes Doc now. Let's ask him."

"Something smells good in here," remarked Doc, a young man with thick, blond hair. He pushed his wire spectacles higher on his nose.

"It's the chicken soup you ordered," Minnie said, hands on her hips.

"And I just mixed up the cough medicine, too."

"Good. We'll start treating our sick children and pray it works."

Evangeline looked skeptically at the new doctor. "You haven't used the cough mixture before now?"

"Actually, no. It's an old remedy my grandmother used. I copied it down once and placed it in one of my medical books. When I was leafing through them the other day, it fell into my lap."

"I find that the old ways are better than the newfangled treatments," Cassandra added.

"In this case, you might be right. Anyway, it's worth a try," Doc said rather sheepishly as he took a taste of the cough mixture. The women exchanged glances at the new doctor who came to the mission directly from medical school. He hadn't won their confidence yet.

"Not bad," he said. "I thought it tasted terrible when I was a child. You can dispense this mixture as often as the children need it."

"We'll give them all some at lunch," Bea said.

"That'll be just fine. We'll see by evening if the coughing subsides, so we all can get a good night's sleep. I'm going to make my rounds to some of the families. I'll be back before dark," he said, reaching for his hat.

"Stay for lunch. We are about ready to serve," Minnie said.

"Well, I suppose I can have a quick bite." Doc sat next to Evangeline during lunch. He leaned over and whispered, "I'd like you to come by my office for a visit. You certainly look healthy enough, but I'd like to check you over and see if the baby is growing properly."

"I have been meaning to ask you about an appointment. I'm so glad you're here. Frankly, I have been worried about the delivery since I'm so far from any medical facility." She wanted to ask him how many babies he had delivered and if he had studied the procedures with extra care.

"Don't worry. I will take good care of you and the baby," he said as though he had read her mind.

––––––

After another round of chicken soup and cough mixture for supper, Evangeline stopped by the dormitory to see how the flu treatment was going. Minnie, Bea, and Cassandra had just finished the dishes and were relaxing and drinking tea.

"How's the cough mixture working out?" Evangeline asked.

"Believe it or not, it's working. Maybe we can get a good night's sleep. These tired bones need one," Minnie said.

"Minnie, you're working too hard. Do we need more

help?"

"Lily is a great help. It's just this blasted flu season. Once we get past that, we should be fine."

Minnie is always so positive, Evangeline thought. But she was concerned everyone was working far too hard. After finishing her cup of tea with the ladies, she returned home to find Elijah relaxing in his rocking chair.

"How's it going at the dorm?"

"Doc's cough recipe seems to be working. What a relief. The students are rolled up in their quilts, snoozing away. What a sight."

"That's good news. I was worried," Elijah admitted.

"I'm glad we have a doctor here, but he's going to have to prove himself. I know he feels self-conscious about his lack of experience, and I'm afraid the ladies are just working too hard."

"An experienced doctor would have been better, but I don't imagine many of them were up to the challenges so far from home."

"I wonder about how the families are receiving him."

"I'll have to ride along with him one of these days and give him some moral support," Elijah said. "As you know, it might take a lot of doing to win the confidence of the Lakota families. They're not going to give up their old treatments that easily."

"I'm afraid your mother was quite curt with him today."

"What did she say?"

"Oh, something about the old remedies being better than the new medicines. She seems to be out of sorts since you told her about Ben. Has your mother mentioned Ben after you told her you found him?"

"No, but I've noticed she's often deep in thought about something."

Evangeline smirked. "We should bring them together somehow. Call it woman's intuition, but I feel she would like to see him again."

"She will never forgive him. I know her that well."

"Now, Elijah, give her some credit," Evangeline said, laughing. The noise of a buggy and horses brought Evangeline to the window. "The doctor is home."

"I wonder if he had any luck."

"I hope so." Evangeline frowned. "If he gets discouraged, he might leave. I want him here when my time comes."

"I'll talk to him tomorrow," Elijah said.

CHAPTER 17

After winter lost its frosty grip on the landscape, Elijah lost no time in seeking out his father. He found him living at the Cheyenne Agency with one of his old friends. When Elijah presented the idea of heading up a rodeo, Ben's face lit up like a bright, sunny morning. Ben packed up his few belongings, including the canvas and the tepee poles. When father and son arrived at the mission, Cassandra and Evangeline were preparing the garden for planting.

Cassandra shaded her eyes, seemingly entranced as the men came closer. Evangeline had no idea how her mother-in-law would react to seeing Ben after all these years.

"Shall I go with you to meet Ben?" Evangeline offered.

Cassandra remained silent, almost as though she hadn't heard what Evangeline had said. Evangeline was just forming the words again when Cassandra replied, "Yes, I might as well get this over with. I see that my wishes are being ignored."

Evangeline followed, afraid of what Cassandra might say to both Elijah and Ben. Cassandra assumed a stance as rigid as stone. Elijah gently folded his hand over Evangeline's arm when Cassandra and Ben faced each other. Evangeline drew near Elijah and held her breath. They were all waiting to see who would speak first.

Elijah cleared his throat. "We'll leave you two alone."

"Wait," Ben said. "What's said between us can be heard by you." The silence among them was deafening. Evangeline wished that Elijah would say something—anything.

Finally, Cassandra spoke, forcing the words from her lips. "Why did you leave us?"

"It's hard to talk about."

"Try," she said through clenched teeth.

At that moment, Evangeline doubted there was any hope for reconciliation. She hoped that at least they would speak to one another and dispel some of the anger that had been boiling inside of Cassandra for years.

Ben took in a deep breath and began. "I was confused when I married you. At that time, I thought the white way was the road I needed to go. The mission convinced me of it. But after a time, I knew I had let my own people down, and I wanted to help them."

"But we are helping them," Cassandra protested.

"I'm not so sure anymore. You say our way of life is no good. My people are forced to change and are so unhappy and confused."

"But what of your family? You deserted us without a word."

"I did, and I'm sorry for that. But, I knew the mission

would take care of you. Besides, you didn't have any love for me, Cassandra."

She hung her head in agreement. "Not in the way I should have."

"I would like to know my son."

"I see I have no choice in the matter," she said, walking away.

"It will take her awhile to come around," Elijah said, awkwardly. "We have an extra room in the dormitory for you."

"I brought my tepee," Ben said. "I'll pitch it and stay there." He pointed to a place on the perimeter of the mission.

"If that's what you want. You can eat your meals in the dormitory. We serve three a day. The rodeo grounds are nearly completed. You can look them over whenever you want. And, if you see anything that should be different, let us know."

"I will."

"Evangeline and I are going to take our daily walk. If you need anything, we'll be happy to help you out."

Ben nodded and left to set up his tepee.

"I hope he'll be happy here," Evangeline said.

"I don't guarantee he'll stay here forever, but he will definitely help us during rodeo season," Elijah said. "Where'd you like to walk on this glorious day?"

"Let's explore the progress they're making with the rodeo grounds, and then maybe we'll walk up to the cemetery. I'd like to see the irises blooming."

"Should you walk that far?" Elijah asked.

"I should be alright." She beamed at his concern.

"A rodeo will be a good ending for the school year. I

think Sol has come up with a good idea," Elijah remarked as he and Evangeline toured the new rodeo grounds Sol and the boys were constructing. They stopped to look over the corrals.

Evangeline caressed her enlarging midsection. "I just hope I'll be able to see some of the action before the baby arrives."

Elijah smiled at her. "You'll have plenty of your own action pretty soon."

"That I will," she said smiling. "According to the letter I got today, Mama and Father are going to be here when the baby arrives."

"What exactly did she say?"

"Are you sure you want to hear it?"

"I can just imagine what she says. Go on, read it to me."

Evangeline took the letter from her pocket and read a section to Elijah.

"Since you won't take my advice and come to Boston (I think you're making a huge mistake), your father and I have been discussing coming West. I would have never considered the trip, but I want to see my grandchild and make sure you get the proper care during your confinement. I just hope I'm up to the journey. Of course, your father is most anxious to see you, but he'll have me to contend with this time."

Evangeline refolded the letter. "I am a little worried about Mama's reaction to the mission."

Elijah stiffened. "What do you mean? We've come a long way since it was first established. We have a nice church, a new dormitory, and now even a doctor."

"Oh, I agree. I didn't mean that we haven't made progress, but my mother doesn't always look at progress that way. She tends to compare everything to Boston."

He softened a bit. "We need to give her more credit. She has come a long way in her thinking."

"That she has, but I am always wary.

Elijah bent down to kiss her. "I give thanks every day for being able to serve here, especially with you by my side."

"All this excitement and rodeo preparation reminds me of the church conference we hosted the year I was here." She sighed, recalling good memories. "The tepees and the tents covering the prairie left such an impression on me. I will never forget it," she said, gazing at the grass as it danced in the wind.

"I expect a large attendance at the rodeo, too." Elijah said. "It's an opportunity for families and friends to come together, which is important since that allotment act attempted to break up their communities. I don't think they will ever give up their communal living, but it certainly broke up the tribal land base."

"I agree. It's a part of them, woven into their very being."

"They'll bring their tents, stay a few days, and thoroughly enjoy the celebration," Elijah said. "Kind of like the church conference."

"You say that with a shine in your eyes. You do think the rodeo is a good idea?"

Elijah nodded. They stopped and sat on the grandstand benches. "Sol reminded me the other day that horse racing and wagering is a part of Lakota history. It's a way for them to display their riding skills, as well as their bravery. Of course, we won't encourage wagers," he said, laughing. "Sol says the participants will compete for money collected as an entrance fee instead. The fees won't cost much, but will give a little to the winners."

"Are we being unconventional again?" She grinned. "What do the other missionaries think of rodeos?"

"Some probably aren't for it, but we have always done what we think is best for all. I see no harm. The Indian agents aren't too keen on the idea, either."

"Why not?"

"They feel it promotes laziness and takes them away from their work on the allotments."

"Aren't rodeos dangerous, too?"

"They can be," Elijah said. "The men like it that way, so they can show their courage and bravery. That's what it's all about."

"I don't know if I'll like that. How many rodeos are we talking about?"

"As many as Sol can get together in a season."

"I hope Ben enjoys his job helping Sol."

"I'm pretty sure he will, as long as he can live in his tepee on the outskirts of the mission. Maybe I can eventually convince him that he's welcome to use one of the dormitory rooms."

"Maybe we can convince him in the winter." Evangeline laughed.

"We'll see. Are you ready for the hike to the cemetery?"

"I'm ready," she said as he helped her to her feet.

The green grass waved in the breeze as they ascended the hill. They laughed as they watched the birds dipping overhead, rejoicing over the beautiful day.

"I can see the purple irises from here," she said as they neared the hilltop.

"The cedars have grown, too."

"I like to hear the wind whisper through the trees." Halfway up the hill, Evangeline stopped to rest then resumed the short climb to the top with Elijah's help. The sego lilies nodded their creamy, white blossoms on the sunny slopes. The large, wooden cross, designed for the cemetery by the mission boys under Elijah's guidance, still stood straight. She loved how it overlooked their mission.

She went to each grave and ran her hand over the smooth gravestones she had ordered for Red Bird, Swift Bear, and Angeline. "I'm happy with the way the headstones turned out," she said to Elijah, who was pulling the weeds that had intruded on the blooming irises.

Evangeline had chosen a special symbol for each headstone. For Swift Bear and Angeline, she chose flying birds—the flight of the soul. A sprig of ivy had been carved on Red Bird's stone. Evangeline knew that ivy signified friendship, which she had shared with Sara's grandmother, even though they could not speak each others' language fluently. Somehow, they had communicated their love and concern for Sara. She didn't want her friends to be forgotten.

Evangeline stooped to smell the iris bending in the wind. "It's really pretty from up here."

"It is."

"Have you thought of any names for our children?" she asked as she read the names on the markers.

"Not really. My father said the names of children born to his people are chosen at birth."

"Is that what we're going to do?" She broke off a few blossoms to take with her.

"It's just an idea."

"And maybe a good one. How will we know if the name fits if we don't hold the baby in our arms and get to know him?"

"I agree."

"It's lovely up here, but I should get back. It's nearly lunchtime, and I have done nothing to help."

CHAPTER 18

Evangeline was soaking her swollen feet in a pan of cold water. She, Cassandra, Lily, the students, and the remainder of the ladies had finished the Coat of Many Colors quilt that day, and she had been on her feet too long.

Evangeline heard a commotion outside, and Elijah peered through the window. "Your mama and father are coming in the buggy," he told her. "They've stopped at the dormitory, probably asking where we live."

"I look terrible," she wailed, grabbing a towel to dry her feet. "Detain them a few minutes so I can at least get my shoes on," she pleaded.

Elijah managed to stall Maud and Frederick for only a few moments after they knocked on the door. Maud burst into the house, pushing past Elijah.

"Evangeline, there you are!" she said breathlessly. "I was worried you might be bedridden. I got the feeling Elijah didn't want me in the house."

"No, I'm fine. Just uncomfortable."

Maud glanced at the wash pan and the water that had spilled out of its sides. She then paced around the room. "I suppose you're working too hard. You should have someone waiting on you. Well, anyway, I'm here to help you out. That is, if I remember how. It's been years since I held a baby."

Evangeline didn't know how much help Maud would be, but she was genuinely glad she was there. Her father entered the kitchen with his endearing grin and embraced her.

"Let me look at you," he said with pride. She knew he had always admired her courage and determination to do what she had set out to do, even though he didn't always agree with her choices. "Where should we put our baggage?"

"You'll be staying with us. You can have the baby's room. It's the one with the cradle. Elijah made it," she said proudly. "The baby won't need the room for a while."

"And what about Sara?"

"She'll be staying in the dormitory."

"We don't want to put anyone out." Maud peered through the house. "You did keep it simple, like you said in your letters."

"We're comfortable here." Evangeline stiffened at Maud's remark. "Would you like to see the mission? Elijah can show you around. I'd rather remain here and rest." She stifled a yawn. "Minnie said for us to come to the dormitory kitchen for supper," she added.

"Shouldn't I stay here with you?"

"No, I want you to see the mission. Stop by when you're finished and we'll go to supper together," she said, although she had no appetite.

As soon as they left, she sat in her favorite chair and propped up her feet. She suddenly realized her back ached, too. *It's too early for the baby,* she thought. *I must have overdone it today. I'll have to be careful in the future.* She dozed off and awoke with a start when her parents and Elijah returned from their mission tour.

Frederick praised the work that had been accomplished. "There are even rodeo grounds. You never mentioned that project," he said to Evangeline.

"That's a recent idea inspired by Sol, our local cowboy. They've been working hard to get it done."

Frederick's face brightened. "Will we be able to see a rodeo while we're here?"

"I certainly think you shall."

Maud frowned at her husband. "The dormitory is first class. I can see you had a hand in designing it, Evangeline."

"Thank you, Mama, but I had a lot of help."

"If everyone's willing, let's walk over to supper," Elijah suggested. "You'll be able to meet my father."

Maud tilted her head at him in surprise. "Your father is here?"

"I was lucky enough to find him, and I asked him to help with the rodeo."

"Where has he been all this time, if I might ask?" Frederick said.

"He's been performing in Wild West shows. He was injured, and he's not able to perform anymore. But he has experience with bucking broncos, horse racing, and other things connected to rodeos."

"My, this still is the Wild West," Maud concluded with a raised brow.

Elijah laughed. "Are you up to supper, Evangeline? You look tuckered out."

"I'm fine." She stood and winced; her shoes pinched her swollen feet. She managed to wend her way over to the dormitory where they found Ben and Sol discussing their latest rodeo project. Evangeline ate little while she and her parents caught up on all the months they had been separated. By the time they returned to the house, her back ached worse than before.

"I think I am going to turn in for the evening," she told everyone.

"Are you all right?" her mother asked.

"Yes, just tired, I guess. See you in the morning. Elijah has promised to make breakfast for us." She winked at her husband.

—————

During the night, Evangeline woke with back pain that intensified before the morning light peeked through their window. She remained in bed without waking Elijah. There was nothing he could do at the moment anyway. But when she heard him stir, she shook his shoulder.

"I think you should wake the doctor."

"Is it time?" he asked groggily.

"I believe I have been having contractions all night." She sat up and kneaded her back.

He shot out of bed. "Shall I wake your parents before I go?"

"No, let them sleep. It will be awhile yet."

Her prediction was correct. As the day slowly ebbed, Evangeline suffered the throes of childbirth. Maud eyed the young doctor dubiously when she came to check on her daughter.

"Do you know how many babies he has delivered?" she asked Evangeline after he left for the fourth time.

"He really didn't say. I think he has attended births, but he has always assisted. Actually, I'm afraid he has never delivered one by himself." She was more frightened than she cared to admit.

"Maybe you would have been better off with a midwife, although I can't say I have a lot of faith in them, either."

Evangeline grimaced as another contraction escalated. "Are you praying, Mama?"

"Yes, I have been, but you should have taken my advice and come to Boston."

By evening, the doctor had difficulty concealing the worried look on his face. Maud picked up on it immediately.

"We have to do something," she told Evangeline.

Sara had just joined the group when she overheard Maud's concern. "I know a woman who might be able to help. When she was young, she helped deliver babies in my tribe."

"A native woman?" Maud blurted.

"Yes. Her name's Josephine."

"Do you know her, Evangeline?"

"She comes to our sewing circle," Evangeline said through clenched teeth. "She's quite old, but I trust her."

"Where could we find her? Do we have time?" Maud asked.

Sara left her chair. "She lives in the old camp. I can go fetch her if you like."

Maud searched her daughter's eyes for approval, and Evangeline looked to the doctor.

"I trust the herbs." He shrugged. "Some of them actually work."

"Why not, then? I'll go with Sara," Maud volunteered. "We'll get Frederick, too."

Sara placed her hand on Maud's arm. "No, you stay with Evangeline, Maud. She needs you here."

"Oh, alright. But please hurry," Maud whispered to Sara.

———————

To Evangeline, it seemed like Frederick and Sara had been gone for hours but, in less than an hour, they returned with Josephine. Evangeline watched the old woman take herbs out of the bag she brought and mix them into hot water.

"Is Evangeline going to drink that stuff?" Maud asked Sara. "Is it safe?"

"It will hasten the labor pains," Josephine said. "We have used it for generations."

The doctor shrugged. "It's up to you, Elijah."

"I trust Josephine. Give it to her."

Evangeline managed a weak smile and sat up to drink the concoction of herbs. The bitter taste made her shudder.

"Now, let's leave her to rest the best she can," Josephine said. "In about two hours, I believe the labor will get harder for her."

Maud rolled her eyes in disbelief and cast the doctor a disappointed look.

Elijah, exhausted, left the room and sank into his rocking chair just as Jeremiah came to the door.

"We haven't heard any news, and we couldn't stand the waiting anymore. Is everything all right?" Jeremiah asked.

"We don't know. The labor is taking too long, so Sara and Frederick sent for Josephine, who gave Evangeline an herbal tea to hasten the labor. We have to wait to see if it works."

"I see. While we wait, I suggest we all go to the church." Jeremiah said.

"You're right. We'll leave Josephine and Doc here, and the rest of us will go on over."

"I'll stay here, too," Ben said right after he walked in the door.

"If you wish," Jeremiah replied. He motioned for the others to follow him outside.

After her well-meaning family left, Evangeline sunk back into the pillows to regain her strength. The new baby quilt she had made was tucked neatly inside the wooden cradle Elijah so tenderly made. She prayed with all her might that her unborn child would arrive safely. Another contraction wrenched her body into agony, and another, each one worse than the last. Josephine and Doc rushed to her side.

In a moment of relief, she heard Elijah's voice. "Is that a baby crying?"

"Yes! Yes! I think it is," Maud cried.

She heard Elijah call through the door, "Evangeline, Evangeline! Are you all right?"

"I'm fine...the baby's fine," she yelled back. Doc opened

the door and let him enter. "No need to worry." Her weak words intended to dispel his fears. Elijah bent down and kissed her before he kneeled beside his wife and daughter.

"I was so concerned. We prayed so fervently for your safety."

"Isn't she beautiful?"

"She is. Just like her mother."

"May we come in?" Maud asked softly.

"Yes, everyone come in and meet our daughter," Evangeline said.

All the grandparents and Sara quietly entered the bedroom where Evangeline held the sleeping baby girl.

"Oh, how precious," Maud gushed as she squeezed in beside Sara to see the newborn granddaughter. "What's her name?"

"We don't have one picked out yet," Evangeline told her.

Ben said, "In the old days, a name wasn't given until birth. Then we waited for a sign to name the child."

Maud shrugged off his suggestion. "Oh, there are so many lovely names for a sweet girl. How about Daisy, Constance, Ethel, Agatha…the list goes on and on."

Cassandra stood silently on the other side of the bed. She looked down at the baby and smiled. "I always wanted a girl. Could I hold her?"

"Of course." Evangeline gently passed the sleeping child to Cassandra, who cradled her in her arms.

"Oh my, she's so little. I don't think I can hold her without dropping her," Maud said.

"Don't fret, Mama. She will grow."

"May I hold her next?" Sara's face beamed.

Evangeline laughed. "You may."

"Sara will be a great help to you. I can see that already," Cassandra crooned to the baby.

Ben moved closer to Cassandra and held the small hand of his new granddaughter. "When I came to your house from my tepee this morning, I was drawn to the shimmering willows bending in the wind. I walked toward them and listened. They were speaking to me."

Elijah shifted his gaze from his wife and daughter to his father. "Are you trying to suggest a name for your granddaughter?"

"If you see it that way."

Evangeline caught his meaning. "Willow! We'll name our daughter Willow."

Maud looked at Frederick, who gave her a stern look in return, and she held her tongue.

―――――――

Willow woke Evangeline early, just as the sun was just beginning to rise. Evangeline padded over, lifted her out of the snug cradle, and wrapped her in her quilt.

"Are you hungry, little one?" She nestled into the rocking chair to nurse her. She enjoyed the early morning hours with her baby. Elijah had already left to help organize the rodeo, so she didn't need to concern herself with making breakfast. Instead, she warmed water on the stove for Willow's bath.

After Evangeline finished bathing Willow, she nuzzled her while she dressed her in a long dress Cassandra had made. Willow cooed and made funny faces.

"You are so cute and getting so chubby."

She wrapped Willow in a soft blanket and carried her over to the sewing room so that Grandma Cassandra could watch her while Evangeline and Maud went to see the mission's first rodeo.

"I'd stay and visit awhile, but I told Mama I would meet her at the rodeo grounds. We want to get there early and watch the arrivals."

"We'll be just fine. If she sleeps, I'll do some sewing. Otherwise, we'll make use of the rocking chair here." Cassandra took Willow from Evangeline and planted soft kisses on the baby's forehead.

"Are you sure you don't mind missing the rodeo? It's a first. You might not want to miss it."

"I'm not interested in rodeos."

"Or Ben?" The question popped out of her mouth to her own astonishment.

Cassandra visibly stiffened, but merely shook her head in surprise that Evangeline spoke so candidly. "I have all I need right here."

Feeling abashed, Evangeline left the sewing room for the rodeo arena. Before she found a place to sit, she walked up to her father who was talking to Ben and Sol. Frederick held his stopwatch in his hand. The fact that Frederick carried a large, gold stopwatch apparently didn't go unnoticed by the rodeo crew. As she approached them, she overheard Ben and Sol talking Frederick into being the official timer for the upcoming rodeo event.

"I would be delighted to help out," he told them. Frederick acknowledged Evangeline with a nod. "Now, what exactly do you want me to time today?"

"Have you ever been to a rodeo or a Wild West show before?" Sol asked.

"I did attend a Wild West show once," he answered with

pride.

"We'll give some of those events a try today. We'll start with horse racing. You don't have to time that one. Whoever gets across the line first wins," Sol said.

"Will you be racing, Sol?" Frederick watched the jerky movement of the second hand on his watch face.

"You bet. I got myself a fast horse."

Ben cleared his throat. "Don't count me out."

Frederick laughed. "Ah, this should be a good event to watch. What's after horse racing?"

"Ben and me have planned a *travois* race, too."

"*Rom* race?"

"Yeah, you know, a pony drag. Two poles are attached to the horse with rawhide stretched across them."

"Oh, yes, I have heard of them. Will you two be competing against each other in that event?"

They both shook their heads.

"I don't time that one either?"

"No, this is what you will time," Sol said. "I have some good bucking stock from my ranch. First, we'll do the bareback riding and then the saddle bronc. You'll have to time each rider to make sure he stays on eight seconds. We'll watch your hand signal when the eight seconds is up, and then we'll blow a horn. The one with the best ride wins. I have already chosen several men to judge that part of the event."

"I see. I should be able to do that. What else do you have scheduled?"

"After the riding, we'll have some trick roping. I know some fellers that can rope real good."

"Excellent."

"Any questions before we begin?" Sol asked.

"Nope, I think we got it," Frederick said.

"Looks like you have a job," Evangeline said after Ben and Sol left.

"It does, but I don't mind. Just think of the stories I can tell my friends when I get back home. They'll never believe I actually helped out at a rodeo."

"I'm sure they'll be very interested and impressed." She laughed. "I'll get out of your way and find a seat. Talk to you after the rodeo." When she had settled herself on a bench, she looked up to see Maud traipsing over to meet her. "What is she wearing?" Evangeline asked aloud.

A powder blue gown fluttered in the stiff breeze. Maud tenaciously hung onto a matching hat and parasol as she leaned into the persistent wind. "My, what a blustery day," she said when she approached Evangeline. She struggled to open her parasol.

"Mama, do you realize you will probably be covered with dust before this is all over?"

"I will?"

"Certainly. Just think of all these horses kicking up dirt and dust, let alone the wind doing its damage."

"Oh, dear. Horses are so smelly. I hope I can endure this. Frederick insisted that I attend. He thinks everything about the West is so fabulous," she said, somewhat disgruntled.

"You have time to change if you want."

"No, I'm not interested in getting undressed and dressed again." Maud squirmed and wiggled until finally she settled in, oblivious to the blatant stares. "Oh, what's that?" She pointed to a procession of Indians dressed in their feathered warbonnets.

"It's just like the Wild West show we saw in Denver. Members of the surrounding tribes have put on their finest beaded regalia and bone breastplates, feathers and all."

"You don't think they mean us any harm?" Maud asked fearfully as she shrank deep into her fluffy dress.

"No, Mama. It's an opportunity for them to dress up in their finest. Sort of like you." She suppressed a grin. "They enjoy horsemanship events, these displays of courage and skill."

"If you say so. I didn't know there were so many of them around here." Maud tried not to stare, but she couldn't help herself.

"We're on the reservation, remember?"

Maud nodded. "Oh, yes, how could I forget?"

It wasn't long before the horses came tearing down the stretch, each rider bent forward, shoulders rounded, intent on winning the race. A cloud of dust drifted toward the stands. Maud coughed and brushed the fine dust off her dress. She didn't appear especially impressed as she searched for a handkerchief. Between choking on the dust and batting the air with her hand, she squeaked, "Do we know anyone racing?"

"Oh, sure. I do believe Sol won!" Evangeline jumped up and cheered. "And I don't think Ben was far behind him."

When the contestants lined up with the horses and *Rom*, Maud nudged Evangeline for an explanation.

"They're called travois. The Indians used them to carry their belongings. Elijah tells me they also transported those too ill to walk or ride a horse. They invented the travois using the materials they had available." Maud merely nodded. "Of course, today they use wheeled carts like we do, but they still race with travois. Watch!" Again, there was a flurry of excitement until one contestant outdistanced the others to the finish line.

"I can't imagine being stretched out on that traw—"

"Travois, Mama."

"Oh. Well, I think a travois would be very uncomfortable." Maud wrinkled her nose. "And too close to the back end of a horse."

However, the trick riding held Maud's attention. The young Indian boys were very adept at this event, demonstrating a skill that took hours of practice over many days to acquire.

"I don't know how anyone could judge this one," Maud said.

"I wouldn't know how to judge the winner, either. The boys practically live with their horses.

After all of the trick riding contestants had performed, three horses roared across the arena abreast of each other. The horse on the left held two riders, and the horse on the right only had one. The middle horse, without a rider, was snorting and bucking to break free. Then a rider from the horse on the left slipped onto the back of the middle horse. The outside riders broke free, leaving the bucking horse and rider to their own struggle. This inaugurated the bucking bronc event.

Evangeline glanced over at Frederick who was carefully watching his stopwatch. The rider managed to stick while the horse whipped his body in all directions. Frederick's hand went up, and the horn was blown. The crowd cheered for the good ride. Evangeline gazed over and smiled at Maud, who was glued to the action.

"Do people ever get hurt?" Maud asked. "It looks so dangerous."

"Yes, they say riders are even killed sometimes."

"Then why do they do it?"

"It's a display of courage and skill. They can't count coup anymore."

"And what's that?"

"When the Indian rode up to his enemy in battle and touched him without killing him. It was considered a very courageous act."

"My, that's too wild for me." Maud caught sight of Doc walking up to the arena. "I see the doctor's here."

"I hope we won't need him this afternoon."

Several more riders managed to complete their rides, but others bit the dust unhurt. Evangeline could clearly see the rodeo was a hit with the crowd. It provided excitement and many anxious moments for the spectators. It gladdened her heart to know that Ben and Sol's efforts were worthwhile. It seemed there would be many more rodeos to follow.

Each day during that summer blended into another joyous routine. Just when Evangeline had decided nothing could spoil the euphoria everyone was feeling, her entire world collapsed between the lines of the short letter she had just read.

This just can't be, she whispered to herself again and again. *Why did it take so long to learn that no money remained in James's estate?*

The creditors had sucked it dry. She could have ignored

this news if she had been the only one affected, but the mission was going to use that money to pay the bills for the school's new dormitory.

Why did I wait so long to pay them all? If I hadn't waited, the money would have been in the account before the creditors demanded their share and depleted the funds. Worst of all, how am I going to tell Elijah? He hadn't wanted to use her money in the first place. She had let him and mission down.

She couldn't seem to rouse herself into action. Night shadows crept through the windows, jolting her to the realization that her beloved house wasn't paid for, either. No matter how she read the letter, it delivered the same news. She folded the paper and placed it into her pocket before she peeked out the window to see if Elijah was coming from the church for supper. She hadn't even begun to prepare anything. Her mother and father were eating at the dormitory tonight, so she hadn't given supper much thought. She and Elijah had agreed that they would eat together tonight, just the two of them. Absorbed in a mental fog, she absently mixed pancake batter while pondering how to break the news to Elijah. He would be angry and distraught for sure. She had jeopardized Elijah's dream, her dream, too.

Evangeline had just heated the griddle when Elijah entered the kitchen. He kissed Evangeline and pumped water to wash for supper.

"These rodeos have been such a good idea. I'm so glad Sol brought up the notion. And my father is such a help. I think his participation has made him feel younger."

Evangeline's heart sank. How would they pay for the rodeo grounds? Guilt and uncertainty stabbed at her heart as she set the pancakes on the table. She sat across from him and let him eat his fill before obliterating his dream.

"I received a disturbing letter today."

"You did? Tell me about it. Nothing can mar my joy today."

"The letter is from James's estate."

Elijah looked up from his plate. "Is there trouble?"

Evangeline nodded. "The letter says that the creditors have demanded payment for horses that James bought. They have filed a judgment against the estate. When the bills are paid, there will be nothing left. Some of those horses were drowned at sea." Evangeline dropped her head into her hands. "Elijah, we haven't paid all the bills for the construction of the boarding school."

"But you did pay some?"

She nodded.

"There must be some mistake." Elijah pushed away from the table, leaving half-eaten pancakes on his plate and paced the floor. "How could horses cost that much? Something else must be draining the funds."

Evangeline tapped the letter in her hand. "That's all the letter says." She handed it to Elijah. "What else can there be?"

"Horses may be expensive, but I can't believe he went through a fortune like you said he did. Not just by buying stock. Did he gamble? Bet on the horses?"

"I don't know. Toward the end of our marriage, he paid little attention to me. He was more focused on his horses and not being able to win the steeplechase. I knew very little about his affairs."

Elijah grabbed the letter. "I shouldn't have accepted your money," he said harshly. "Or should I say James's money?"

"I'm sorry. I thought I was good for it. I had no reason to believe I wasn't."

"We dreamed too big, Evangeline. I should have followed my instincts." His fist hit the table.

Evangeline had never seen Elijah behave this way. Was he blaming her? It certainly appeared that way. "Elijah, I've never seen you like this before."

"Probably because I never was about to lose something I worked all my life to build."

"We cannot give up now. There must be a way out of this predicament."

"I don't see how."

"There's no way I'm going to let this setback affect the mission."

Elijah slumped down in the chair. "We're talking about a lot of money. Sure, we can make payments, but that will take forever. In the meantime, we will need funds to keep the mission running."

"My parents could help out some. But Father has already given to the construction of the church."

"We can't ask them to pay off our debt."

"You're angry with me, aren't you?"

"I trusted you, Evangeline. I thought you knew what you were doing."

"I won't let you down. I promise I'll come up with a way. Please don't hold this against me."

"I...I'm going to the church. I have to think."

Evangeline watched him turn his back on her and walk out the door. They had never had a major quarrel until tonight. A dark fear enveloped her. She was alone with her

THE BOARDING SCHOOL QUILTS

problem, and only she could fix it. Feeling deserted, just as she had with James, she let the tears of heartbreak flood her eyes.

———————

How long she let the tears flow she could only guess. It was dark, and her parents would be coming soon. She washed her face and willed her tears to stop. When she wiped the last one away, she realized her catharsis yielded clarity. She realized she had always depended on someone else for her happiness. Perhaps it began with her parents, who had shielded her from the world to ensure her happiness. It was same with James and Elijah; she had depended on them for her happiness. Now she could see that she was solely responsible for her own joy. No matter how Elijah felt about her at this moment, she had to fix this dilemma and move forward. Elijah had told her once that her source for happiness was inside her. He was right. She now knew what he had been trying to tell her.

Evangeline paced the floor awaiting her parents' return from supper. She needed her father, but not as she once had. Determined not to ask him for money to assist the mission, she would ask him for legal advice only. Over and over, she told herself not to break down in front of them. If she did, her mother would seek the easy way out and tell her father to step in and save the day.

A portion of the redness had disappeared from her eyes by the time her mother and father arrived. Evangeline deliberately averted her gaze. "How was supper tonight?"

Her mother removed her shawl and draped it across the back of a chair. She lowered her voice. "Delicious, as usual.

Is Willow asleep?"

"She is. We'll bring her out of the bedroom when you're ready to retire. Elijah's at the church."

"At church? Did something come up? It's rather late," her father said.

Evangeline handed him the letter. "You could say that. Here, read this."

He perused the seemingly innocuous piece of paper and dropped it in his lap. "I can't believe what I just read."

"What? What's happened?" Maud's voice swelled.

He read the letter to them, the harsh realities penetrating Evangeline's soul once again.

"Evangeline, I don't like the sound of this letter. There's something else going on here."

"That's what Elijah said."

"You need to see a lawyer, preferably my Boston lawyer, and get to the bottom of this. Surely some debts need to be paid, but not to this extent."

"That means I would have to make a trip to Boston when I'm needed here. I just don't know if I can do that now."

"You will have to. I could possibly loan you the money for a period of time," he offered.

"No, Father. I need to do this on my own to prove I can fix the damage I've done."

"Whatever you wish. Consider coming back to Boston with us."

———————

As each day passed, Evangeline distinctly felt Elijah had placed the blame on her. They no longer shared cozy evenings by the fireplace. After supper, he made excuses to return to the church. She was usually in bed by the time he chose to come home, and he didn't attempt any conversation with her when he arrived late. Instead, he crept noiselessly in bed beside her.

It broke her heart that Elijah was behaving in much the same way James had. A year earlier, she would have fallen into a heap of despair, but after returning to the mission, she had regained the courage and confidence in herself that she had lost. She would just have to go it alone. Perhaps Elijah would forgive her someday. It hurt to think about the rift in their marriage, but she would persevere.

An important decision faced Evangeline as she assumed her morning walk before the heat of the day. Should she return to Boston and seek a lawyer? Her father was shrewd. She should act on his advice. She had discussed this with Elijah, who didn't seem to have an opinion one way or the other. Her husband did express disappointment that Willow would go with her, however. She had vowed never to leave the mission again, yet here she was, considering it once more.

Ben was outside his tepee, painting at his easel. After Willow's birth and the rodeo, she was beginning to feel closer to him. She would never entirely understand him, but at least she could carry on a conversation with him. She eased up to Ben, trying not to startle him, for he seemed absorbed in his work.

Quietly she said, "Good morning, Ben."

"Good day to you," he replied as he saluted her with his paintbrush.

"Nice morning to paint," Evangeline continued.

"Don't like it when it's hot. You're out and about early,"

Ben said.

"I have a lot of thinking to do."

"Elijah told me about the mission's predicament."

"Elijah's blames me, doesn't he?" she blurted without thinking.

"You'll have to ask him."

"Yes, I suppose. Do you mind if I look at your painting?"

Ben stepped aside to allow her to view his progress. A beautiful prairie scene stretched out before her. "How can you paint the buffalo so lifelike when they aren't even here?"

"They're in my mind."

"Fabulous. I've never seen your work, other than what you showed us in Denver. Do you have more?"

"I do. Come inside the tepee and I'll show you." Ben led Evangeline into the dimly lit tepee. From behind a large, canvas covering, he pulled out about a dozen paintings. Each painting he showed her was more beautiful and realistic than the last.

"My, how gorgeous. When did you change to realism?"

Ben glanced at her puzzled.

"Your other works were beautiful, but rather...primitive."

"Oh, that. My boss, Jack Benton, talked me into painting another way—this way. I painted many pictures for his home."

"He did pay you, didn't he?"

"Some."

"I shouldn't say this, but he got a real deal."

"What do you mean?"

"You could sell these back East for good money. Many easterners are infatuated with the West."

"You know of such people."

"A few. My father has good contacts with art dealers. In fact, he might want to buy of few of your works himself."

"I just paint because I like it."

"You have talent. No doubt about it." Evangeline mulled over an idea while Ben applied a few more strokes to his painting. "I'm considering returning to Boston for about a month or so to tend to legal matters concerning my late husband's estate. I could take some or all of your paintings and see if I can sell them, if you wish."

Ben put his brush down and rubbed his chin. "A few I can part with. A few I will give to the mission. Let me think about it."

"Fair enough. I just thought you might want to make some money."

"Money has no value to me. I'm happy. But if you need money for the mission, I'll send some pictures with you. Your mission can have what they bring."

"Oh, Ben, I didn't mean it like that."

"Don't worry. My gift to the mission," he said.

"But that's too generous."

"The mission is not important to me. It is to Elijah, though. I haven't done much for my son." Ben's face remained expressionless.

Her face saddened. "It is important to him."

"I see myself in him. I left my family to search for something. It wasn't worth it. Elijah is doing the same."

———

Evangeline shaded her eyes and watched geese fly overhead in perfect formation. They honked their farewells and dipped their wings with a final adieu.

I hope to return before you do, she thought.

Evangeline had packed the last of the trunks she was taking with her to Boston. Willow's things took up much of the trunk's space, and Ben's paintings filled another. She had promised to arrange an exhibition and do her best to sell his art.

She had just eaten breakfast at the dormitory kitchen and said her good-byes to all who were there. Cassandra, Sara, and Elijah were at the house waiting for her. Cassandra had come by the house every day to snuggle her grandchild. She held Willow in her arms as Evangeline entered her own kitchen.

"I'll miss an entire month of her growing up," Cassandra lamented. "I'm sorry that things are strained between you and Elijah. I don't know what has gotten into him lately. I shouldn't have interfered with your lives in the first place. I thought I knew what Elijah wanted."

"It isn't your fault. It seems to be beyond our control," Evangeline reassured Cassandra. She wasn't sure what had happened, either, but her conversation with Ben may have had the best answer yet. The mission was Elijah's driving goal. She and Willow were secondary. She had been aware of that fact, but she didn't realize it was the same kind of consuming passion that had driven Ben away from his family. She did not want to face this side of Elijah, but now it loomed before her, threatening destruction.

"I promise I'll be back as soon as I determine what's going on with James's estate," Evangeline stated emphatically.

"I'll say my good-byes here," Cassandra said. "I can't watch you and your parents drive off. It's just too painful." She hugged Evangeline briefly and then squeezed Willow.

After she handed her granddaughter back to Evangeline, Cassandra left without looking back.

Evangeline forced a smile. "Don't fret, my little Willow. Have faith; it will work out for the best." Evangeline turned to Sara, who had moped and hardly left her side for the past week. She placed her hands on Sara's shoulders. "I will never again make the mistake of leaving you behind for any length of time. No matter what happens, I promise you will be with me."

Sara paled at her words and pleaded, "You're scaring me. What's happening between you and Elijah?" She reached up and held Evangeline's wrists.

"I honestly don't know," replied Evangeline, "but I do know I have to save the mission first and then patch up the differences between Elijah and myself."

"I want you and Elijah to be together—you're my family." Sara wailed.

"I'm sure everything will straighten out when I return," Evangeline consoled. "Be strong and good luck with your teaching. I feel so much better knowing you'll be here with the students. Try not to worry."

Sara nodded while tears spilled down her face.

Elijah and Frederick entered the house, hefted the trunks outside, and loaded them in the wagon. Evangeline followed them with Willow in her arms and Sara close behind. Her gaze passed over the browning prairie, the church, and the graveyard with the small cedars stretching toward the sky. At last, she allowed herself to scrutinize the dormitory, which was causing her so much pain.

How could this be happening to me? Why am I being tested now? She wanted to scream. The mission she sought as a place of refuge was rejecting her once again.

Elijah stepped beside her, taking Willow in his arms. He hugged and kissed the infant as if he would never see her again. Then he leaned toward Evangeline and pecked her on the cheek. "I hope you find the answer," he said.

Evangeline gently placed Willow into Maud's arms and exclaimed, "Wait, I forgot something." She rushed into the house, rolled up the Job's Tears quilt that had been draped over the chest, stuffed it in an unused satchel, and pulled the strap tight.

More Books from AQS

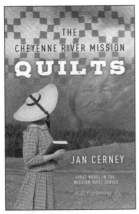

#1544 $14.95

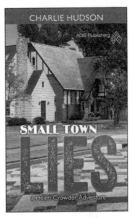

#1258 $14.95

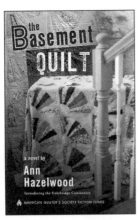

#8853 $14.00

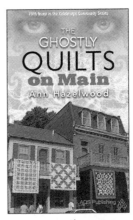

#1643 $14.95